SHERLOCK HOLMES

A Betrayal In Blood

MARK A. LATHAM

TITAN BOOKS

Sherlock Holmes: A Betrayal in Blood
Print edition ISBN: 9781783298662
Electronic edition ISBN: 9781783298679

Published by Titan Books
A division of Titan Publishing Group Ltd
144 Southwark Street, London SE1 0UP

First Titan Books edition: March 2017
2 4 6 8 10 9 7 5 3 1

A CIP catalogue record for this title is available from the British Library.

Printed and bound in the United States

What did you think of this book?
We love to hear from our readers. Please email us at:
readerfeedback@titanemail.com, or write to us at the above address.

To receive advance information, news, competitions, and exclusive offers online, please sign up for the Titan newsletter on our website.
www.titanbooks.com

For Steve Lymer, who's always wanted to be in a
Sherlock Holmes book, and now he is.

"I want you to believe… to believe in things that you cannot."

Abraham Van Helsing

CHAPTER ONE

A STRANGE TALE

"Good heavens, Holmes," I said. "You're not really reading those, are you?"

I was astonished, upon rising for breakfast, to find my friend Sherlock Holmes already busying himself with a large dossier, a plethora of newspapers, and numerous case-files. Holmes was not known for rising early, and certainly not for working at such an hour.

Holmes made some utterance and waved me away, and I looked about the room in despair. He had clearly been active for some time, given the abject disarray of the Baker Street rooms, which had been put back to order only days ago following the rather trying events following his return to London from his long exile. Since then, I had resolved to spend some time at Baker Street, to ensure no further attempts might be made on Holmes's life.

The object of his latest obsession was queer indeed; that the sceptical and pragmatic Sherlock Holmes I had known for so long would pay any heed to the so-called "Dracula Papers" was a puzzle.

This collection of documents detailed the battles of a crew of "vampire hunters" against a fiend who took the form of a Transylvanian nobleman; the events had unfolded between May and November of the previous year, 1893, in London, Whitby and Transylvania itself. Composed by numerous hands, collected together the Dracula Papers exonerated the hunters themselves, whilst damning the late Count Dracula. Four young men had accompanied one Professor Van Helsing and Mrs Mina Harker, *née* Murray, on a mission to rid the world of Count Dracula, purportedly a blood-sucking vampire from Transylvania. This much I knew from the newspapers, which called the men "intrepid vampire hunters", or the "Crew of Light". Of these men, one had perished in the adventure—a Quincey P. Morris of Texas. The others still lived in England, and had become celebrated in the public eye: Jonathan Harker, a solicitor, and husband to Mina; Dr Jack Seward, who had the running of a lunatic asylum at Purfleet; and Arthur Holmwood himself, now Lord Godalming. This last was a tragic figure, for there was a deceased girl in the case, Lucy Westenra, who had been Lord Godalming's betrothed, and he himself had cut the head from the poor girl's corpse in order to stop her rising from the grave. The affair had taken a great toil on the young lord, who had not been seen in public since, though he had married surprisingly soon after Miss Westenra's demise.

Only the most sensationalised versions of events had thus far made it to the public attention. The inquest into the facts of the case had dragged on for no small time; most people expected the Crew of Light—particularly its illustrious leader, Van Helsing, to be exonerated of any wrongdoing, and perhaps even to receive some honour for its role in Count Dracula's defeat. I had heard a little more of the details from idle chatter at the club, but it was certainly not the kind of thing that Sherlock Holmes would normally concern himself with.

I sighed, and rang for Mrs Hudson.

"You will take breakfast, at least?" I asked.

"What? Oh, if you like."

My friend, so generally enervated by his work, was tired, that much was plain to see. Dark rings had formed around his eyes, and his sharp features were more drawn than ever, his skin almost luminous in pallor. Holmes had been back at Baker Street not even a fortnight after his miraculous return from "death" and the capture of the dangerous villain Colonel Sebastian Moran. Yet it appeared that a case had already presented itself to Sherlock Holmes, and a strange one at that.

A soft rap came at the door, and I opened it for Mrs Hudson. She craned her neck to peer in at Holmes, and frowned when she saw him crouched on the floor in his dressing gown, marooned upon an island of crumpled papers. Then her frown swiftly changed to a smile of unexpected warmth.

"It's good to have him back, Dr Watson," she said softly. "For all he has driven me to distraction over the years, it was quite something else without him, don't you agree?"

"I… yes, quite something indeed."

"I still can't believe he's here, large as life. Back from the dead."

Her words provoked memories within me—painful memories of one I had only recently lost; one who would not be returning. The sudden thought of Mary took me by surprise in its forcefulness. My expression must have betrayed my feelings, for the landlady looked momentarily distressed. "Forgive me, Doctor… Did you ring for breakfast? Will Mr Holmes eat?"

I appreciated the change of subject, even if her concern was more for Holmes than myself, and the moment of awkwardness passed.

"Yes, Mrs Hudson, I think so. Breakfast would be excellent."

"Mrs Hudson!" Holmes exclaimed, and in two large bounds he was at the door in all his dishevelled splendour, looking like the ghost of the great detective. "You may need to be quick about it if breakfast is to be had, for I am expecting a visitor this morning. Early, I should think. Dr Watson may have to wait for his toast."

Mrs Hudson closed the door behind her, and I turned to Holmes, who had already begun to pick up his newspapers in great armfuls, throwing them over the back of the sofa in an apparent attempt at tidying up.

"Holmes, why are you reading this stuff about Count Dracula with such relish? And why on earth would you expect a visitor this morning in connection with it?"

He paused abruptly. "Watson, I believe I shall make a detective of you yet. You have deduced that the visitor and the curious case of Dracula are connected?"

"Your absorption in those papers could indicate no other reason, for you are always single-minded in the pursuit of a case. My questions stand, however—why the interest in this matter? It is, after all, already solved."

"Is it?" Holmes's mouth twisted into a little smile; his eyes fair sparkled from within the purplish-black sockets born of his months in Europe tracking down Moriarty's circle of confederates. But there was strength there still—Sherlock Holmes may have been physically exhausted, but his brilliant mind worked as rigorously as ever.

I could see I was walking into a trap, but I was so intrigued that I did so willingly, for it was often the only means of extracting the juice of a tantalising case from him.

"As I'm sure you have seen from yesterday's *Times*, Holmes, Sir Toby Fitzwilliam himself has exonerated Professor Van Helsing of any wrongdoing, and has spoken in the highest possible terms of the professor's associates. The Count is dead, though a string of poor victims lie in his wake. The full contents of the Dracula Papers are set to be made public any time now—although I see you have found a copy already. What is there to be gained by looking over the facts again?"

"My dear Watson, there is always something to be gained by looking over facts, especially when they have been presented to me in such a strange fashion. Indeed, while there is nothing here that has not already been seen by the highest authorities in the land—I include Sir Toby Fitzwilliam, whose judgement I believe to be impeccable—the most intriguing fact is that they came to me at all. Just look where they came from, Watson."

Holmes handed a card to me, upon which was printed neatly, "The Diogenes Club, Pall Mall". On the back of the card was written, in royal blue ink, a single initial: "M".

"Mycroft," I muttered, my interest at once piqued. Sherlock's brother requested aid but rarely, and when he did it usually heralded excitement, or danger. "Did he attach a note?"

"There was no need, Watson. It was clear from my brother's very involvement that I was intended to read what he sent me and find something that the authorities had failed to notice. The Dracula Papers contain twenty-seven journal entries, letters, telegrams, articles and sundry reports. In addition, the version Mycroft has given me includes several police reports that will not be included with the papers to be made public. There is also some interesting marginalia, not all in Mycroft's hand. I have read every word twice over, and several yards of column inches in the popular press besides, and I believe I have hit upon the crux of the matter."

"Twice over… When were these delivered, Holmes?" I asked. I had dined out the previous night, but I had returned at a quarter to ten while Holmes was playing his violin—there had been no sign of any papers in the rooms then.

"Shortly before midnight," he replied.

"Then… you must have been up all night. Really, Holmes, you

must learn to look after yourself. As a doctor I—"

"Come now, Watson, there will be time enough for that later. Tell me quickly—what do you know of the case of Count Dracula?"

I disliked the way Holmes dismissed my concern for his well-being, but knew there was little to be done. "As much as anyone," I said, sighing. "This Dutchman, Professor Van Helsing, and a small group of other men—"

"And a woman," Holmes corrected.

"I was getting to that. Yes, and a woman, too, a Mrs Harker, I believe. They uncovered a plot by a… a… well, it is too terrific to describe."

"A vampire," Holmes interjected again.

"Yes, well, *humph*. A plot by a vampire, indeed, to gain a foothold for his reign of evil here in London. The professor put a stop to it, and has been lauded as a hero. Why, all of London is stirred up over the story."

"Very true," said Holmes. "But tell me, how much credence do you give to the tale?"

"Why, had it not been for the ruling of Sir Toby in the courts yesterday, I would have scoffed at the notion of a vampire, here or anywhere else for that matter. But you yourself said that Sir Toby Fitzwilliam's judgement is impeccable. So…" I shrugged, not wanting to admit the existence of the Un-Dead to my sceptical friend. Sir Toby was one of the most respected judges in the land and, some said, a member of a secret intelligence agency. I wondered in which capacity Mycroft Holmes was acquainted with him.

"Indeed. Which is why there must be more to this story. For as we know, vampires do not exist."

"The evidence suggests something to the contrary," I said. "Unless you yourself are now the one twisting facts to suit theories." I tried not to look smug. Holmes somehow managed to look smug enough for both of us.

"And you believe that is what we have? Facts?"

"Well… are you suggesting that Sir Toby has been hoodwinked?"

"I am asserting most confidently that he has allowed a popular version of events to become known to the public, because he lacks the evidence to disprove it."

"A man in his position does not need evidence to renounce the word of a Dutch professor," I scoffed.

"Ordinarily, no. But Abraham Van Helsing is no ordinary academic. I have heard his name several times in the past, most recently while I was on grave business in Austria. He is a clever man, Watson. A cunning man. There must be more to the story—there must be some reason for Sir Toby to lend his assent to this… poppycock, and for my brother to involve me. I believe I have the nub of it from the papers, what there is of them."

Such strong terms from Holmes suggested he was ruffled. I abandoned any further questioning about Van Helsing for the time being.

"You do not have all of the papers?" I said instead.

"Oh, yes. I have all of the official material."

"Then what, Holmes?"

"All in good time, Watson. First of all, be a good fellow and open the door for Mrs Hudson."

A quiet knock came at that moment. There was no elementary trickery in this—Holmes's hearing was sharper than a bat's, and I knew he must have heard the tea tray rattling a good few seconds before I did. I opened the door, and bade the landlady come in.

No sooner had she set the tray down than the bell rang downstairs.

"Oh dear me," said Mrs Hudson. "Now there's someone at the door. Might I leave you with breakfast while I go and see who it is?"

"Indeed you may, Mrs Hudson," said Holmes, already exchanging his battered dressing gown for a jacket, "but I can save you the bother of an identification. It will be Inspector Bradstreet of Scotland Yard."

Mrs Hudson, to her credit, did not look surprised. She went downstairs, and a few minutes later, the bearded Inspector Bradstreet was ushered into the room. I shook his hand, and bade him sit, casting a rueful look at the toast-rack that would have to go ignored for now.

"Your landlady said you expected me, Mr Holmes," Bradstreet said, "though I cannot guess how."

"I was thinking the same thing," said I.

"A simple matter of timing, Inspector," Holmes smirked. "I received the Dracula Papers late last night from a certain person in government. The dossier was marked with the stamp of Scotland Yard's B Division, and given our previous working relationship it seemed obvious that you would be selected for this interview. As to the timing—the subject matter is of pressing import, otherwise the papers would not have found their way to me at such an unusual hour. Someone wished to give me a head start on the reading, it seems. As such, I knew you would head to Baker Street as soon as you reported for work today at, I suspect, eight o'clock. The traffic at this time is heavy, to say the least, and so I estimated forty minutes for the journey. You took thirty—I congratulate you."

"Well I'll be blowed. But as it happens, Mr Holmes, the journey took forty-five minutes, it's just that I left a bit earlier than you thought. I'm an early riser, you see. Force of habit. I'm afraid you've made a second mistake, also," the inspector said, drawing a raised eyebrow from my friend. I confess I rather enjoyed that moment, for I do not believe Holmes had accounted for a genuine error.

"Oh?" Holmes said, pleasantly enough despite his obvious—to me—chagrin.

"You said I would have been sent, on account of us working together on that blue carbuncle case, among others; but that was some time ago, Mr Holmes, and there are few at B Division now who'd remember it. No, when I got in this morning, Mr Holmes, there were some already talking about you because of this Dracula business, and I requested the assignment."

"Might I ask why?"

"On account of a friend. A very old friend."

"Cotford," said Holmes.

At this name, which was new to me, Bradstreet's mouth dropped open. Presently, he replied, "Why... yes. But how?"

"One Detective Inspector Cotford is mentioned very briefly in the dossier, scribbled faintly in pencil and clumsily erased. It was a small matter to me to discover that he was formerly with B Division before serving for some short time in the Purfleet constabulary, which would almost certainly have brought him, a senior policeman, into contact with Professor Van Helsing and his merry band. I could find no further reference to Cotford, nor any police report originating from Purfleet, which is one of several notable omissions in the narrative. I now hope you can illuminate these matters, Inspector—a hope that I did not entertain when first you arrived at my door."

Bradstreet beamed as though Holmes had paid him a compliment, though I was fairly sure it had been a slight. I poured some tea and handed a cup to the grateful inspector as he relaxed and began his story.

"Frank Cotford is an old friend, as I said, Mr Holmes, and a colleague of some long standing. We worked together in Whitechapel, cut our teeth on the worst vice and murder to be seen in this or any other city, before we both made our way out of that pit—me to Chelsea, and him to Purfleet. Over time we drifted apart; duty and locale have a way of doing that. The last time I saw him, he was in a bad way. He'd taken to drink, and was speaking in riddles about some 'Dutch devil' who had set himself in opposition to the law."

Holmes shot me a glance. "How long ago was this meeting?" he asked.

"It must have been November last. Frank said he'd had a run-in with some gents, including the Dutchman, and... well, to tell the truth I couldn't get much sense out of him. All I know is something happened—something to do with this 'Dracula'—and it was the ruin of Frank Cotford. Twenty years on the force gone up in smoke."

"You must have seen him again, or else why seek my counsel?" Holmes said.

"I saw him in the distance two weeks ago, though he was gone before I could speak to him—I admit I was a little afraid to approach him, his expression was so severe. I made a few enquiries as to why he looked so down at heel. The regulars in his local pub said that he rants and raves about vampires and crooks and devils, and swears they'll come for him before long. I think the loss of his position has taken its toll on Frank's mind, Mr Holmes, but even so—if I ever called myself his friend, I would be remiss in not making a few discreet enquiries on his behalf."

Holmes pressed his fingers together and stared straight ahead, thinking hard. Finally, he spoke. "Where is the former Inspector Cotford now?"

"Back where he started," Bradstreet said ruefully. "Whitechapel."

"Then that is where we shall begin. Drink your tea, Inspector."

"We're going now?" I asked, giving voice to the inspector's expression.

"There is no time like the present, Watson. And on the way, I shall educate you in the discrepancies of the Dracula Papers. There is a mystery to be solved here, a very great mystery. More importantly, I believe I will soon have the opportunity to match with a truly worthy adversary. And so soon after the last one— such fortune should not favour a man twice in one lifetime."

"You are on your second lifetime," I said.

Holmes's eyes lit up as he considered the jest approvingly, and at once his tiredness seemed to melt away. "How right you are, Watson," he said. "How right you are."

CHAPTER TWO

INSPECTOR COTFORD

Bradstreet insisted on accompanying us to the home of his former friend, not only to make the necessary introductions, but also to offer some protection. Cotford had apparently been forced into early retirement on the grounds of deteriorating health, and his meagre police pension afforded him a flat on Wentworth Street, just a stone's throw from some of the worst doss-houses and black thoroughfares that the East End had to offer.

Even as our coach clattered along the cobbled roads, Holmes's hawkish eyes darted about, taking in every detail of the locale. But it was not the squalling children in the gutters nor the gin-soaked sots sleeping upon heaps of rubbish that he was interested in.

"Up ahead there, is that not Chicksand Street?" Holmes asked the inspector.

"It is, sir. What of it?"

"Chicksand Street is noted in the Dracula Papers as one of the Count's lairs, discovered by one Jonathan Harker of Van Helsing's infamous group. Strange that Inspector Cotford would retire to a residence just a few minutes' stroll from that place, is it not?"

"Curious, I'll grant you," said Bradstreet, as the police carriage came to a halt outside a squalid terrace, black from soot and filth. The smell of rotten vegetables, stale beer and things far worse drifted into the confines of the coach. "Cotford was always adamant that the whole Dracula affair had been his ruin, and seemed somewhat fearful of all involved; perhaps he dwells here out of necessity. It cannot be good for his state of mind, that being the case."

Holmes was first to step out of the carriage, and bade the inspector make haste to the door. I was still unclear on the exact details of the papers my friend had read, and knew I would have to digest them soon if I were to keep up with Holmes. I could tell from the spring in his step and that familiar gleam in his eye that he had the scent of villainy, and would stop at nothing until the wrongdoer was brought to justice.

Bradstreet rapped hard on the front door of the downstairs flat, the sound almost masked by the infernal clattering and bumping of a dray passing close by.

We waited a moment on the doorstep before Bradstreet rapped again. This time, a growling expletive was fired from somewhere behind the door, instructing us in no uncertain terms to make ourselves scarce. Holmes raised an eyebrow and looked at Bradstreet. The inspector grimaced, before leaning into the peeling paintwork and shouting in his bullish fashion, "Frank? It's Roger. I'm here on official business. Better open up."

Seconds later, the door was yanked open with such force that it cracked upon the hallway wall. Before us stood a tall, grey-haired man, with narrow flinty eyes beneath dark brows, tanned-leather skin, and a bushy moustache. He looked more like a rangy cowboy from the cover of an American dime novel than a policeman of Whitechapel, former or otherwise.

"I've got no official business to answer, Roger Bradstreet," the man growled. His fists were clenched, and he rocked unsteadily like he was on the deck of a ship. A waft of gin-breath emanated from him, though it was barely past nine in the morning.

From the look on Bradstreet's face—and his uncharacteristic loss for words—I guessed he had not expected his old friend to look in quite such a state, nor to face him so belligerently. It was Sherlock Holmes, not Inspector Bradstreet, who spoke up.

"Detective Inspector Cotford, is it not? Sherlock Holmes at your service. I have never had the pleasure, though I have heard nothing but good about your police work."

Cotford's face crumpled into a frown. "Sherlock Holmes, is it? The great detective himself, risen from the grave and come to my door, perhaps to investigate the sorry affair of my missing fortunes. Take a good look, sir, and then take your leave, for there is naught you can do for me now."

"On the contrary, Inspector," said Holmes, continuing to use the defunct title. "Your good friend Bradstreet here has employed me to take up your case; to assist you where Scotland Yard cannot, or will not. I am no martinet, I am not bound by legal duty, by political machination, or by petty jurisdiction. If there is a case to answer, I am apt to discover the culprit. And there is at least one culprit who has thus far evaded your long arm, is there not? You know of whom I speak."

"The Dutchman," Cotford muttered, with venom.

Holmes nodded.

"You'd best come in, Mr Holmes."

"So y'see, it has to be Van Helsing. That devil pursued the Count halfway across the world, and murdered him in cold blood." Cotford offered around a tarnished hip flask for the third time, and we all politely declined again.

Cotford's flat was something of a hovel, but for his bookshelves, which were filled with neatly ordered volumes, mostly journals. They looked singularly out of place; it was easy to forget that Cotford had once been a respectable man of the law.

"Why would he do such a thing?" Holmes asked. His eyes were closed, his fingers pressed together, his lips pursed as he concentrated on every word of Cotford's slurred testimony.

"How should I know? But you only have to look at him to know his sort. A schemer."

"So you have no evidence to support your suspicions?"

Cotford made a sound that was half belch, half snarl. "Confiscated, the lot of it. Van Helsing made a complaint to the powers that be. Someone bent the ear of the assistant commissioner; the assistant commissioner slapped me down. That's how it works, Mr Holmes. Politics, as you said. They took all me files and handed them over to that little Dutch devil, and I bet he burned the lot. 'Cept…" he stopped abruptly.

"Except for what, Inspector Cotford?" Holmes said, opening his eyes and fixing the man with an expression of intense scrutiny.

"The journals," Cotford replied, with some reluctance. He waved his flask at the bookshelf. "I write everything down, always have. I copied every letter, every note, plus my own observations, o' course."

"You mean to say that those journals contain copies of the entire Dracula Papers?" I interjected.

"All that I saw, or held in my own two hands, at least. And s'far as I know, some of the things I copied down, and some o' the statements I took, never did make it before the courts."

"Such as?" Holmes asked, a hard edge entering his tone.

"I'll show you," Cotford said with an air of defiance, and staggered to his shelves to fetch a slender volume. He flipped through the pages before handing the open book to Holmes. "Record of an exchange of letters between one Miss Wilhelmina

Murray—later Mrs Harker—and Miss Kate Reed, a schoolmistress at the Blackall School for Girls, Exeter. The letters were written between 23 and 26 May last year, 1893, while Mr Jonathan Harker was in Transylvania. You'll remember his own account in the Dracula Papers tells us he was being held prisoner by the Count at the time."

"You are a credit to your profession, Inspector," said Holmes. "The contents of the letters are not here noted. You have them?"

"I do not."

"But you know their contents?"

"I do not."

"Then what leads you to suspect anything is untoward?"

"I am a thorough man, Mr Holmes. I see something of that same thoroughness in you." (I tried to hide my smirk almost as hard as Holmes tried to hide his annoyance at the comparison.) Cotford went on, "I spoke to Miss Reed, and though she would tell me nothing, there was something in her manner that put the bit between my teeth. She was hiding something, and it was to do with gossip regarding Miss Murray and Miss Lucy Westenra."

Holmes's interest visibly piqued again. "Miss Reed knew the late Miss Westenra, of Hillingham?"

"They were all three of them at school together. And there was something more—I would stake my claim on it that Miss Reed was afraid of Miss Murray."

"This is your policeman's intuition?"

"You could call it that."

"But you have no evidence. Indeed, you never saw these letters at all."

"No, but I did check with the local post office. It is a small enterprise and the postmaster's wife there knows every coming and goin'. Said she'd known Miss Reed and Miss Murray since they was nippers. She confirmed that the letters were sent, and recalls that it was the last time the three girls exchanged letters at that post office, s'far as she knows, presumably on account of Miss Westenra's untimely demise."

"A garrulous soul is a true virtue in detective work, Inspector."

"She confirmed that, beyond the letters to Miss Reed, Miss Murray had sent only one other letter that week of the 23 May—to Miss Lucy Westenra." Cotford looked proud of himself.

"You already told us that," I said, now thinking that the man was merely a delusional drunk, and that perhaps we should not be humouring him so.

"No, Watson!" exclaimed Holmes, excitedly. "The inspector has answered a question that I had not yet got around to asking."

I exchanged a glance with Bradstreet, who shrugged.

"Why did Miss Mina Murray," Cotford said, with some swagger, "not write a letter to her fiancé, all the way in Transylvania. We have seen the journal transcripts. We know she was worried about him. We know she wrote to Miss Lucy about him. But she never tried to reach him directly."

"Perhaps she did not have the address of this remote Transylvanian castle," I said with a frown.

"But Mr Harker's firm surely had it, and they could have provided it," Cotford retorted. "If she was so concerned, she certainly would have tried. Hardly seems like the actions of a doting sweetheart, now does it? S'why the postmaster's wife remembered it so clear—said she asked Miss Murray about her gentleman, and received short shrift in reply."

"And so what is your conclusion, Inspector Cotford, based on these findings?" Holmes asked.

"Not just based on these findings, Mr Holmes. Based on many more like 'em." He gesticulated toward the shelves again. "And my conclusion is that we have a conspiracy, the product of which was several murders."

"You believe Lucy Westenra was killed by someone other than Count Dracula?"

"I certainly do."

"Mina Murray?"

"No, although I think she knows more than she's telling. I think the Dutch professor did for the girl, and the Harker woman, her simple-minded husband, and that Arthur Holmwood covered up the mess."

At that name, Inspector Bradstreet sucked air through his teeth. Holmes's lip twitched upwards, on the cusp of a knowing smile. I could not see any good coming of throwing around such accusations.

Sherlock Holmes now addressed Cotford firmly. "You are bold to implicate Lord Godalming in this matter. I ask again for your evidence, or is this also intuition?"

"And again I say everything I have is in these books. If you have read the Dracula Papers, then you should surely be able to work it out, 'detective.'"

Holmes scowled.

Cotford took no notice, and went on, "A fine matter indeed when a peer of the realm, within days of inheriting his father's estate due to the sudden death of the old man, finds himself without his betrothed and his mother-in-law soon after. And a finer matter, too, when said peer of the realm inherits the Westenra estate, due to a most unusual and ill-advised clause in the elder Mrs Westenra's will. I say Holmwood had motive and means, Mr Holmes. What say you?"

"You mentioned conspiracy, *Mr* Cotford," said Holmes. "A serious charge in itself."

"If you truly mean to take on this case, Mr Holmes, then you'll know what I speak of soon enough. The famous vampire hunters are thick as thieves, and no mistake."

"And what of their illustrious mentor, the good professor?"

Cotford spat. "There's nothin' good about him. Thinks himself the lord o' Carfax now. Another rum deal, of which the law cannot make head nor tail. He has inherited the Count's newly acquired property, where he lives like a king. So I'm told."

"You have not been tempted to see for yourself?"

"I have not." It was plain from Cotford's demeanour, even to me, that he was lying. "I—"

"You cannot, can you, Frank?" interrupted Bradstreet. He turned to us to explain. "It was a condition of Frank's honourable acquittal from his duties that he would leave Van Helsing well alone, on pain of arrest. No charges have ever been brought against the professor, and it seems, after the court ruling, that none ever shall."

"And that's final, is it, Roger?" Cotford grumbled.

Holmes stood quite abruptly and said, "Mr Cotford, may we borrow your journals, so that we might make a thorough comparison between them and the official papers?"

"You may not, sir."

"Oh?"

"I don't know you. I will not entrust such a body of work to a stranger, even one so famous."

"Then how about me, Frank?" Inspector Bradstreet asked.

"Nor you neither, Roger Bradstreet. 'Specially not you. It was the law that brought me low; the law that ignored my testimony and handed what evidence I had to that Dutch devil."

"But what use are they to you now?"

"More than you could know, but that is my own business."

I interjected, seeing an opportunity. "Mr Cotford, we have no desire to bring more police into what is now a private matter. But your cooperation would be appreciated. Otherwise, perhaps the police could be informed of your continuing investigation. You have visited the property on Chicksand Street, have you not?" It was speculation on my part, but from Cotford's reaction I saw that

I had guessed correctly. From the look on Holmes's face I also saw that I had acted out of turn.

"You would dragoon me, sir, in my own home?" Cotford growled, drawing himself to his full height and balling his large fists. "All of you will kindly leave this instant. I withdraw my 'ospitality."

"Frank, out of friendship—" Bradstreet started.

"Out!" shouted Cotford. "If you want friendship, you come for a drink down the Ten Bells—you don't come 'ere with no detectives poking into my business and issuing threats. Out!"

"I'm sorry, Holmes," I said, as the police carriage trundled away from those squalid environs and bumped along Whitechapel High Street. "I rather put my foot in it."

"Yes, Watson, you did," Holmes remarked. "But it is not to be helped. Besides, it was not a total loss." He pulled a notebook from his jacket pocket.

"You stole a journal!" said Bradstreet.

"Borrowed, Inspector, borrowed. This is the book that Mr Cotford selected as a prime example of discrepancies in the Dracula Papers. It stands to reason, as it was the first volume he searched for, that it is the most important. When his disposition towards us turned sour, I knew I could not leave without it. When we are done, I shall of course place this book in your hands, Inspector, and you may return it to your former colleague as you wish."

Bradstreet did not look overly happy; possibly he disapproved of Holmes's subterfuge, but more likely he did not relish returning the book to Cotford and explaining its removal.

"So where now, Holmes?" said I.

"To Baker Street. You have much reading to do, Watson, if you are to be of any use to me. Inspector Bradstreet, might I ask a favour of you?"

"Of course, Mr Holmes."

"Poke your nose into the business of as many detectives as you dare, and find what notes you can—however scarce—that were made regarding the Dracula investigation. Raid the police files, also. Coroner's reports, witness statements, charge sheets—whatever you can dredge up, no matter how tangential to the case. Bring them to Baker Street at your earliest convenience." At mention of home, my stomach rumbled, and my thoughts turned to my abandoned rack of toast.

"And what will you do with them, Mr Holmes?" Bradstreet asked.

"It seems to me that, despite the best efforts of your division, the Dracula Papers are incomplete or, at best, edited deliberately to obfuscate the facts. I intend to reconstruct them as they were originally intended, with no omissions. I plan to stitch together the true story of Dracula."

CHAPTER THREE

GLARING ERRORS

Much of the day and part of the evening was spent in study of the Dracula Papers. It was tiresome research, made tolerable only by Mrs Hudson's frequent visits with a fresh tea tray. My concentration was sabotaged at every turn by Holmes, who would periodically rush over with a newly transcribed sheet that he had copied from Cotford's book, or a newspaper article that he had clipped carefully from its page, and stuff these amidst the papers I held. More often than not, Holmes forced me to reorder the pages and go over the same ones time and again, bringing the new details to light.

"You must fix the sequence of events correctly in your mind, Watson," Holmes repeated. "The devil—Dutch or otherwise—is in the details."

Twice during the day, a police constable arrived with folios of notes from Bradstreet—first from B Division, then from H Division. Later, a courier came with pages of court transcripts, including the summarising speech of Sir Toby Fitzwilliam before the Lords, naming Professor Abraham Van Helsing an "honourable man" who had "taken his duty to his fellow man and his oath to heal the sick to their utmost extreme. Any wrongdoing in the eyes of the law whilst in pursuit of this noble cause must be overlooked by the courts of England on this occasion, or the bedrock of justice upon which this great nation is built will be eroded." It was clear that Holmes believed not a word of it. He finished ahead of me, and sat at the window, silently smoking his pipe for some time, until I had caught up with my reading.

By the time I had completed the endeavour, our rooms were an eyesore, strewn with papers, discarded notes and drained teacups. When Mrs Hudson returned in the early evening with a platter of bread and cheese, she tutted and shook her head at the mess, before dutifully collecting what seemed like a week's worth of tea-things and retreating downstairs.

"Finally, Watson!" Holmes jumped to his feet and stretched theatrically. "I never took you for a slow reader."

"Really, Holmes," I grumbled, "were it not for your constant interruptions…"

"As far as I can see, Watson, we have here the most complete copy of the Dracula Papers in the land. And yet you will have observed, I take it, references to events and personages, herein unnamed, that are still not present in the official papers. Mislaid narratives, do you think? Or suppressed ones?"

"Suppressed by whom?" I asked.

"Aha! What do you make of it all? Do you still believe what you read in the newspapers?"

"The testimonies as they are now arranged do shed a somewhat different light on the matter," I conceded, "but still not enough to accuse anyone of conspiracy to murder."

"What do you make of the inconsistencies?"

"Many of them can be put down to editorial error. The original notes were handwritten by the hunters or recorded on to wax cylinders via a phonograph machine, and then re-typed by Mrs Harker. Any number of innocent mistakes could have crept in."

"True. The most damning is an exchange of letters between Mina Harker and Lucy Westenra, dated August last year, at a time when Mina was supposed to be in Buda-Pesth. As you say, perhaps it is all innocent enough. Of course, if Mina Harker wished to disguise her real movements, it would be the ideal way to achieve that goal. She was, after all, entrusted with all of the diaries and correspondence, of which few originals remain."

"Cynical, Holmes. If we take even half the accounts of Mrs Harker at face value, she is a remarkable woman, as noble as Count Dracula is villainous."

"And what of the Count? Are you a believer in vampires now, Watson? *Tsk, tsk.*"

"I am merely willing to give their account the benefit of the doubt, Holmes. Have you not always instructed me to do just that?" My friend had always advised me to keep an open mind; that once you have eliminated the impossible, whatever remains, however improbable, must be the truth. His father's adage, I believe. And yet, where the supernatural was concerned, Holmes's mind was a castle door, locked and barred against possibility. I did have misgivings, though. "Admittedly, the Count's terrible powers are somewhat inconsistently portrayed. Again perhaps this is due to the various perspectives of the witnesses."

"An example, Watson."

"Van Helsing and Harker speak independently of Dracula's aversion to sunlight. And yet Mrs Harker very clearly states that she and her husband saw him in London, during the day, and she did not mention any severe weakness in his demeanour on that occasion. Quite the opposite, in fact. Likewise, Van Helsing claims that Dracula can transform himself into a wolf, or a bat, or even mist—and yet several times Dracula fails to do these things when they would be eminently useful to his cause."

"Very good. It is almost as if Van Helsing's endless postulation and critical fact do not quite tally. Anything else?"

"There were certainly some lapses of judgement on the part of these vampire hunters, and some... questionable methods, particularly from a medical standpoint."

"Go on."

"I speak of Lucy Westenra's general health. There was an argument in court that she may have suffered dyspnoea, although I think anaemia is the most likely cause of her ills. A pity there is no chance to examine the subject. Mina Murray notes herself that Lucy had an anaemic look about her, and we see that she was prone to bouts of listlessness. I suspect she was anaemic before the visit of the Count, and any doctor should have been able to see it."

"I dare say."

"You will note that Seward analyses Miss Westenra's blood, however, and finds her in rude health after the transfusion."

I scoffed. "Seward is an alienist, although we are supposed to believe that he studied practical medicine. Any doctor could tell you that a 'qualitative analysis' of anaemic blood such as Dr Seward conducted, simply cannot confirm vigorous health or otherwise."

"What would you have done, Watson, had you been confronted with a patient showing all of Miss Westenra's symptoms?"

"I would have administered an ioduret of iron to begin with, and a simple glass of porter once a day before attempting anything more dramatic. I might add ammonia to that prescription later if required, but would hope not to."

"And yet Seward and Van Helsing immediately jumped to the conclusion that a vampire was to blame, and administered a potentially dangerous treatment. Is that fair to say?"

"It is."

"But what of the other symptoms, Watson—what about her

sleepwalking, supposedly triggered by the hypnotic power of the Count?"

"Balderdash!"

"Really, Watson!" Holmes feigned a censorious tone.

"It seems to me," I went on, encouraged by Holmes's sudden interest in my professional opinion, "that at every turn, this Dr Seward allowed himself to be misled by outmoded, superstitious bunkum. He states his belief, in his own journal, that the poor Westenra girl's sickness is one of the mind, and yet at Van Helsing's behest he carries out several transfusions of blood—transfusions that simply cannot work in the way they are described here. When Lucy's end came, she was discovered in a state of near torpor, freezing cold due to blood loss. The very first thing Van Helsing and Seward prescribed was a heated bath to warm her, before administering yet another transfusion. This is the worst possible treatment; in such a state, the heat would have encouraged the flow of blood away from Lucy's brain. I am afraid that, had she survived much longer, her faculties may have been irreversibly diminished."

"You are speaking of malpractice, Watson."

I paused. "I suppose I am."

"And to what do you attribute this shocking malpractice?" Holmes went on.

"As a young man of modern medical training, Dr Seward has little excuse, save one. His complete devotion to his former teacher, Van Helsing, appears absolute. A young man of limited worldly experience might defer to his beloved teacher's wisdom, especially in times of great stress. He evidently loved the Westenra girl, and in his worry he was easily led."

"But why would Van Helsing lead him so?"

"Because the old man is superstitious, and believed in a supernatural cause for Miss Westenra's illness. He believed she had been repeatedly drained of blood by a vampire, and that the instant transfusion of blood—any blood—would suffice in restoring her to life. He was misguided."

"Was he?" Holmes said quietly, lips curled into a thin, facetious smile, though the subject of his amusement was a touch too morbid for my tastes. "Because he believed in vampires?"

"Why... yes."

"Of course, if he had motive to kill the girl..."

I frowned, and suddenly felt very sorry for the fair young lady who had been so nobly described in the journals I had read. "Then the professor's actions would have been a sure way to commit murder, and shift the blame in the process," I said solemnly. "But tell me, Holmes, other than the suspicions of Frank Cotford, what evidence here suggests any such motive?"

"Ah, Watson. You have read, but you have not understood. I will not, however, foist upon you a half-formed hypothesis. You know that is not my way. No, soon enough we will see if my suspicions can be proven as fact."

"But that is the crux of it, then? We are investigating not just the death of Count Dracula, but also that of the Westenra girl?"

"And not just her! Watson, have you absorbed nothing today? Cotford was a drunk, yes, but a mind as thorough as his could not be so easily misled. Within these papers we have the deaths of Mr Peter Hawkins, the solicitor who sent Jonathan Harker to Transylvania; Mrs Westenra the elder; Miss Lucy Westenra; Lord Godalming the elder; the lunatic R. M. Renfield of Purfleet Asylum; the American Quincey P. Morris; and, of course, Count Dracula himself. That is supposing the mysterious deaths of the crew of the ship *Demeter* are either incidental or accidental. They add to the supernatural narrative, I grant you, but I have not yet made up my mind on the matter."

"Of those," I said, "Lord Godalming would seem to me to

have died of age and infirmity. Renfield was obviously taken by the Count. The rest, I grant you, are questionable."

"We will see about Renfield in good time!" exclaimed Holmes. "As for Lord Godalming, you know by now that I do not believe in coincidence when murder and motive are close by. As Cotford pointed out, albeit crudely, one man stood to profit by at least three of those deaths, perhaps more, if we can find the trick of it."

"Arthur Holmwood," I groaned, realising that Holmes would not be put off, and that we would almost certainly be harassing an important peer before too long. Given Cotford's fall from grace after doing the same, I could only hope that Holmes's immense reputation would save us a similar fate.

"Sharp as a tack, Watson, as ever. Our next port of call must be Ring, in Surrey, where the young Lord Godalming has become something of a recluse."

I looked at the mantel clock, which was obscured by a thick haze of pipe smoke—how many bowls Holmes had consumed throughout the day I could not tell. It was almost nine o'clock in the evening. "You surely aren't suggesting we leave now, Holmes?" I said. "You have not slept for over thirty hours."

"We cannot leave now, Watson, for we would never make the last train. We depart for Surrey first thing in the morning."

CHAPTER FOUR

LORD GODALMING

I felt a certain trepidation as our cab swept up the long, gently curving drive of Ring, that great country pile that had been home to the Godalming family for centuries. I wondered just how Holmes was planning to question the reclusive Lord Godalming; I hoped he would not be in one of his more brusque moods. I doubted very much that Mycroft Holmes, who had set us on this path, would appreciate answering questions at Westminster as to why his brother had insulted a peer of considerable import.

Holmes was quiet for much of the journey, his mind doubtless back at Baker Street, envisioning those many pages of notes and type that had led us to Surrey on a cool April morn. He certainly had no mind to take in the spectacular first glimpse of Ring, which swung into view, with its imposing finials, parapets and buttresses. For all its glorious embellishments, however, the vast house had a bleak and forbidding aspect about it. Jagged shadows reached across the gravel drive towards our carriage like clawed fingers, and uncountable black windows stared at us menacingly from the ancient, grey walls.

We came to a halt in the shadow of that severe stately pile. A butler came to meet us, and bade us inside before waving the coachman on. "We wish to speak to the master of the house," Holmes said, his voice echoing around the grand, but rather dingy, marble entrance hall. "My name is Sherlock Holmes, and this is my associate, Dr Watson. We have come from London on business of great import."

"The master rarely grants audiences to unannounced visitors," the butler replied haughtily.

"Then I suggest you go ahead and announce us," Holmes retorted, with great authority.

The middle-aged servant, no shrinking violet by the look of him, squinted at Holmes with suspicion. Eventually he told us to wait, and closed the door. There was something odd about the butler; I noted a certain weariness to his manner, and dark rings about his eyes that would rival Holmes's.

Some minutes passed before the door opened again, and the butler reappeared, this time with a haughtier aspect about him. He looked down his nose at us, and gestured formally for us to enter.

"You may wait here," the butler said, waving a hand towards a pair of benches in the large hallway. With that, he took to the stairs, before disappearing across the landing.

Holmes at once took the opportunity to examine the hall, and poked his head into the adjoining rooms. He made only the most cursory inspection, and I wondered if he had come to any private deduction in that short time, such was his great skill at observation.

He had just set foot on the great stairs, and their curiously threadbare carpet, and was looking at the family portraits that covered the walls, when a woman's voice sounded above us.

"Why, is it really the famous Sherlock Holmes? How thrilling!"

We looked up to see a slender, dark-haired woman in perhaps her middle twenties, wearing a casual gown of emerald green, an ostentatious string of pearls, and a flowing chiffon house-coat. For a moment I wondered if we were in the presence of Mina Harker, for she certainly fitted the description of the young woman from the Dracula Papers. And yet this lady was possessed of great confidence, a girlish exuberance, and less than the usual sense of propriety I would expect from a resident in such a house. She fair skipped down the stairs, her feet barely making a sound upon the treads, before giving a small curtsey.

"Mr Holmes," she said. "I am Genevieve Holmwood, Lady Godalming. And this must be Dr Watson." She turned to me and smiled. I confess she was a pretty thing, though my observation at the time was that, though she certainly had a youthful energy about her, she acted in a manner much younger than her years. Not only that, but there was an immodesty about the woman that made me rather ill at ease; I wondered if we had not entered the house of some hedonists. This naturally went unsaid, and I instead gave a small bow. "My lady," I said.

"Please, call me Genevieve, everybody does. Won't you come through to the drawing room and take tea?" She was already leading the way, picking up a small china bell from a hall table and ringing it as she went. "I'm afraid Art will take a while to make himself presentable, but you both must be tired and hungry if you came from London this morning. Mainwaring?" At the call, the butler appeared on the stairs.

"M'lady?"

"Bring tea. We shall be in the drawing room."

This room was dark and closed up, but Lady Godalming set about opening the curtains. At once, light streamed in through tall windows, though their unfavourable positioning caused dark shadows to gather in every corner of the room, hanging like cobwebs out of reach of the sun's touch. The fire was unmade and unlit, leaving the room a trifle chilly, and the room had the faint odour of stale tobacco smoke about it.

"Might I ask, Lady Godalming," Holmes said, "what ails his lordship?"

"Call me Genevieve," she said again. "And Art? He suffers dreadfully from nervous prostration. Ever since that awful business with Count Dracula."

"It must have been a… most trying time, all told."

"You needn't tread on eggshells around me, Mr Holmes." As if to illustrate her assertion she reclined languidly upon a chaise by the window, as though posing for a penny stereoscope or Parisian painter. I felt the colour rise to my cheeks, and found myself averting my eyes despite myself.

"I can see that," Holmes said, straight-faced.

"You are alluding to Art's former fiancée, the late Lucy Westenra, I suppose. Well, it is true, of course, one can never really recover from a loss like that. But I am here to pick up the pieces; I love him, and he me, and I give him the care he needs." A flicker of sadness crossed her flawless features, but evaporated in an instant.

"You are his nurse as well as his wife," Holmes said. It was not a question.

"A wife has many duties, Mr Holmes."

"Is Lord Godalming attended by a physician?"

"There is no need. Besides, some things require a more tender touch, don't you think?" There was something strange about her manner when she replied, but I could not decipher it.

Mainwaring returned, carrying a tray of tea. He placed it down, and Lady Godalming dismissed him. I saw Holmes scrutinising the butler closely as he left the room.

"I hear you do tricks, Mr Holmes."

"Tricks, Lady Godalming?"

"Call me Genevieve."

"I am sorry, Lady Godalming, but I would rather not. Over-familiarity can be a distraction in my business."

Some other expression played upon her features then. Annoyance, perhaps, and one I could empathise with after my own long association with Sherlock Holmes. But like her sadness, it was gone just as quickly, replaced by something more mischievous.

"Tricks," she repeated. "You can tell everything there is to know about people, just by looking at them."

"There is no trick, Lady Godalming. My method relies purely on observation, on things that most would discount as trifles. I make educated guesses, little else. Those guesses just happen to be right, most of the time."

"What can you tell of me, Mr Holmes?"

"I would not be so presumptuous."

"I insist." She darted to her feet and moved over to Holmes sinuously, like a cat approaching a canary.

"Holmes," I warned, sounding as cheerful as I could. I knew he would never turn down a challenge, but I also knew that he rarely shied away from telling the truth. In this case, I was not sure that would be wise—even I intuited a strange feeling about Genevieve Holmwood, and it was not altogether favourable.

"Very well." Holmes closed his eyes for a moment. When he opened them again, they were fixed on Lady Godalming's. "You are an ambitious young woman. You are well educated, and have certainly never been without comforts, though you were not born into great wealth. I expect you had an occupation once, and would not be surprised to learn that you worked in the theatre in some capacity. You have known Lord Godalming much longer than most people think, as you were acquainted with his late friend, the Texan Quincey Morris. Your reaction to that name tells me not only that I am right, but that you perhaps once harboured feelings for the brave Mr Morris. You are also acquainted with one Professor Abraham Van Helsing, who, if I am not mistaken, has visited here quite recently. Did he mention me, I wonder?"

"Why should he?" A look of indignation came over Lady Godalming, and then annoyance—probably at herself for confirming Holmes's last, rather wild speculation. Again, her expression cooled so swiftly it looked as though she had practised it. "Bravo, Mr Holmes. You are correct, on all but one point."

"Which is?"

"First tell me how you did it, and then I shall teach you how not to make the same mistake again."

I groaned inwardly, but Holmes merely smiled thinly and bowed. "Of course, my lady. I called you ambitious, a simple and obvious guess of a young woman who has risen so high up the social strata. You wear pearls even in the house, privately, because you are proud of them; they are a symbol of your achievements. I say you were not born into wealth and title, because a lady born would never curtsey to a lower-ranked gentleman, not even Sherlock Holmes, although it may well be a long-formed habit of an aspiring heiress out to impress. You are well educated, this is evident from your manner, but also by your bearing and enunciation. It is learned, not inherited; you have the measured step of a finishing-school girl, and a slight burr on the vowels that, though well disguised, I would take for Yorkshire, were I pressed. Your ability to mask your emotions, to project your voice, and your lightness of step, coupled with your confident bearing all suggest time spent on the stage, a fact confirmed to me by your hairstyling and make-up, which have evidently been administered without the aid of a lady's maid, and rather expertly, I might say. Added to that your tendency for fun and mild gossip would spring most naturally from evenings spent in the company of girls, doubtless in the chorus-line dressing room, and your unconventional ease of manner around gentlemen, particularly older ones, suggest that you have been used to patrons, directors, stage-hands and managers passing through that dressing room.

"I said that you knew Quincey P. Morris—I confess this was conjecture on my part, which was solely down to the fact that you call Lord Godalming 'Art' as, I believe, did the Texan. However, when you do so it is with a softening of the accent, almost in homage to the man. I overstretched when I suggested some deeper feeling, and for that I apologise; and yet your reaction, quickly covered with the guile of an actress, confirmed my speculations. Really, it was all quite straightforward."

"And Professor Van Helsing?" Lady Godalming said coolly.

"Given the professor's well-known fondness for your husband, and his equally well-known high opinion of his own abilities, he would allow no one else to attend to Lord Godalming, save perhaps Dr Seward, who is currently engaged at Purfleet Asylum. That, and the cigars in the ashtray over by the window, rather sloppily left by the maid this morning, would suggest he was here as recently as yesterday. The professor is known to smoke cigars; your husband doubtless would not in his present condition, and I doubt you are entertaining often with the house in its current out-of-season state. If you would be so kind, Lady Godalming," Holmes said, "would you educate me in the details I misread? My method relies on continual correction."

"You said I was in the chorus line, Mr Holmes—that does me a great disservice. During my time in the theatre I had my own dressing room, I'll have you know. I was, however, engaged as an artist's model for a time. Can't you tell? Aren't I just the very image of the Rokeby Venus?" She gave a sly wink in my direction, which I confess made me more uncomfortable than I already was, if that were possible. "Perhaps that is what accounts for my comfortable manner around gentlemen," she concluded.

I was relieved when there came a quiet knock at the door, and Mainwaring appeared.

"M'lady, his lordship is ready to receive our… guests."

"Good," Lady Godalming replied. "Then we had better go up, to see what tricks Sherlock Holmes can perform for poor Art."

Whatever I had expected to see upon meeting Lord Godalming, I could not have prepared myself. The Dracula Papers had painted a picture of a vigorous man who would now be but thirty years old, who had been on many adventures with the equally athletic Quincey Morris, and had played sports with Dr Seward. The fellow who lay now beneath an excessive number of bedclothes for the season, in a stuffy, panelled room reduced to almost total darkness by thick curtains, was a shadow of that portrayal. Arthur Holmwood was now every bit as frail as I had heard, and more besides. His skin had a ghastly pallor about it, his hair prematurely greying, and the purple bags beneath his eyes would give even Holmes's a run for their money. His forehead was beaded with sweat, and he appeared to find it a great exertion to do anything for himself. I confess to feeling a certain dread at approaching his bedside, for his pallid complexion, dark eyes and cracked red lips put me in mind of Mina Harker's description of the vampire count himself. The stench of sickliness hung about the room, barely masked by a faint floral odour, although I could see no flowers about.

Holmes perhaps saw my reticence to approach the sick-bed, and as a medical man I felt ashamed when he stepped forward boldly and bowed to the invalid peer.

"Lord Godalming, I am most pleased to make your acquaintance. My name is Sherlock Holmes and this is my associate Dr Watson. We are here to ask a few questions about a case we are investigating, and would be most appreciative if your lordship could assist us."

"Q… questions?" Lord Godalming's voice was a thin, papery rasp, a winter's breeze through a hollow. It was followed by a quiet, dry cough, as though the effort of speech was too much for him. I thought it quite possible that Lord Godalming was a victim to the same anaemia that had troubled his late fiancée.

"Mr Holmes is a detective, my darling," Lady Godalming said, her voice soft and melodic. "He is investigating… oh, that is curious, I rather forgot to ask. Just what are you investigating, Mr Holmes?" Her question was delivered with a flourish of rather insincere interest.

"The death, under mysterious circumstances, of one Lucy Westenra."

Holmes delivered this story with a straight face and cold eyes. Genevieve Holmwood's eyes widened just a little. It was almost all I could do not to cough and splutter at Holmes's sheer audacity— Lord Godalming, on the other hand, did exactly that, hacking and groaning like a man gasping for his last breath.

"Really, Mr Holmes," Lady Godalming said after an exasperated pause, "such a thing is not for my husband's ears at this time."

"Then whose ears are they for, my lady?" Holmes said, his barbed words oozing cordiality. "There are many details of my investigation that require clarification, and his lordship is the only man living who can provide the answers we seek."

Lady Godalming began to speak, but Holmes cut her off at once, addressing the bed-ridden viscount directly.

"Lord Godalming, I have read the Dracula Papers as part of my ongoing enquiries into the death of poor Miss Westenra, and I know that you loved the girl dearly. As such, I am certain you will want to help us as much as you are able."

"I… I…" Lord Godalming croaked, gasping for air. And then he ceased to struggle, and simply nodded.

"Thank you, my lord," Holmes said. "I understand that this is painful, but I would like to take you back to when you first met Professor Van Helsing at Lucy's bedside. Did it not strike you as odd that her family physician had not been consulted first?"

Lord Godalming seemed quite confused, but made a concerted effort to respond. "I… no. Jack…"

"Jack Seward?"

"Yes. Seward. He… vouched for the professor… as an expert."

"An expert in blood diseases?"

Lord Godalming nodded.

"In anaemia?"

"No. In more… unusual diseases."

"Ah, so, my lord, do you know whether or not Lucy Westenra was ever treated for any more commonplace condition. Say, anaemia?"

He shook his head.

"No she was not, or no, you do not know?" Holmes persisted.

"I… do not believe so. But why would she…" He stopped, shoulders sagging, struggling for breath. He appeared frustrated and upset in equal measure. "You cannot understand."

"Understand what? Vampires?" Holmes asked. "Or the vagaries of medical malpractice?"

"How dare you?" Genevieve said, though she lacked conviction, I thought. "Professor Van Helsing has been like a father to Art. Might I remind you that he is a respected professional?"

"Ah yes, a professional medical practitioner, and a professional lawyer, also," said Holmes. "Did the good professor have any hand in the legal affairs of the two Westenra women? By which, I mean Miss Lucy and her mother?"

"How would I know?"

"Lord Godalming?"

The man in the bed shrugged weakly. He looked as though he might faint.

"It is just that the legal circumstances surrounding the dissolution of the Westenra family's many holdings are most curious. That his lordship should benefit so richly from the will of the elder Mrs Westenra, when he and Lucy had not married, is of singular interest to a detective. I believe Mrs Westenra's solicitor, Mr Marquand, of Wholeman, Sons, Marquand & Lidderdale, expressed great concern over the transactional nature of the settlement. I suppose it was lucky for the 'Crew of Light' that they counted amongst their number a solicitor – Harker."

Lord Godalming began to cough incessantly. Genevieve Holmwood set her jaw and stared directly into Holmes's eyes.

"Mr Holmes, on this one occasion I will grace your impudence with a reply. Mr Marquand himself gave Professor Van Helsing his blessing, and agreed to his consent being published in the Dracula Papers, as I am sure you are well aware."

"Thank you for clarifying the matter, Lady Godalming," said Holmes. "Your testimony is most valuable, given that Professor Van Helsing saw fit to confiscate the legal documents. Thankfully, you are remarkably well informed considering the delicate, private nature of the proceedings." Holmes smiled—his audacity never ceased to amaze me. His display of insincere charm was worthy of the stage.

During the exchange, Lord Godalming's coughing had increased in severity and regularity, and Lady Godalming had made no move towards him. With no servants on hand, I went to his side.

"This man should be in a hospital," I said.

"Impossible. Art is in no state to travel," Lady Godalming said. "Besides, Professor Van Helsing assures me he is on the mend."

"On the mend?" I asked, exasperated. "What exactly is the professor's diagnosis?"

"Oh, it is far too complicated for me to understand. Some nervous disorder due to the great constitutional shock poor Art received at the hands of Count Dracula."

I stood upright. It sounded to me like quackery, and I saw the look in Holmes's eyes clearly. I knew I had his support.

"That, my lady, is impossible," I said. "The first thing this man needs is good clean air."

I marched at once to the window, aware that Lady Godalming had begun to protest, and that her husband had become rather distressed. I pulled the curtains aside, allowing light to stream into the room. I stopped in disbelief even as Lord Godalming's piteous cries and his wife's angry rebuke reached my ears.

The great sash windows were fastened shut with large iron nails, and hanging from the frames were dozens of posies of dried garlic flowers. I turned to face the viscount and his wife.

Lord Godalming had almost fallen from the bed, and was shielding his eyes from the sun. Lady Godalming ran to his side, and then fixed me with a look of fury.

"Get out!" she cried. "Both of you—get out!"

The door opened and the butler entered. He ushered us from the room. I could tell at once that the man was eager to frog-march us bodily from the house, but it was not necessary. Holmes strode along the corridor and down the stairs, but stopped abruptly on the lower landing. He looked up at the portraits that lined the wall, studying them intently.

The butler was clearly considering wrestling Holmes down the stairs when his mistress flew from the bedroom, appearing on the landing above us.

"Didn't you hear me?" she screeched, her accent slipping into what Holmes had astutely recognised as a northern one. "Get out!"

"Well, a fine result," I grumbled as our carriage moved off down the gravel drive. "I half expect to find us ruined by morning. I wonder,

Holmes, if we might have gleaned more had you not earlier insulted Lady Godalming with your… indelicate observations." I was still bristling from the manner of our exit from Ring, while Holmes simply assumed a demeanour of relaxation, leaning back in his seat and lighting a cigarette; his nonchalance was infuriating.

"Indelicate?" Holmes appeared amused. "Watson, if I were being indelicate I would not have masked my deductions with falsehoods. I should have told her the true observations I had made."

"Which were?"

"That a woman who would greet two strange gentlemen with no appointment, in person, while wearing nothing but a casual dress and a house-coat is no lady born. She had time to prepare for us; no lady would feel obliged to meet us in such a fluster, and the butler could have simply instructed us to wait. Her attire and manner were chosen very carefully for our benefit. Second, the hint of Yorkshire accent I detected in her voice is particular to the coastal towns of Whitby and Scarborough. This leads me to believe that she not only knew of Miss Lucy Westenra, but possibly met her during Lord Godalming's courtship of the deceased lady. I would have said that there were two cigars in that ashtray, one of which had the faintest trace of pomade upon it, and was undoubtedly smoked by Lady Godalming—a rather unladylike habit, probably picked up from her association with Quincey Morris—and that the reason Van Helsing's cigar was still in the ashtray was because the house is in ruin, bereft of servants. There was not even a maid-of-all-work present to clear the ashtrays, open the curtains, air the room or light the fires. When we arrived, no groom was on hand to see to our carriage. The butler himself greeted us at the door, rather than the footman, and that same butler served us tea."

Holmes took a long, imperious draw on his cigarette to indicate that he was done, and doubtless most pleased with himself to boot. I would have challenged him, perhaps due to some misplaced impulsion to defend Lady Godalming's virtue, but I thought better of it. I had noticed the woman's brazen manner from the moment I'd laid eyes on her—how could I have failed to? And the lack of servants had played on my mind since we had arrived at Ring. When Holmes stated it, it was like scales had fallen from my eyes.

"How can they be so poor if they have seized the Westenra estate?" I asked. "Unless they have sent all the servants away in order to conceal their collusion with Van Helsing."

"Van Helsing has been exonerated, nay, honoured, Watson. No subterfuge from mere servants would be necessary. There are no servants here because they are destitute."

"Holmes, how can that be? This house is palatial! The Westenra estate at Hillingham is worth a fortune in itself."

"Arthur Holmwood would have inherited Ring regardless of any criminal act. But the facts speak for themselves. The lack of servants, the threadbare carpets in the hall, the missing silverware in the drawing room as evidenced by marks in the dust upon the sideboard. I put to you, Watson, that Lord Godalming does not own the Westenra estate any longer."

"Sold? But then where did the profits go? Is the family in such debt?"

"Watson, though I laud you for staying clear of the gossip columns and keeping your mind on higher endeavours, sometimes I do wish you would keep your eyes and ears open. No, if the Holmwoods carried debts of such magnitude, someone in society would have heard of it. They survive on the income of Ring's great estate, but a wretched survival it has become. With her husband in a poor state of mind, and only a skeleton staff at their disposal, Lady Godalming must rely on someone to keep their affairs in order, for she is certainly unused to the many trials of running such a household. There is one man, close to Lord Godalming, who I am sure is only too happy to take care of matters."

"Van Helsing?"

"If Van Helsing is not the direct beneficiary of this scheme, he is certainly involved."

"Then Van Helsing is taking advantage of their misfortune?"

"You say 'their' misfortune, Watson. Surely you do not think Genevieve Holmwood an innocent party?"

"It is crass to slur a young woman so, Holmes, simply for marrying above her station."

"Oh, I do Lady Godalming no such injustice, Watson. There is far more to her than that. She took us—strangers both—to the bedside of her sick and troubled husband, so that we could see for ourselves the fear in which he lives; to convince us that the things of which he is afraid are very real, at least to him. But did you note the most important detail when she came to greet us?"

I wracked my brains, but in the end I could think of nothing.

"Of course not, for I suspect her attempt at distraction worked a charm upon you. She did not ask us why we had come, Watson."

CHAPTER FIVE

A TELEGRAM

*Genevieve Holmwood, Lady Godalming,
to Professor Abraham Van Helsing,
10 April 1894*

The detective has been and gone. He
asked of you a lot, but I played my
part beautifully. G.

CHAPTER SIX

A BATTLE OF WITS

"So what now, Holmes?" I asked. Holmes had been pacing back and forth so much I worried that he would wear a hole in the hearth-rug.

"Hmm?" As was so often the case, Holmes was so deep in thought that he barely acknowledged my presence, let alone my question.

I shuffled through the Dracula Papers, which I had been reading again. "I expect we shall need to interview the Harkers," I said. "Perhaps we should find the girl that Inspector Cotford mentioned. Kate something-or-other? Although I am tired of all this sneaking around, Holmes."

"Sneaking around?" Holmes stopped pacing. "Whatever do you mean, Watson?"

"I mean that the full weight of suspicion clearly falls upon Professor Van Helsing. You obviously believe him to be involved in some great conspiracy, though I cannot tell what that might be—it all seems a rather elaborate and dangerous way to obtain property. Regardless, Van Helsing is not a million miles away. According to the newspapers he is here, in London; I do not understand why we don't just find him and get the measure of the man."

"Sometimes, Watson, I do believe the consistent simplicity of your approach is the very making of our little enterprise."

"Thank you… I think."

"Don't mention it. Our tip-toeing around has not been in vain, old fellow. Indeed, it has provided us with a great deal of information about the professor and his wiles."

"It has?"

"Oh, indubitably. If Van Helsing is half as clever as we are led to believe, then he is already aware of our involvement—and if I was wrong about that before, I am sure Lady Godalming would have warned him of our investigation by now."

"What makes you so sure?" I asked.

"If she is not in league with the man, then she is at least a friend to him. To that end, I engineered the situation so that she would feel compelled to contact Van Helsing even were she not in his employ. I made certain to disparage Van Helsing's good name, while encouraging you to cast doubt upon his medical expertise."

"Well, I wouldn't say—"

"Don't be modest, old fellow," Holmes went on, before I could say that I meant no disrespect at all to a fellow practitioner. "Professor Abraham Van Helsing must surely now be following one of three possible courses of action."

"Oh?"

"He will either be gathering intelligence to use against us, making arrangements to flee, or, if he is innocent, preparing to defend his honour against any accusations that may come his way."

"But what accusations, Holmes? We have the word of Mr Cotford, a disgraced former policeman who is now an inveterate drunk. We have some papers that may have been misplaced, but which you obviously think were suppressed somehow… Perhaps there's an argument that he has defrauded Lord Godalming, though there is no evidence. Do you think he killed Miss Westenra? Is that it?"

"You're right, Watson, of course. We are lacking hard evidence, but have faith that it shall come. We have no body to examine, no crime scene to scrutinise. We have simply the details of a fantastic tale, already concluded, and an insinuation of guilt. However, you must look deeper. There are numerous crimes detailed in the Dracula Papers, not all of which may at first be apparent to the untrained eye. If Van Helsing is not responsible for them, I would stake my reputation that he is intimately involved. Mycroft must believe it also, or why involve us at all? To believe otherwise is to believe in the existence of vampires, and that, Watson, is absurd."

I frowned, for Holmes appeared for a moment to be far from himself. I half wondered if Frank Cotford's little witch-hunt against Van Helsing had not influenced my friend's thinking unduly. "Very well, Holmes, let's say you are correct. And if he flees the country? If you really believe Van Helsing to be guilty of some crime, then surely our delay can only work in his favour."

To my surprise, Holmes seemed to consider this. He took one more draw on his pipe, and sat down in his armchair before replying.

"Watson, the Dracula Papers give me a singular impression of Professor Van Helsing—the impression of a man absolutely assured of his own genius, who has taken great pains to cover his tracks and produced a dazzling, nigh-impenetrable story to do so. Such a man would not run from us, even if my modest reputation were brought to his attention. No, such a man would look us in the eye and scorn us, and that is what I am waiting for. Each moment we hesitate before confronting him is a moment for his confidence to grow, and our case to build, do you see?"

"You think he will make some mistake that will cast doubt on his character?" I asked.

"Perhaps, though I do not underestimate him one jot. More likely, he will soon move against us."

Holmes spoke so gravely that I felt my chest tighten. I thought of the tales of the vampire count, draining blood from his victims. I thought of the ghastly visage of Lord Godalming, so recently a man of vigour and adventure. I wondered if Van Helsing had been responsible for the horrendous crimes discussed in the Dracula Papers, and did not relish becoming an enemy of such a man.

"What makes you so sure of this?" I asked.

"Because Van Helsing, by reputation at least, rather reminds me of another professor with whom I played a deadly game not too long ago," Holmes responded, somewhat distantly.

The thought of Moriarty had not been far from my mind during the past day. I loosened my collar as Holmes spoke of his old nemesis.

"You think it will come to that?" I asked, somewhat hoarsely. I remembered all too well my time without Holmes, believing he was dead at Moriarty's hands.

"If we allow it," Holmes replied, wistful and almost sad. His melancholy passed abruptly, and invigorated by some train of thought perhaps, he leapt from his chair. "Watson, you are right, of course. If I have learned one thing from my time abroad, it is that dancing with the devil is not a task for those faint of heart. We shall pay a visit to the professor this very evening and get the measure of the man."

"Tonight? I…"

"Tonight! Now, Watson, I need to think. I am sure you need to make yourself ready. Be sure to pack a small case with a change of clothes for dinner; there's an excellent fellow."

And with no further word, Holmes exchanged his brier for his violin, and began to play.

* * *

We arrived at Carfax shortly before dusk. It was a larger property than I had imagined, and grander, too. Perhaps it was testament to the change in tenancy, but the house was not quite the gloomy, tumbledown pile that had been described in the Dracula Papers. It was, however, clearly unoccupied.

Holmes and I had left our cabbie waiting at the road, and traversed the drive on foot. The gardens were large and tree-lined, and the house sizable and square, its tall mullioned windows and whitewashed walls a testament to early Georgian design. Though a high wall surrounded the property, and ivy clung to the north face of the house, there was none of the haunting gloom that we had expected.

"It appears no one is home," I said.

"Of course not, Watson. The renovation of Carfax is not quite complete, and Van Helsing divides his time between this house and an apartment at the Savoy. Besides that, tonight he has an invitation to a Royal Society gala, which I am certain he will attend. Again, I must remind you of the value of reading those inches of society columns."

I sighed. "You knew all that, and yet you still brought us out here? For what purpose, Holmes?"

"Knowing that the professor is not at home, and that the house is unlikely to be staffed at present due to its state of disrepair, I decided this would be a good time to reconnoitre the lair of the enemy."

I recalled from the Dracula Papers that the hunters came to Carfax on the trail of the Count, and broke in. They found only Dracula's coffins, filled with Transylvanian earth.

"You don't mean us to force entry into the man's house, do you, Holmes? There is absolutely no legal recourse for us to—"

Holmes raised a hand to silence me. "Of course not, my dear fellow. I mean only to explore the lay of the land, and to follow in the footsteps of another character from our fanciful tale of Dracula."

"Another? Who—"

Before I could finish, Holmes had bounded across a sheltered lawn, his long, thin legs carrying him in great strides, until he reached a boundary wall covered in aged honeysuckle. Even as I rushed to follow, Holmes was up and over the wall, leaving me agog at my friend's sudden wellspring of energy.

For a moment I stood alone, in the dark shadow of Carfax, uncertain what I should do. Then from above me came the scuffing of boots and the scuttling of loose mortar, and Holmes appeared, offering his hand over the wall.

"Come on, Watson, no time to dawdle."

In a trice I was hoisted upwards, and as I swung my legs over the aged capstones I saw the object of Holmes's little jaunt. Ahead of us, across a wide lawn and expansive courtyard, was Purfleet Asylum.

I dropped down beside Holmes, who was skulking behind the bushes in a most ungentlemanly fashion.

"Really, Holmes, if you wanted to see Dr Seward I am sure you could have just made an appointment."

"I do not want to see Dr Seward, Watson. I want to see how the lunatic, Renfield, so easily managed to escape the asylum and enter the grounds of Carfax on more than one occasion. And now we do see."

"I agree; it's hardly the most secure perimeter to contain such dangerous patients."

"The fact that the wall still has not been raised, or a more secure fence installed, begs an interesting question. Are the inmates of Purfleet Asylum really as dangerous as Dr Seward stated? Or rather, was it just the one inmate who was dangerous?"

"Does it matter?" I grumbled, dusting off my trousers.

"Of course it matters," said Holmes. "If this asylum is one of the strictest security, then not only would Renfield's escape have been implausible, but this wall would be considerably higher for the sake of the general public. If, on the other hand, the asylum is designed to accommodate only those lunatics who pose no great threat, then why was Renfield here at all? Here is a man severely disturbed and possessed of great physical strength. And yet he was so poorly guarded that he could flee his cell, wound an orderly and pass through the hospital corridors, before escaping through the—presumably locked—doors?"

"Seward as good as admits in his diary that it was his own hubris that was to blame," I reasoned. "That he was so fascinated by Renfield as a case study that he allowed himself to become remiss in his duties."

"But of course, Dr Seward was not the only doctor on the staff. Could he have been so negligent without his fellows noticing?"

"You're right, Holmes. There was another doctor mentioned— Irish-sounding fellow. Hennessey?"

"I think you're right, Watson. I tell you something, this Dr Seward really does hold together so many parts of our puzzle. He knew both Van Helsing and Lucy Westenra separately. He coincidentally operates an asylum contiguous with a property bought by Count Dracula. Dracula could not possibly have known Lucy, could he? And yet when he first arrived in England it was to her he went, in distant Whitby. Van Helsing then pointed the finger of blame at Dracula. And then—"

"And then Seward convinced Renfield that the object of his ravings was Dracula," I said, thinking of the man's tragic end. "If Renfield believed that Count Dracula was the imaginary 'master' he both worshipped and feared, then learning, even accidentally, that the Count was moving in next door would surely have intensified his delusions."

"A first-class deduction, Watson! A more believable scenario than the one presented to us, don't you think? And although I am certain Seward or the professor would wave away your theory with talk of psychic suggestion and other such esoteric notions, it is a sequence of events I am partial to investigate. When next we return here, it will be to speak with Seward directly, but that can wait. It is with his mentor that we have business tonight. You brought a change of clothes, as I suggested?"

"Why, yes, Holmes."

"Very good. Our next stop is the Royal Society, and we can't very well go there with Purfleet dirt all over our suits, can we?"

How Holmes managed to secure our admittance to the exclusive Royal Society gala I do not know, but I would hazard a guess that his brother was involved. The event was an exclusive one, open only to fellows, patrons and esteemed guests drawn from the upper echelons of society, academia and government. And now, of course, myself and Mr Sherlock Holmes.

The great vaulted hall of New Burlington House fair fizzed with life and light. Sage, white-haired scientists mixed with titled dilettantes, powerful financiers, members of Parliament and even royalty. Twice I almost walked into a guest as I fumbled my way through the crowd in pursuit of Holmes, and twice I was stunned upon looking up: the first time to recognise the Queen's personal physician, and the second time a princess. Holmes himself had no trouble gliding through the assemblage as though born to such functions.

When I caught up with him, Holmes was engaged in conversation with the baronet Sir Maugham Jarsdel and his wife, who I recognised as former clients from the strange case of the Elgar rosette. It could be said that their continued influence in society was in part due to Holmes's success in resolving that rather scandalous affair, and the pair greeted me warmly as I approached.

"Ah, Dr Watson, so good to see you well. Mr Holmes was just saying that you were looking for an introduction to Professor Van Helsing. Well, look no further—we have had the pleasure of making his acquaintance, and would be only too pleased to introduce you."

"You are too kind, Sir Maugham," I said.

"Then do follow us, Doctor," said Lady Jarsdel, "and we shall see what we can do."

The couple led us through the hall, pausing at intervals to greet other acquaintances, before entering a great chamber off to the side of the main gathering. The room was decked out ready for a dinner address, with a dozen or so large round tables set out before a stage, complete with an almost ecclesiastical pulpit beneath a Gothic arched ceiling. The room was less crowded than the hall, but a fair number of people—mostly older gentlemen— were gathered. These, I guessed, were fellows of the Royal Society, and at the sight of a few familiar faces from the scientific community I felt singularly out of my depth.

"Don't worry, Watson," whispered Holmes. "Let me do the talking."

I had planned to do nothing else, although I confess to feeling some trepidation as a small press of guests parted before Sir Maugham and Lady Jarsdel to reveal our first glimpse of Professor Abraham Van Helsing.

He was unmistakeable both from the physical description we had read in the Dracula Papers, and the barking, heavily accented tone of his voice that cut through the air as we drew near. He was not a tall man, but a formidable-looking one, broad of shoulder and square of jaw, with tufty, reddish hair flecked with silver-grey, and bushy brows over intense blue eyes. As he held court over the small group, he puffed on a cigar, marking his frequent gesticulations with trails of smoke.

"And this, gentlemen," Van Helsing was saying, "is how we are knowing the fundamental truths, that so-maligned metaphysical influences may exert dominion not only over the flesh, but over the very soul. The nature of the human being is a thing fragile, no? If we to the left or to the right stray from the path of righteousness, we risk more than just the health. *Mein Gott*, we risk all, as my friends most dear risked all."

The men standing about the professor nodded in agreement, though it was hard to tell what they made of Van Helsing's strange beliefs. As we came into their company, Van Helsing's dark blue eyes fixed first upon me, and then upon Holmes. If he knew who we were, he showed no sign whatsoever.

"Professor Van Helsing," Lady Jarsdel said, holding out a hand, which Van Helsing took and kissed gently.

"Dear lady, welcome," he said, and then shook Sir Maugham by the hand in turn.

"We come to introduce an old friend, Professor. This is Dr John Watson, who has been dying to meet you."

Van Helsing's gaze turned upon me, so impassive that I almost fumbled my lines.

"Indeed, Professor," I managed. "It is a singular honour."

"The honour is mine," he said, in his thickly accented voice. "I see that you are a man most practical, Doctor, and from your bearing perhaps a military man also?"

"For my sins," I said.

"We all of us should be thankful to our soldiers, no? And our soldiers, they are thankful for their doctors. For too many years my work has taken place in the lecture theatre, in the laboratory, and in the library. Respect must always be given to the practitioner, he who help the patient every day, in the office, on the battlefield." He cast his eyes to Sherlock Holmes, and any warmth that had crept into his expression as he had addressed me now drained away. "And this man—wait, tell me not. He look upon me as if to make a study. I recognise that look, for it is the one I deliver myself to the enigma. This man, he is no physician, but a man of science, certainly. Or a policeman? Yet no mere policeman would be here at the Royal Society, and in company with the good doctor here. Wait! I have it. What a fool I have been not to see, that the great Sherlock Holmes is here."

This drew approving laughter from the group. Holmes smiled his thinnest smile and bowed his head to his adversary.

"A magnificent deduction," said Holmes. "It is almost as though you knew we were coming."

"Ah, but the deduction is a child's play, Mr Holmes. Observation, supposition… mere guessing games. It is science, yes, but a poor science that seek always to unlock a mystery of circumstance, never the mystery of existence. It is to the greater problems that the finest minds turn always their attention."

I looked uncertainly at Holmes. To the casual observer, Van Helsing was merely espousing some philosophical argument. To anyone who knew Holmes as I did, however, it would be obvious that the professor had just given the great detective the gravest possible insult.

"It is a matter of science that I had hoped to discuss, Professor," Holmes said, seemingly unruffled. "If you could spare us a few moments I would be most grateful."

"Mr Holmes, the dinner it begin soon, and I speak to these good people after that. Time is the thing most short at present."

"That is a pity, for it concerns a mutual friend, and one of your patients, or so I believe. I hate to be the bearer of bad news, but I must inform you that Lord Godalming has taken a turn for the worse."

Lady Jarsdel and her husband looked concerned. Van Helsing's large eyes narrowed a fraction.

"I am sure it is nothing," he said with a smile, addressing the guests around us as much as Holmes. "An effect of the illness most unfortunate, but one that I instruct Lady Godalming how to treat. But if it concern you so much, Mr Sherlock Holmes, I give you five minutes. Gentlemen, my lady, please to excuse us for a moment."

We withdrew to the edge of the room near the service door, while the rest of Van Helsing's associates left us to some scant privacy.

"Professor Van Helsing," Holmes began, "your reputation precedes you, and as such I am loath to question your judgement. But do you think it wise to leave Lord Godalming unattended by any physician while he is in such fragile health?"

"Arthur is attended by me, Mr Holmes, and he need no other physician while Van Helsing draw his breath. I know what is best."

"That's as may be, Professor, though Dr Watson here would beg to differ. Isn't that right, Watson?"

That rather put me on the spot, but having seen Lord Godalming's condition, my dander was sufficiently risen for me to question Van Helsing's assessment of his patient. "That is correct. The idea that shock could account for Lord Godalming's present condition is outdated thinking. Why, the man should be—"

"Tested for anaemia," Van Helsing interrupted. "You do a disservice to me, Dr John Watson, and I think you are not so much a follower of my teachings, as Mr Holmes suggest, no? As you both are aware, my expertise—gathered upon a lifetime of study—is in the field of exotic and what you call metaphysical disease. These diseases are the so-rare killers of men, that even your Royal Society are knowing nothing of. I come to educate them, Dr Watson, to remove from their minds the cloud of ignorance. But ask to yourself: if these men so wise cannot accept the facts of the world beyond their five senses, what chance does a poor woman have? A woman like Genevieve Holmwood."

"Are you suggesting that Lord Godalming's condition is caused by some… supernatural means?" I asked.

"If you have read the papers I have put before your courts, which I assume you have, how could you doubt it?"

"He sits in darkness, his windows nailed shut, and garlic flowers hang in his windows. The Count is dead. Did his evil not die with him?"

"These so-simple methods of protection comfort Arthur, and that is enough. He fight not for his life, but for his soul, for even with the destruction of that great monster, Count Dracula, there is evil abroad. Evil in the very blood!"

"And Lady Godalming does not understand that her husband's immortal soul is at risk?" Holmes asked.

"I tell her not these things," said Van Helsing. "She is but one spark of light in his dark life, and it is her spirits most high that provide to Arthur the comfort he need."

"It seems unlike you, Professor, to do such a disservice to a woman who, in my opinion, is most strong of character. I have read the Dracula Papers, as you guess, and in that tragic tale did you not take women of similar presence into your confidence?"

"Similar? *Nein!* There is only one woman in the tale of Count Dracula who I would have trust with such knowledge as this."

"Wilhelmina Harker," Holmes stated.

"A woman such as Mina could have helped Arthur more, perhaps," Van Helsing said, somewhat wistfully. "I love Mina like a daughter, and Arthur like my son so long-lost. Alas, their paths are separate, Mr Holmes. Mina has a duty to her own husband. My dear Arthur has the sweet girl Genevieve to care for him, and she needs more help than Mina. Do not fear for Arthur Holmwood,

Mr Holmes, for he is one of my company, and he has friends still who will provide that help."

A slight frown crossed Holmes's features. I found Van Helsing's words puzzling, but if there was one thing I had gleaned from the Dracula Papers, it was that the Dutchman was eccentric and rambling.

"Professor," I interrupted. "Forgive me, but as a medical man I wish only to understand. You say it is a metaphysical disease, but what exactly is it that ails Lord Godalming?"

"Ah, there is the question that lead perhaps to wisdom, if you so allow," Van Helsing said. "But for now, I have not the time to explain, for you are not ready to understand. One day, God willing, you shall, and perhaps sooner than you think."

"Professor," said Holmes. "Watson here, I am sure, would be fascinated to study your methods one day, but I have methods of my own. Methods that I am obliged to employ in the solving of a most perplexing mystery."

"Mystery? Please to tell me, Mr Holmes, what your elementary methods are failing to find." Van Helsing gave a patronising chuckle.

"Just that a certain Lucy Westenra could not have met her end in the way that you described in the Dracula Papers. Which rather begs the question: how did she die?"

"You dismiss the truth out of the hand, Mr Holmes. Why? Because your mind is filled with your so-small world of deduction that you neither see nor feel what stare you in the face."

"As you may or may not have heard, Professor, while you were tangling with your alleged vampire, I was myself 'dead', for all intents and purposes. While walking that twilit path between life and death, I discovered many transgressions against justice, and witnessed many things that lesser men might consider 'supernatural'. But all of them—every one—could be resolved through rational deduction as the work of men."

"And you expect, Mr Holmes, that you are to uncover some injustice here? Some plot that your great detective brain can unpick?" Van Helsing took a heavy draw upon his cigar.

"In my experience, where there is true villainy, there is also overconfidence. Many of my opponents have underestimated my methods, Professor Van Helsing, and few of them have escaped justice. To underestimate one's opponent is the gravest mistake one can make in the fight between good and evil."

"Ha! Then at least we are agreed that there is a thing such as good, and a thing such as evil. But it is you who is sounding overconfident, Mr Holmes. You would do well to taking your own advice, I think."

"I shall instead, for the time being, heed the advice of the estimable society in which we now find ourselves," Holmes replied, raising a hand towards the podium. There on the ceiling, emblazoned in gold lettering upon a classical mural, was the motto of the Royal Society. *Nullius in verba*: "Take nobody's word for it."

Van Helsing stared for a moment, and then chuckled. He held out his hand, and Holmes shook it firmly. Van Helsing leaned in, and muttered coolly, "Mind your step, Mr Holmes. When one has used his luck as you have, extra care must be taken."

"In my experience, Professor, there is no such thing as luck. We merely play the odds, and the best man wins."

Van Helsing nodded and stepped back. "Then I am forward-looking to the commencement of our game. Do let me know when you are starting, hey? Now, Mr Holmes—Dr Watson—you must be excusing me."

With that, Professor Van Helsing was gone.

"Well, Holmes, that was a tricky dance and no mistake," I said. "Should we stay for his speech and see if we can spot any of his associates?"

"No, Watson. I doubt very much he would collude with

anyone of interest in so public a place, and we cannot follow him closely while he is so on his guard. We have learned everything we can this evening."

"I'm not sure we learned much at all."

"Nonsense, Watson, we learned a very great deal. For instance, we have confirmed that Van Helsing—despite his name—is most certainly not Dutch, but German."

"I don't see how you come to that conclusion, Holmes," I said. "He uses German phrases when excited, yes, but many Dutchmen are fluent in German, and the two languages are not so very different."

"To the untrained ear, Watson, correct. It is not the words he uses, but the ordering of them. When I read the Dracula Papers, I thought perhaps Seward was mocking his old teacher when recounting his words in such a strange fashion, but now I see that Dr Seward recorded his mentor quite accurately. You see, the Dutch language may be closely related to German, but its construction has more in common with English. A Dutchman would not make so many grammatical errors when speaking English—indeed, he would have to go out of his way to do so. If that were not proof enough, I noted the very particular odour of his German cigars just now—a brand that is uncommon here in London due to the great expense of importing them."

"Very well, but I don't see the significance," I replied.

"Nor do I," said Holmes. "But I shall."

"So what now? I suppose it's too late to dine…"

"Not at all, I have already secured us a table at the Café Royal—we will need to be quick if we are to make it. Thankfully we are already dressed for dinner."

"You mean to say you planned the exchange down to the minute?"

"May we press on, Watson? I would rather not be late, for we have another early start tomorrow."

I sighed heavily. I had been hoping to arrange a few appointments for my patients the next day; they had been rather neglected of late. "Where to this time?" I asked.

"Exeter," Holmes said, already turning back to the main hall as the Royal Society guests began to file in for dinner. "If our man has a close accomplice, I believe I now know their identity."

CHAPTER SEVEN

THE HARKERS

"If I may say, Mr Harker, it is a testament to your faithfulness that the name of your former employer, Mr Hawkins, still hangs above the door." Holmes beamed as he shook the hand of Jonathan Harker, whose greying temples and furrowed brow looked out of place on a man who should by rights be in his prime.

Harker nodded, somewhat gingerly, and walked around the large desk of his office, taking a seat and, as an afterthought, waving a hand indicating we should do the same.

"You are lucky to find me unengaged, Mr Holmes. It is a long way to come without a prior appointment." His voice was thin; like Arthur Holmwood, it appeared to me that Harker was in poor health. Given the many trials he had endured as described in the Dracula Papers, that was perhaps understandable.

"Of course it is, Mr Harker. I realised that error already this morning, when I called at your home and found it uninhabited."

The wrinkles upon Harker's brow deepened. "My home? Then am I to assume this is not a business matter?"

"Oh, it is certainly business to me," said Holmes. "But it is not the business of your firm. Trust me when I say it is a matter of utmost seriousness upon which I call. I had rather hoped to speak with both you and Mrs Harker—tell me, would it be convenient to do so today?"

Harker's hands trembled a little at Holmes's words and, noticing this, he pressed his palms upon the leather inlay of his desk to quell the shaking.

"My wife is visiting an old friend in the north, and will be unavailable for a week or more. But this all sounds rather serious—should I be worried?" He tried to offer a reassuring smile to make light of the situation, though it was a feeble attempt.

"You say your wife is in the north," Holmes said, avoiding the question entirely. "Surely she has not returned to Whitby, home of so many painful memories?"

Harker hesitated, his thought processes writ large across his features. "She has, as it happens," he said eventually. "You could call it a pilgrimage, I suppose. With the court ruling in our favour, and that dreadful business put behind us, she has gone to… make her peace."

"A strange choice of words—'make her peace'. Lucy Westenra, rest her soul, was killed in London. What is left to do in Whitby?"

"I…" Harker paused, and sighed. He stood, looking more frail now than I had previously noticed, and went to gaze out of the office window. "Mina wanted to see the place where she and Lucy stayed, one last time, and help set Lucy's affairs in order."

"And what of Hillingham, Mr Harker?" Holmes asked. "Would your wife's time not be better spent assisting your good friend Lord Godalming with the affairs at the Westenra estate?"

A tremble again—Harker did not turn to face us when he replied. "No, Mr Holmes. We own Hillingham now, although I doubt we shall keep it. It's all above board, I assure you."

I saw the twitch of Holmes's lip as he clicked another piece of the puzzle into place. I myself was taken aback that the Harkers—who less than a year prior had been hard-working people of middling income—now had considerable wealth in property, and enjoyed a status surely beyond their imaginings.

"Why should I think otherwise? But it is a generous gift for Lord Godalming to give, considering his… predicament."

At that, Harker turned to us, his face pale. "Predicament?"

"You must be aware, given your great bond of fellowship… why, Arthur Holmwood is gravely ill, and his finances are in a parlous state. It would seem that the inheritance of Lucy Westenra's property would have been exactly what he needed to maintain the legacy of Ring, and yet he gives one such property to his good friends the Harkers. Truly he is a big-hearted man."

"Arthur is… the very best of men," Harker replied. He stumbled awkwardly, resting his hand upon the back of his chair. I thought perhaps he might faint, and stood to assist him. He waved me away at once. "Mr Holmes, why are you here?"

"A perfectly reasonable question, Mr Harker. The Dracula Papers, which I and Dr Watson here have read, contain details of a number of deaths, some apparently at the hands of a Transylvanian vampire. The highest court in the land appears ready to accept these papers as truth. I, however, am less inclined to accept them, for one very simple reason."

"Oh?"

"I do not believe in vampires."

Harker stared at Holmes, beads of perspiration forming upon his brow.

"So who do you propose killed my friend Quincey Morris?" he asked at last, setting his jaw firm, though the quaver in his voice betrayed the steel in his eyes.

"Gypsies, as stated in the papers," Holmes said, quick as a flash.

"Controlled by the Count!"

"As you please."

"And the lunatic, Renfield?"

"Unknown. We have only one man's word for those mysterious circumstances."

"The word of a respected and eminent professor," Harker snapped.

"Again, as you please."

"And—and dear Lucy?"

"I am glad you asked that question, above all others, Mr Harker. For I believe that, should I find the true cause of Lucy Westenra's death, I shall solve this perplexing case once and for all."

"There is no case to solve!" Harker snapped. "Lucy was… taken. By the Count. He… he—"

"Transformed her into a vampiress, according to Van Helsing—who stalked Highgate Cemetery until you and your friends cornered her in a tomb and cut off her head. Yes, I read that also. If you bear in mind what I told you, Mr Harker, that I do not believe in vampires, then either Lucy was not the woman walking about Highgate, or she was not dead when she was entombed. In the latter case, we have written accounts from your fellows that it was most assuredly not Dracula who cut off her head."

Harker's mouth worked noiselessly—Holmes was pressing him, perhaps more than he could bear. How the man managed to run a law firm when his wits appeared so frayed was beyond me.

Holmes went on, "Of course, Miss Westenra's legal affairs were so tightly controlled that not only did her property fall under control of her fiancé upon her death, but all other legal claims. There is no chance to exhume the body of the deceased—"

"Exhume the… Are you mad?"

"—Without the permission of Lord Godalming," Holmes went on, ignoring the now frantic-looking solicitor, "which I doubt very much he will give. And so I take it upon myself to gather such evidence that will rather force the hand of the authorities on the matter. I suppose, Mr Harker, that the deaths of the elder Mrs Westenra, and of the late Peter Hawkins of this very firm, were also wrought by this Dracula's hand?"

"No… Look here, what are you saying?"

"I am saying that those two deaths in particular proved most beneficial for several members of your little fellowship. Arthur Holmwood, and yourself, principally."

"How dare you?" Harker's eyes blazed, but his words again lacked conviction. He clutched the back of his chair tightly. I became at once concerned for Harker's mental and physical state. Holmes's questioning was of the hard kind that he so often reserved for low criminals and scurrilous blackmailers. Harker did not fit that description by any stretch of the imagination.

Holmes shrugged. "I simply state facts. If my investigations uncover evidence that Count Dracula was indeed behind this string of unfortunate events, then I shall offer you a full and sincere apology for any distress I may have caused you. I hold no vendetta, Mr Harker, I simply wish to satisfy myself that no wrongdoing has occurred."

"If you had seen the things I had seen…" Harker said, somewhat distantly, and now he did retake his seat.

"Ah, yes. In Transylvania. I understand you were kept prisoner in Castle Dracula for an extended period. Tell me, Mr Harker, did you at any point confront the Count and demand to be set free?"

"I… I tried but once, and saw that it was folly. That is, it was impossible to oppose the Count's will. You cannot understand the terrible hold he had over me."

"The same hold that he had over those women who lived within his castle?"

"God no! They were… something entirely different. Oh,

God…" Harker buried his face in his hands.

"Holmes…" I said gently, fearing that Harker might have a relapse of the brain fever brought on by his ordeal. Holmes was referring to the three vampire women who had supposedly tried to seduce Harker with their hypnotic allure.

"I imagine," Holmes said, "that your wife is a forgiving and trusting woman, with a generous heart."

"My wife?" Harker asked, hoarsely, not looking up.

"Yes. After all, even though the incident at the castle was not your fault, it is a painful thing to a woman to hear of her husband's infidelity."

"I never… she…" He faded.

Holmes stood, and moved over to the far wall, upon which hung various photographs, certificates and trophies that I had barely noticed until that moment. One of the photographs was of four men, standing at the site of a part-built railway line against a dramatic background of some exotic, mountainous location; I thought I recognised Harker in the group, but could not see it clearly. At first I believed that was what had grabbed Holmes's attention, but I quickly realised I was mistaken. I saw now amongst the articles two large knives: a kukri knife, with its wicked, curved blade, and an American bowie knife, both hanging upon a wooden plaque.

"This bowie knife," Holmes said. "An interesting blade to find in an Englishman's office."

"It… it belonged to Quincey. Mr Morris."

"Then the kukri knife—surely it is not the very same blade with which you cut the throat of Count Dracula?"

Harker's eyes took on a haunted aspect. "The same," he said.

"Did the Count bleed?"

"Holmes!" I baulked at my friend's insensitivity.

"He… yes. He must have recently glutted himself."

Holmes gave a wry smile, and merely nodded. He examined the knives for a few moments more, before returning to the desk.

"Mr Harker, might I ask when would be a good time to call upon both you and your wife? I would very much like to complete this little interview, and then I shall leave you be."

"I can think of no opportune moment in the forthcoming weeks," said Harker. "Mina and I have busy schedules."

"A pity."

"I have a question for you, Mr Holmes," said Harker. "You are a consulting detective, they say. With whom do you consult on this business, that you would go to such impertinent lengths to pry into the affairs of others?"

That was spoken more eloquently than I would have expected from the pasty-faced solicitor. I imagined he had been girding himself to ask the question for much of our interview.

"Mr Harker, my clients vary from the meek and wronged to the powerful and stately, and every last one of them relies upon my utmost discretion. All that matters is that I am here."

"Yes… here you are. Well, Mr Holmes, I am afraid I can be of no assistance to you."

"Nonsense, Mr Harker, you have been most helpful already. Although might I ask you for directions before we leave? If you could point us to the Blackall School for Girls, we would be most grateful."

"The school?" If Harker had conjured some pluck in the last few minutes, it now drained visibly.

"Yes. We need to speak with a certain Miss Reed. Unless you could provide her home address?"

"Why should I know her address?" Harker snapped abruptly.

"You know the woman, do you not?"

"I… she is an old acquaintance of my wife's."

"Acquaintance? I had heard they were great friends."

"The school lies over the river," Harker said coolly. "I suggest you take a cab—I am sure the driver will steer you well. Now, Mr Holmes, Dr Watson, you really must let me get on with my appointments."

We did not impress upon a cabbie for directions, for Holmes knew the way perfectly well after all. His question about the school's location had been intended only to rattle Jonathan Harker, and in that he had certainly succeeded. We took off for the school on foot, a rather pleasant stroll that crossed the River Exe.

"Jonathan Harker is a sick man," I said. "He was not up to such stern questioning."

"Perhaps," Holmes replied. "However, his strange behaviour was due more to the fact that he was hiding something."

"Hiding what?"

"The state of his relationship with his wife, for one thing."

"How could you possibly know that?" I asked.

"Because, Watson, among the pictures upon his office wall was a photograph of himself, with Jack Seward, Quincey P. Morris and Arthur Holmwood. It was signed by all four men. There was no picture of Mina Harker among them, nor was there one upon his desk. I wonder if his wife's absence is due to an estrangement, perhaps the very estrangement that sees her travel to Whitby without her husband."

"Now I concur that is strange, Holmes," I said. "If Mrs Harker is helping to settle her old friend's affairs, it is one thing. If she is actually taking charge of the house—which I thought was a boarding house, in any case—that is quite another. How could she bring herself to do it?"

"It could be grief, or some misplaced sentimentality to be near the place where she and her late friend were once happy. Or it could be something more sinister. Nevertheless, the only way to be sure is to visit Whitby at the earliest opportunity, and hope we can catch Mrs Harker unawares."

"Oh, Holmes," I groaned. "Must we continue on these laborious door-to-door enquiries? Though you have now told two suspects that we are investigating the death of Lucy Westenra, might I remind you that we do not actually have a client?"

Holmes laughed, and I reddened. "Watson, dear Watson!" said he. "Of course we have a client. When Mycroft sends a titbit of information to me, however veiled, it is not for nothing. Our client is the British government. We rattle cages on their behalf, because they, for reasons as yet unclear, are unable to. Do you understand?"

"Not entirely," I grumbled.

"You shall, Watson, you shall. Now, look there, the Blackall School. I have a feeling this is where we shall find some quite intriguing answers."

I looked ahead to where Holmes pointed with his cane. Set back from a cobbled road, beyond a tall wrought-iron rail, was a grand old building of grey stone. It was ivy-covered across most of its southern face, and above the tangles of greenery shot a church-like spire. Dozens of girls in white pinafores ran across the cobbled yard to their lessons, overseen by a rather stern-looking mistress. It was she who we approached. The woman was reluctant to summon Miss Reed to speak with us, but before too long she relented, in no small part due to a sudden turn of charm on Holmes's part. So it was that we were directed to a cosy staff room.

The young woman who eventually entered was plain of appearance, slight of build, and neatly attired. The rose blush of her cheeks and slight shortness of breath suggested to me that she had made great haste to meet us. She sat down opposite us.

"You are a detective, Mr Holmes?" Miss Reed said.

"I do my best," said Holmes.

"Then you are here to ask me about Count Dracula, of

course—a subject about which I know little, beyond what I have read in the newspapers."

"Tangentially, perhaps. But tell me, Miss Reed, what led to your assumption."

"You are not the first to come to me," she said, somewhat angrily. "I will tell you what I told the others—I know nothing of use."

"Others?" Holmes said, leaning forwards in his seat. "I imagine you have spoken to Inspector Cotford of Scotland Yard; but who else?"

"I would rather not speak of it."

"You have been threatened?"

"I… no…"

"Miss Reed, your appearance, which I first mistook for fatigue after some physical exertion, now seems to me to be a form of nervous peroration. You are attempting to disguise your fear. Moreover, you plainly have not heard of me, but you guessed that I was a detective. Perhaps your colleague said something to that effect, but it is equally likely that you have been warned not to speak with me should I pay you a visit. Am I near the truth?"

"I should not be speaking with you," she said, and stood abruptly, turning for the door.

"Please, Miss Reed, whatever has been said to you, know that we are not your enemies. We seek only justice for your old friend, Miss Westenra."

Miss Reed stopped, and turned back to us. Her eyes darted uncertainly between me and Holmes.

"Lucy?" she said.

Holmes stood, and invited Miss Reed to take her seat again. He spoke to her in a gentle tone. "I rather expect that your previous visitors were somewhat unconcerned with justice for Lucy," he said. "But have no doubt, Miss Reed, that justice is our only motivation. I am certain some villainy is afoot, and I intend to uncover it."

Miss Reed sat down, and looked at Holmes imploringly. "I do not know how I can help, though I am certain you are right. But, Mr Holmes, I am not a strong person. My friends are… gone. What I mean to say, Mr Holmes, is that I have been warned against speaking to you, and I am afraid of what might happen should I tell you anything."

"If you have nothing of import to tell, what have you to fear?" Holmes asked.

"I do not think that will matter to… *them*."

"Before we continue, Miss Reed, are you certain that this room is private?"

"Why… yes. There is no one here who would eavesdrop on us."

In just two strides, Holmes was at the door, and opened it suddenly. Outside was a short, bare passage, which led to another corridor. There were no adjoining doors, and no persons present.

"Everyone is at their studies now," Miss Reed explained. Holmes closed the door and returned to his chair.

"Just a precaution, Miss Reed. Now, first of all, describe these men who were so unnerving to you. No, there is no need to protest. I have friends in the police force who will stand guard at your door day and night should I ask it of them. No harm shall come to you, you have my oath on it."

She breathed deeply. "Very well, Mr Holmes. The men were tall, fair, and well dressed. They spoke in foreign accents, which I took for German, only because the German mistress here at the school is possessed of a similar diction. They told me that should I ever breathe a word of my correspondence with Lucy or Mina— that is, another friend, Mina Harker—then it would go badly for me. They said that if I did not care for my own safety, then perhaps I should fear for the girls in my charge."

"Why, the devils!" I interjected, feeling my colour rise at once.

"You are sure that they were German, and not, say, Dutch?" Holmes asked.

"Certain. Like Miss Breckendorf, one of them had a peculiar lilt, which I believe is Bavarian, and not common elsewhere."

"Excellent, Miss Reed!" said Holmes, his admiration for the woman's observational skills brimming over. "What else can you tell me? When did they visit? Was it on more than one occasion?"

"I remember the timing of it well, Mr Holmes. It was late September last year, just a few days after poor Lucy's funeral. A week later, Inspector Cotford called upon me, saying confusing things about the 'bloofer lady' of Highgate Cemetery, and asking all kinds of frightening questions about vampires, Dutch professors, and… and…"

"And Mina Harker," Holmes said.

"How did you know?"

"I have spoken to Cotford, and in his opinion there was something between you and Mrs Harker that he could not explain, but which made him suspicious."

"Cotford is a boorish, unpleasant man. He scared me."

"I can well understand your feelings towards him. However, he is no longer with the police, and any further dealing you may have with Scotland Yard shall not be with him, but with men in my confidence, you have my word. Now Miss Reed, forgive my insistence on what must be a delicate matter, but I must ask the current condition of your friendship with Mrs Harker."

"To be frank, Mr Holmes, Mina and I have not spoken for some time. I saw her but briefly at the funeral of Mr Hawkins—Jonathan's employer, who I had known since I was a girl. Lucy, it seems, represented the last true bond of friendship between Mina and me—with her passing came the end of our long association."

"Might I ask why your friendship ended thus? From what I understand, Lucy and Mina spoke of you warmly in their correspondence, though you are not explicitly named in the letters we have read."

She blushed slightly at that. "I do not know what you have read, Mr Holmes, but I assure you any warmth would have come only from Lucy. Since we were girls, Mina has always beheld some sense of competition between us, which I think was her own imagining."

"On what matters?"

"Oh, everything really. Academic achievement, the obtaining of a station as qualified schoolmistress, and… other things that I would much rather not discuss. Throughout my youth, whatever I strove for, Mina had to have first." She stopped, evidently finding it difficult to keep her composure.

"I think I understand," said Holmes. "Tell me, Miss Reed, when your courtship with Jonathan Harker came to a close, were you betrothed?"

"How could you possibly know about that?" Tears welled in her eyes.

"It was evident, first from his words, and then from yours."

"We… we were not betrothed. Our courtship was in its infancy."

"But you cared deeply for him?"

"I did."

"And he for you?"

"Apparently not, for within weeks of him breaking off whatever… arrangement… we had, he and Mina were stepping out together." A tear rolled down her cheek, and she dabbed it away delicately. As one who had fairly recently lost a love, I felt for her keenly.

"Yet you remained friends with Mina?"

"I had no true claim on Jonathan's heart. I knew Mina had always admired him, although I never realised how much. I gave them my blessing."

"And if you were so magnanimous, it seems strange that Mina would choose to dissolve that friendship, and at such a difficult time for you both. Tell me, Miss Reed—and please be frank, for even the smallest detail could be of utmost significance—could jealousy, no matter how misplaced, have been the cause of her sudden change of disposition?"

"Partly, yes. We had long had an agreement that Jonathan and I would maintain no friendly contact, as it seemed inappropriate. But at the funeral…"

"Such contact was unavoidable," Holmes finished for her. "But there was another matter, perhaps; one that Mina referred to in her letters to Lucy, and I wonder if you could elucidate it for me, Miss Reed."

"If… if I can."

"The letters were written while Mr Harker was on business in Transylvania. In it, Lucy notes that 'some one has evidently been telling tales'—referring to some titbit of gossip about herself and her involvement with Lord Godalming and… others. For all his faults, Inspector Cotford believed that someone to be you. It would be of singular assistance if you could tell us those same tales, Miss Reed."

"They are of a most private and sensitive nature, and belong to the confidence of one who has gone to the grave," Miss Reed replied, her voice earnest.

"Miss Reed, I am sure that I need not explain how great an injustice has been done. I believe Lucy Westenra to have been murdered, not by a marauding vampire from foreign lands, but by someone known to her. If it were not so, you would not have been threatened by those strange German fellows. I know this is painful for you, but any minor detail from those letters could be of the utmost importance in uncovering her true killer."

"Very well, Mr Holmes. I do not know why, but I trust you.

But I do not need to tell you the contents of the letters, for I still have them."

"You kept them from the police?"

"I did, but please do not think ill of me. I did it only to protect Lucy's good name; by the time I came to realise something more was at play, I had told a lie too many, and could think of no way to hand the letters over without coming under suspicion myself. None of that matters now, Mr Holmes. I can spare you a little more time to fetch the letters, if you would be so kind as to escort me, and then perhaps it will feel like a great burden has at last been lifted from my shoulders."

We stood across the road from the school, beneath the shade of the elms that lined the road. I had the letters tucked under my arm, for both Holmes and I agreed it would be unseemly to read such private memoranda on the street. Some were in plain white envelopes, which Miss Reed identified as being from Mina Murray, as she was then. The remainder were from Lucy Westenra, and were all in lavender-scented envelopes, tied together with a pretty ribbon. Holmes paced back and forth, drawing the last of his cigarette and exhaling the smoke in a great plume.

"It all fits into place! In her diary, Mina wrote that Jonathan was particularly shaken on the day of Mr Hawkins's funeral. She postulates in the note that perhaps it is her husband's recent brain fever, coupled with the sombre funeral, which makes him so nervous. I should have seen it instantly."

"What?" I asked. "Surely it was just sentimentality—the Harkers were much attached to Mr Hawkins, after all."

"Jonathan Harker was shaken because he had a tryst with Miss Reed on the day of the funeral. I cannot prove it, but I know now from Miss Reed's words that it is so."

"Holmes, that is a scandalous accusation. The poor girl was most upset, and your questions were singularly intrusive."

"They were, and yet they were necessary. She may well have confessed all when I asked her about the funeral, Watson, or it may have been that the private moment she undoubtedly shared with Harker was purely innocent, but I saw no reason to disgrace the poor girl by making her relive any wrongdoing on the part of herself or Harker.

"If Harker was shaken on the day of the funeral, I would guess he was discovered in the act, probably by Mina, and that somehow this detail was later discovered by Professor Van Helsing. From that day forth, the professor manipulated Mina's jealous nature, which we have today heard a great deal about, and turned her against her husband. It does not matter if Harker and Miss Reed were acting purely innocently; we know from Miss Reed's testimony that Mina Harker has a jealous nature, which could easily be manipulated by mere insinuation. Coupled with the story of the strange, seductive women of Castle Dracula, and we have a very solid reason for Mina's estrangement from her husband.

"Perhaps Harker himself believes his tale, due to his long spell of delirium shortly afterwards. Whether the encounter happened as he described, or even at all, is another thing entirely. What matters here, however, is what Mina Harker believes. And that, Watson, is almost certainly whatever Van Helsing has told her."

"It seems to me that Mina Harker is a wronged woman," I said, "led astray perhaps by the professor. We should feel sorry for her."

"We certainly should not, not yet at least!" Holmes retorted. "If Van Helsing has manipulated her, it is because of worse things than jealousy. The Harkers came into this story before meeting Van Helsing. They came unexpectedly into money, due to the death of Jonathan Harker's employer and his suspiciously generous will, before Van Helsing set foot in England. They knew of Seward, Morris and Lord Godalming independently of Van Helsing, at least by name and, most importantly of all, they knew Lucy Westenra. It was Jonathan Harker who first cast doubt on Dracula's humanity when he asked, 'What manner of man is this, or what manner of creature is it in the semblance of a man?'

"No, Watson, I do not believe for a moment that Mina Harker is entirely a wronged woman. I believe she was already party to a crime, which Van Helsing discovered through reading her correspondence with Lucy. Her jealousy and willingness to throw her husband to the wolves came later, along with the question-mark over his fidelity. Whatever she is doing in Whitby, I am sure it is of great interest to us."

"So you want to travel to Whitby now, I suppose?"

"I have been prepared to do so since yesterday morning. Really, Watson, you ought to keep abreast of developments. Thankfully I had a bag sent ahead to an inn there."

"You mean we aren't returning home first? Holmes, I have a practice, patients, I cannot simply…"

"Then it is well that I need you to visit the telegraph office. You can wire your colleague and then send a telegram for me while you're about it."

"To what end?"

"Wire Inspector Bradstreet by urgent reply. Have him communicate my credentials and a glowing endorsement to the Exeter constabulary. I shall visit them presently and arrange for a policeman to keep an eye on Miss Reed until our business is brought to a conclusion."

"And what will you be doing while I'm at the telegraph office?" I said, somewhat affronted by being sent on an errand, and rather cross at the prospect of more unexpected travel.

"I shall remain here and keep watch for fair-haired German men," said Holmes. "Never let it be said that Sherlock Holmes is not a man of his word."

CHAPTER EIGHT

Letters Between Miss Kate Reed, Miss Lucy Westenra and Miss Mina Murray

The following letters have been reproduced here in chronological order. Upon the advice of Holmes, especially with regard to the more sensitive, personal aspects of the letters' content, I have endeavoured to reproduce only the most pertinent paragraphs.

Letter, Lucy Westenra to Kate Reed, 3 May 1893

My dearest Katie—
Of all the strange things! I confess I have not heard from dear Mina nearly half so often as I should like—she has only written to me once since we all left school. But to think she is experiencing such excitement! What must it have been like to have Jonathan visit her at the school while you were there? Honestly, Jonathan Harker has always been the most oafish, self-centred of men when it comes to the feelings of

girls, as you and I can both attest. You are saintly in your restraint, and an excellent friend to Mina through it all.

You were right to say you should have asked her permission before disclosing such juicy titbits to me, but it is done now, and I shall be the pillar of discretion. I shall write to her this very week, under some pretext, but I swear I won't let on even in the slightest that I know of her engagement to Jonathan. After everything that happened between the two of you, even so long ago, it would be in poor taste to say I'd heard the news from you. I am glad you have both managed to put the matter aside for the sake of your friendship—a man like J is hardly worth quarrelling over. I have no doubt Mina loves him very much, but if, as you say, she really did encourage him to take this trip to advance his career, I half wonder if she did it to have some peace from him for a while. I can think of no further place than Transylvania to send such a frightful bore—I must stop using slang like that, Mother would be most cross with me. And how sly of Mina to gain the confidence of Mr Hawkins so! Clever, too—she is much more level-headed than I could ever be. How delightfully wicked of her, don't you think?

I shall keep this letter short, my dearest, I hope you can forgive me. But we shall see each other at the concert on Saturday anyhow. You can be a scurrilous gossip then and tell me all about Mina and the other girls!

Please do not breathe a word to Mina of my feelings toward Jonathan—not that you would speak to her about him, of course—but I do so want us all to get along when next we meet. And I shall have more news of my own regarding a certain gentleman, I am sure.

Your loving friend,
Lucy

Letter, Lucy Westenra to Kate Reed, 10 May 1893

My dearest Katie—

I must chide you, at least gently, at the start of my letter, for I received correspondence yesterday from our friend Mina, and it seems you have been telling tales about my courtship with Mr Holmwood. You are such a young minx, and I shall tell Mina so!

But oh, I forgive you, for I am sure I am in love and that is all that matters. Mr Holmwood—I shall call him Arthur hereafter—often visits Mother and me, and they get along famously. He is the kind of man who just understands things, if you know what I mean. He sees the part that I must play, and he is always considerate to console me about it. I almost envy Mother sometimes, for she can talk to people whilst I have to sit by like a dumb animal and smile till I find myself blushing at being an incarnate *lie*. And it is so silly and childish to blush, and without reason too. Arthur understands though, he plays his part and I mine, until those sacred moments when we may be alone together, and he whispers sweet nothings to me like the gentlest soul, though with none of the forwardness of a certain friend of his—the American you met at the Pop. He is trying to woo me now in his strange way, and I really do wish you had not rebuffed him so at the dance, for he is now my third suitor and it is all most exhausting.

And yet, it is perhaps lucky for you that you did reject the advances of Mr Morris, for although he is a kindly soul, and most gentle with me, I am sure he is roguish beneath that façade of colonial manners. He and Arthur— who he calls "Art"—have been abroad together many times on hunting expeditions, and I have heard whispers of their exploits in foreign ports that make one's toes curl! But none of that matters, for I shall make an honest man of Arthur and ensure he goes no further astray with the likes of Mr Morris. Whatever his past, Arthur is noble, tall, curly-haired, and true.

I do go on, I know, but only because I am so undeservedly happy, don't you see? I hope with all my heart that you do not begrudge me this happiness, for I am giddy with it. I know that men have not been kind to you, especially the one that now courts our mutual friend. Your goodness makes up for all of us if you bear no ill will to either of them.

But gosh, I am almost forgetting to tell you the real juicy news. You know how you mentioned Mina's ambition regarding the law practice that Jonathan works for? Well, you were absolutely right. Mina went on at some length about how she is completely in the confidence of Jonathan's employer, Mr Hawkins, who now dotes upon her like a daughter. Honestly, she has such plans, for Jonathan to become a partner in the firm, and so young—she positively didn't even mention his long trip overseas. I daresay she is not missing him at all, and I can't say I would either, he's such a bore! Oh, I wrote it again, but I shan't cross it out.

I wrote to you earlier that our American friend, Quincey Morris, would have made you a fine match. Well, I said a similar thing to Mina, about Jack—Dr Seward, I should say. Remember him? You should! He's a doctor at the lunatic asylum now, so I do hope Mina forgives me that little jest at her expense! He's an eccentric sort, who used to play cricket with Arthur, and travelled a little with him and Mr Morris, although I don't think the rugged life is really for him. He's still madly in love with me of course, but he's not the sort of man I could ever take as a husband.

Anyway, I have written much of myself again, and it is a testament to how good you are that you never take me to task for it, even though it is an unbecoming habit. I am inviting Mina to Whitby for the summer, and I hope you will come too. I am not so self-centred in person, and you can tell me all about your life as a schoolmistress, and any scandalous affairs you may be embroiled in. It shall be like old times, the three of us gossiping late into the night!

Ever your loving Lucy

Letter, Mina Murray to Kate Reed, 26 May 1893

Dear Kate,

It has been long since I have put pen to paper to you, and it seems awkward given our proximity, but I think this will be easier to say in writing.

I know that I have been the subject of some gossip about town, and I am sure you know very well why. You must surely know by now that our school is a small place for news, and that the walls themselves have ears—it was you, after all, who set loose the word about Lucy's curly-haired suitor. As a result, I am equally sure that you would not again be the cause of such mischief, and I would hope that you should defend me against tittle-tattle, as any dear friend would.

On the subject of friendship, I have written recently to dear Lucy, who I know has invited you to come and stay with us in Whitby over the summer. I would humbly beg that you stay away for a time, perhaps completely, as I have much to confide in Lucy about Jonathan—my betrothed—and of my anxiety about his business abroad for so long. I should so hate for you to feel at all uneasy about the conversation, given the history that we have so magnanimously put behind us up to now. There is more, of course, for I am not so selfish as to cause upset on purely my own account. Though I am loath to betray a confidence, I must be cruel to be kind. Lucy is secretly afraid of what might happen should the three of us come together—she and I have both recently had our hearts swept away by virtuous men, and at such a delicate time when passions run high, the appearance of a single woman in need of a man may play unfairly upon the impulses of a certain Arthur Holmwood. I am sure you would not wish to be the cause of any anxiety on Lucy's part, however inadvertently, especially given her history of poor health.

I know it will be disappointing for you not to see Lucy and myself this summer, but I am sure you agree it will be for the best. I would so hate for any strain to be put on our long-standing fellowship.

M

CHAPTER NINE

THE GENTLER SEX

It was with no small sense of relief that we alighted from the train and made our way out of the busy little station at Whitby. It was already dark when we emerged onto a thoroughfare. Even from this urban prospect, the chilly sea air blew in from the mouth of the Esk, bringing with it a salty tang and the crying of gulls.

"I suppose you intend to don some foolish disguise now and take up a room in the very crescent in which Mina Harker stays," I said.

"Preposterous, Watson. I have secured a room in the Angel hostelry, just across the road there." Holmes waved his cane to indicate a modest-looking hotel with a peeling and faded biblical scene upon its sign.

"It is certainly too late to go calling on a lady now, Holmes. We should dine and rest, and pay her a visit in the morning."

"Indeed not!" remarked Holmes. "We must strike while the iron is hot. If you must eat, there is an excellent kipper stall just down that hill, if I remember rightly. But we must refresh ourselves and then be on our way."

"What's the hurry?" said I.

"On the train were two tall, fair-haired gentlemen, far too well dressed for the third-class carriage that they occupied. They travelled so to avoid our notice, but I most certainly noticed them! I doubt we shall reach Mrs Harker before they have a chance to warn her of our arrival, so there is no point in trying. However, we must interview Mrs Harker before she has the opportunity to receive instruction from Van Helsing."

"Why, he has humbugged us, Holmes."

"Not yet, I should hope. Our business here should be concluded before Van Helsing's spies are able to report back to him."

"These are the self-same men who accosted Miss Reed then?" I asked. "They strike me as the dangerous sort."

"Perhaps, Watson. And so it is lucky that I took the liberty of packing your service revolver."

The cliff-top guest house stood in a tree-lined avenue, somewhat sheltered from the worst of the elements and undoubtedly picturesque during daylight hours, but was now strangely sinister. Everything about us was still, even though just a couple of hours earlier the entire town had been bustling with traders and day-trippers. From our vantage point we could still see the fishermen's cottages upon the East Cliff, and hear the tolling of buoy-bells beyond the harbour. A purplish haze hung over the distant horizon, providing enough colour to throw the skeletal remains of the nearby Whitby Abbey into relief.

Holmes took the steps to the front door of the house and rapped firmly upon it. I scanned the street in both directions furtively, half expecting two German men to leap out at us from the shadows at any moment.

Before long, we heard the sound of a bolt being drawn back,

and the door creaked open a little, so that a wrinkled, grey-haired woman could peer out at us suspiciously.

"Good evening, madam," Holmes said cheerfully, doffing his hat. "I apologise for the lateness of the hour. I am Mr Sherlock Holmes, and this is my associate, Dr Watson. We have come on a matter of no small urgency, and must speak with one of your guests, a Mrs Wilhelmina Harker of Exeter. May we come in?"

The woman looked formidable, and in many ways reminded me of Mrs Hudson. Our own landlady, however, would not have stepped aside quite so easily as Holmes, with a broad smile and courteous bow, entered the hall before she could utter a word of protest. I followed, rather embarrassed, as Holmes handed the flabbergasted woman his hat and coat.

"Thank you, my good woman," he said.

"Well," said she, "all the years I ran this house, and never did I think it would come to this so sudden. From landlady to housekeeper in one fell swoop; first the other fellow, and now you. I shall be glad to see the back of the old place, and I never thought I'd say it."

"Am I mistaken, Mrs—?"

"Dryden," she snapped, "and most likely you are."

"You are not landlady at this guest house?"

"It's not a guest house no more. It is sold, and I'm only here under sufferance until I find somewhere to go. Not that anyone cares…"

"And who is the owner now, Mrs Dryden? Surely not young Mrs Harker?"

"She's the mistress now, sure enough, although it's some foreign fellow who's bought the place."

"And you did not wish to sell, I take it?"

"Take it how you like. As soon as work is done on my new house, I'll be gone, and not before time. Now, shall I go and fetch 'er, or do you want t'stand there all day asking foolish questions?"

"My apologies; you must be a busy woman. If you would be so kind as to tell Mrs Harker we are here. Is that the sitting room? We shall wait there if we may."

I could tell Holmes was intrigued—he did not say as much, but he must have suspected, as did I, that the "foreign fellow" in question was Van Helsing. But why would Van Helsing have bought the guest house in which the Westenras had stayed? We took our seats as the sound of the housekeeper's chuntered pejoratives faded away down the hall. The room was sparsely furnished, with little more than a table and chairs in what should have been a charming room overlooking the bay. I knew that our visit after dark was unorthodox, and that Mina Harker would be a reluctant hostess at best.

At long last, the door opened, and Mrs Harker appeared. Holmes and I both rose to greet her, but at the very sight of her I became at once hesitant and nervous. Holmes noticed immediately, for I saw the quick dart of his eyes toward me as I bumbled a greeting. Mrs Harker saw it too, and I detected a flicker of a smile as perhaps she sensed a weakness in me. It was then that I realised the curious absence of any physical description of Wilhelmina Harker in the Dracula Papers. Perhaps she had removed this out of modesty when she had transcribed the documents.

I could say nothing, but the simple truth was that Mina Harker, but for her colouring, bore some similarity to my dear Mary. The nearness of my grief for my late wife made me see her image in the most unlikely places, and what a trick of circumstance that I should see her here, in the form of a woman whom Holmes believed to be a villainess.

"Forgive our intrusion on your evening." Holmes spoke for us both. "I am Sherlock Holmes, and this is my associate Dr Watson."

"How do you do," I said, gathering my wits at last.

"Goodness," said Mrs Harker, "the great detective himself, so recently back from the dead, and his equally famous chronicler, here in my presence. And yet, one wonders what the urgent business must be, that it could not wait until morning."

"I am afraid we are in Whitby for only the shortest time, Mrs Harker," Holmes replied. "Our current investigation takes us far and wide, and sets us on a most trying schedule. It was only this morning that we spoke with your husband, for instance. Though we were sorry at the time to have missed you, how fortunate it was that our paths should meet here, so far from home."

"I would scarcely call any part of England far from home, Mr Holmes, not after the distance I have travelled. And if the papers are to be believed, you doubtless feel similarly."

"I have travelled much in the line of my work."

"And what of your work brings you here, Mr Holmes? What could I possibly assist you with?"

"Why, you are surely the very best person to speak with, Mrs Harker. Professor Van Helsing and his Crew of Light held you in the highest possible regard, and you were the organised hand behind the manuscript now called the Dracula Papers. Who else should I turn to, in order to uncover the truth of the matter?"

"The truth, Mr Holmes? That suggests you believe the Dracula Papers to include fabrications."

"Certainly inaccuracies, which I am sure you would like to rectify. We are dealing with testimonies from many sources, each with their own motivations; and there is often nothing so strange and impermeable as the motivations of men."

"Those with whom I travelled were the best of men. There is no subterfuge, no lie to be uncovered. The highest court in the land has declared it so, and thus I cannot see what brings you to my door, Mr Holmes."

"And it is now your door, is it not, Mrs Harker? The house belongs to you now, or rather to Professor Van Helsing."

For a moment Mrs Harker looked irked; she glanced quickly over her shoulder, clearly annoyed that the bad-tempered Mrs Dryden had given too much away.

"I am tenant here for now; is there something wrong with that?"

"Not at all, Mrs Harker. It is just that your husband informed us that you were staying here to sort through the remainder of Lucy Westenra's things. He did not mention that you were now in residence."

"My husband is a private man, Mr Holmes; perhaps he did not want all and sundry to know that his firm is moving north. It is quite an upheaval for all those in his employ, after all, not to mention his clients."

"Is Exeter no longer to your liking, Mrs Harker?"

"What makes you say that?"

"I merely make an assumption that the relocation is at your request. It is simply that your husband appears to have everything he requires there. Except, of course, his wife."

"That is impertinent, Mr Holmes."

"Forgive me."

"Only this once. It is true that I yearned to return to Whitby. Lucy and I shared many moments here in this house; happy ones for the most part. I felt the lure of the sea, if you will, and wished to return."

"It is strange how grief affects the mind," Holmes observed. "After all, this house was surely the scene of more than one tragedy for you."

"The heart wants what it wants, Mr Holmes. There is no denying it. Besides, there are not so many happy memories in Exeter. A change seemed as good as a rest."

"And yet, with all your new-found fortune, you did not buy this house for yourself?"

Mrs Harker frowned. "Mr Holmes, you still have not answered my question why are you here?" It was a question we had been asked several times in the past few days, and one that I myself still did not truly know the answer to.

"I am here, Mrs Harker, to investigate a string of suspicious deaths in the wake of your pursuit of Count Dracula, beginning with the apparent murder of your dear friend, Miss Lucy Westenra, and ending with the slaying of Count Dracula himself, at your husband's hands and by his own written admission."

"M—my husband? No!" Mrs Harker looked panicked. "Count Dracula was a monster; a bloodthirsty creature who claimed the life of dear Lucy, and had to be destroyed!"

Holmes was unruffled. "And if vampires existed, Mrs Harker, that would be a fine mitigation for hacking at a man's neck with a kukri knife. Sadly, as there is no such thing as a vampire, it would seem to me that your husband is guilty of murder, and that you and your confederates are accomplices to the crime."

"You are wrong, Mr Holmes." Mrs Harker stood and turned away from us. "I, better than anyone, know that vampires are real. What that creature did to me… and to poor Lucy…" She sniffed away her tears. I stood at once and offered Mrs Harker a handkerchief, which she took without turning to face us. I did not know what had come over Holmes in the last couple of days—he had never been one to place his faith in the gentler sex, but he had at least always remained gallant. To both Genevieve Holmwood and now Mina Harker he had been almost cruel.

"And to your husband, Mrs Harker," Holmes persisted. "Do not forget him."

She turned angrily to face Holmes, her eyes reddened. "I thank God every day that Jonathan escaped Castle Dracula, and that he recovered from his illness. The spectre of Dracula hangs over him no longer. But for my part, I was for ever changed by my ordeal. And how can I not think of Lucy while standing here, in this house?"

"I merely observe, Mrs Harker, that any marriage would be strained by the things that you and your husband have faced. His—inconstancy—in Castle Dracula was only the first of a number of trials arrayed before you."

"He swore that nothing—"

"And I am sure that he told the truth, Mrs Harker. Even if there is no such thing as a vampire."

I coughed in surprise at the insinuation. If the three beautiful women encountered by Jonathan Harker in that Transylvanian castle were of flesh and blood, then it would take a strong-willed man indeed to resist such sinful temptation. Holmes clearly believed that Jonathan Harker was not such a man.

"I believe in my husband even if you do not. I have ever been a dutiful wife."

"But not such a dutiful fiancé, or so it seems from your journals."

"How dare you!"

"Please, Mrs Harker, the evidence speaks for itself, in your own words. While your journals displayed evident concern for your husband's well-being, at no point did you try to contact him by writing to Castle Dracula. Mr Hawkins's law firm could surely have forwarded any correspondence, and we already know that you were well in the trust of Peter Hawkins himself. Your betrothed was already delayed by almost a month when you finally received a letter from him (which he later said he was forced to write, a letter dictated by the Count), and expressed any concern whatsoever in your own journals. Either the dates set down so meticulously by Mr Harker are false, or you simply cared not for your husband's whereabouts."

"Mr Holmes, I did write to Jonathan, using the very methods

you suggest, only I must have forgotten to include them in the Dracula Papers. And as for my concern, have you not considered that those extracts of the journals expressing my deepest fears for Jonathan's safety contained such private thoughts that I did not wish to publish them?" Mrs Harker replied fiercely, her hands clenched into fists, and shaking. "As soon as I received news that Jonathan was sick, I rushed to his side. It was not the easiest journey for a lone woman to take, as I am sure you know."

"Yes, given the circumstances, your trip to Buda-Pesth and the subsequent wedding was most sudden, and is certainly testament to your prevailing sense of duty. Some might say it was the type of marriage reserved for a man on his deathbed, rather than merely a sick-bed."

"My husband's fever was so severe, the nuns feared he would not survive. So it was a deathbed marriage, if you would put it so, though thankfully Jonathan survived to be a good and loving husband." She dabbed at her eyes with my kerchief.

"I can well imagine the emotion you must have felt. Indeed, in your journal you describe the wedding itself in the most emotional terms; the one passage in your transcript where your deepest feelings for your husband are revealed, perhaps. Indeed, you were most insistent in those lines. 'I could hardly speak; my heart was so full that even those words seemed to choke me.' It appears at first the very image of the dutiful bride. But it could just as easily be interpreted as a heartfelt plea by a woman forced into marriage by obligate circumstance."

Upon hearing her own words recited to her like a phonograph recording, Mrs Harker's eyes blazed for a moment. "To see my husband so weak, so vulnerable, and yet so happy to see me—it was a moment that would have left any bride speechless, Mr Holmes. Happy and sad, and full of love all at the same time. I imagine you are the kind of man who cannot understand such depth of feeling."

"Tell me, Mrs Harker, have you always been so certain of your husband's virtue?"

"Wh—what do you mean?"

"I put it to you that Jonathan Harker was never the man you intended to marry, but a man you courted out of some juvenile rivalry with a schoolfriend. I ask whether removing yourselves from Exeter might be for some other purpose. Perhaps you also sought to remove your husband from temptation?"

"Holmes!" Again I was forced to defend a subject from Holmes's brusque questioning. Here was an ordinary woman—so similar in manner and appearance to my late wife, that I simply could not stand by and let Holmes upset her further.

"It is quite all right, Dr Watson," Mrs Harker said, tears appearing once more in her dark eyes, her colour rising. "Mr Holmes evidently knows already of my husband's past. He perhaps had a wandering eye in his youth, but that was all dead long ago. Now he is married; he has a duty to me as I have to him."

"And would that duty have anything to do with your friend, Professor Van Helsing?" Holmes asked, glancing at me warningly.

"Whatever do you mean?"

"Simply put, Mrs Harker, does Professor Van Helsing know anything about you or your husband that might be… incriminating? Some nugget of information that ensures your continued loyalty to each other, and to him."

At this, Mrs Harker sat back in her chair, threw her small, pale hands to her face, and wept. I turned to Holmes angrily, and remonstrated with him as decorously as I could.

"This is unbecoming of a gentleman, Holmes. Perhaps we should postpone further questioning until Mr Harker may be present."

"Oh, I don't see how that would be any better, Watson. As I said earlier, seeing as how Mr Harker struck the fatal blow against Count Dracula, I still believe him to be guilty of a very serious crime. A crime in which, perhaps, Mrs Harker here is not complicit, and may wish to extricate herself from without any malign influence. If I can prove one murder, then suspicion certainly falls on Jonathan Harker for other crimes detailed within the Dracula Papers, or merely alluded to. Such as the death in suspicious circumstances of Mr Harker's employer, Peter Hawkins."

At the mention of Hawkins, Mina Harker sniffed away her tears and looked up at Holmes with despair in her eyes. "Suspicious circumstances?" she croaked.

"It is suspicious indeed that a man should alter his will, leaving everything to his junior solicitor, just one day before his death, and so soon after Mr Harker returned from his errand to Transylvania. Other than a case of gout, we know of no reason for Mr Hawkins's sudden demise. It is more suspicious still that this strange affair was never investigated by the authorities. But of course, the legality of the will would be beyond question, given that the beneficiary was himself a lawyer. Oh, but I forget, Mrs Harker—you, too, have extensive knowledge of the law. Did you not write in your journal that you studied all of Mr Harker's books, the better to aid him in his work?"

"What are you implying?"

"I am merely trying to paint the fullest picture of events, Mrs Harker. I tend to think aloud, that is all."

"Mr Hawkins was a dear friend, who was almost like a father to me. His passing was one of the saddest times of my life, though I had little time to mourn before losing dear Lucy. You would not say such hurtful things if you had known us before all of this."

"That's as may be, Mrs Harker, but instead I must be led by my observations. It seems to me that you are not simply moving house, but fleeing something."

Mrs Harker fell silent for a moment. Finally, she spoke quietly, the fight drained from her.

"Very well, Mr Holmes. I shall tell you, for if the alternative is to be accused of murder on top of all the other tortures of my life this past year, then what choice do I have? Jonathan Harker is no killer; I shall maintain this with my last breath. But he has a weak will, and a wandering eye. There is someone in Exeter, Mr Holmes—in fact, more than just one 'someone'—with whom Jonathan has had intimacy. He assures me that he has done me no wrong since our marriage, and I suppose I believe that, given his physical state. And yet I have seen with my own eyes the fondness he still holds for another woman—a former friend and neighbour, no less. Professor Van Helsing, out of love for us, secured this property and bade us move here, for the sake of our future happiness. The professor has done us this great kindness for all the multitude of reasons that a true friend could think of, and I fear that you misinterpret this kindness in order to cast a further black shadow over my husband and me."

I was stricken with pity for the woman—no more than a girl, really.

"I see, Dr Watson, that you know how the heart can be broken and remade over and over," she said. "If Mr Holmes cannot understand what it is to love someone unconditionally, then perhaps you can."

"I do," I said. "My dear wife was more precious to me than anything in the world."

"Was?" Mina Harker looked up at me, with sorrow in her dark eyes.

I nodded.

"Watson, that's enough," Holmes said. "I rather fear that we have overstepped the mark this time. Mrs Harker, I am sorry to have caused you any undue distress."

I was as surprised as anyone that Holmes had offered an apology. Mrs Harker, further endearing herself to me, offered

Holmes a forgiving smile by way of acceptance.

We said our goodbyes, though I noticed that Holmes was quick not to let me exchange any further comforting words with Mrs Harker. As we reached the door, Holmes turned back, at which I almost groaned aloud. He was tenacious, like a terrier with a rat.

"I must ask one further question, Mrs Harker, and then we shall leave you in peace. Do you have any idea why Count Dracula would come to Whitby, so far from the home he purchased in London, and single out Lucy Westenra as his victim? He could not have known Miss Westenra, or even of her very existence."

"On the contrary, Mr Holmes. When I wrote to Jonathan, in the letters that you do not believe exist, I told him I was staying with Lucy. She was such a dear friend that I spoke of her in the most elevated terms, which must have drawn the Count to her goodness like a moth to candlelight. He doubtless commandeered the ship—the *Demeter*—for the very purpose of landing in Whitby."

"And Lucy's illness and agitated sleep—this occurred before the Count had even embarked the *Demeter*?"

"Professor Van Helsing explained that the Count projected some strange, psychical influence, that knew not the limitations of borders or even oceans. I felt that influence exerted upon me, and though I cannot explain it to this day, I well believe it."

"And was it a coincidence that Dracula bought a property at Carfax, directly next to an asylum run by Dr Jack Seward, himself a close friend of Lucy Westenra?"

"It must have been, and a horrid coincidence at that. But Mr Holmes, you promised one more question, and I have already counted three. Will you not leave me to my evening?"

"My dear lady, I apologise. Good night to you."

Holmes tugged at my arm, barely giving me time to doff my hat to Mrs Harker before ushering me out of the house. I looked back as we stepped onto the street, and Mina Harker, her face gleaming pale in the moonlight, nodded weakly at me, perhaps in appreciation for rescuing her from Holmes's interrogation.

"It seems our Mrs Harker is a more formidable opponent than I gave her credit for," Holmes said, after we had walked some distance from the house in silence.

"That is the opposite impression to the one I formed," I grumbled.

"Of course it is, Watson, for she managed to find your weakness quickly and clinically, and exploited it. In doing so, she found my weakness also."

"Oh? Does the great Sherlock Holmes have a weakness?"

"Of course. It is you, Watson."

"A fine how-do-you-do!" I remarked. "After all that we have been through, I am now reduced to the weak link in the chain."

"In matters of deduction, Watson, that has always been the case, and here it has played out accordingly. But do you not see how you also lend me strength? You temper my scientific brain with your empathy. And tonight, Mrs Harker's cunning use of your kind-heartedness allowed me to make a close study of her techniques, which I doubt she even realised I had noticed."

I did not quite know what to say, or whether I had been paid a compliment or simply painted once more as another tool in Holmes's armoury.

"I still do not see how she is so cunning, Holmes. Why, you make her sound like another Irene Adler."

"No," he said, quite shortly. "She is brilliant, doubtless, but not quite in the same league as *that* woman. Mrs Harker's motives are entirely different—they stem, I believe, from self-preservation."

"I do not see it. It looks to me as though you are persecuting that poor girl."

"I have only theories for the moment, Watson, and I must ask that you trust me until such time as I can support them. There are a good many questions I should have liked to ask Mrs Harker, but they will have to wait for another time.

"Think further on her journal entries, for instance. Is it not ridiculous to think that she would have returned home after talking to an old man in Whitby, and written down his words in his own dialect, verbatim? It is just like Seward, in his phonograph recordings, imitating Van Helsing's dialect and irregularity of speech. Is it deliberate? There seems to be no real reason for it to be, for in the latter case it has only given away Van Helsing's real nationality. More likely, it is an attempt to lend some 'authenticity' to the accounts, which suggests that many of these passages were made up after the fact. Van Helsing doubtless dictated for Mina directly, and she dutifully recorded his words. The old man she spoke of never existed, or at least not how Mrs Harker described him. His strange way of speaking is lifted directly from Robinson's *Glossary of Words Used in the Neighbourhood of Whitby*, a copy of which I have at Baker Street. Such dialect would certainly have been otherwise unintelligible for an untravelled stranger to these parts, especially a young woman from Exeter. If we were to question the locals about this old man—Swales, she called him— we may find some contradictory reports, for Swales is a common enough name hereabouts. It is just as likely that the name was taken from the obituaries, coinciding with a memorable event— the wreck of the *Demeter*, for instance; so if anyone were to ask, 'Do you recall an old sailor who lived hereabout, whose name was Swales and who died on the night of the *Demeter* wreck?' we would find half a dozen witnesses to swear to his existence.

"Think also on how Mrs Harker became associated with Van Helsing. The Dracula Papers tell us that the professor seized all of Miss Westenra's correspondence upon her death, which is how he learned of Mina and Jonathan. Van Helsing is a clever man;

he would have guessed just as I did that the Harkers played a role in the death of Peter Hawkins. It is hardly a stretch to say that Van Helsing read Lucy's letters and diary during her illness, and thus contacted Mina much earlier, probably to confront her with his suspicions and to discuss the terms of her blackmail. Oh, yes, Watson—it is quite possible that Mina Harker came to this affair because she was impelled to; the reason for the blackmail, however, and the things I suspect she has done since, go beyond mere coercion."

"I think you do Mrs Harker the greatest disservice," I said. "She appeared to be a woman wronged by a callous and inconstant husband; a woman who herself has been manipulated by a group of men who may or may not be unmasked as villains yet. You reduced that poor woman to tears, Holmes, and they were genuine enough." I stopped, realising I had become somewhat emotional in my defence of Mina Harker, and could not think why.

"Oh, Watson, how many times must you be lured from the path of scientific deduction by female wiles. A pretty face and neat ankle never fail to soften your brain. When you passed your kerchief to Mrs Harker, did you not detect a strange odour?"

"No, Holmes. Do you mean her perfume, perhaps?"

"A lady who has settled down for the evening after a busy day, unprepared for visitors, would be unlikely to prepare herself quite so thoroughly—that in itself was a peculiarity. Yet I speak not of perfume, but of what the perfume was meant to hide. If you had not been so well deceived by Mrs Harker's performance, you would have smelled the unmistakeable odour of menthol."

"And what if I had? I often give my patients a little menthol to ease a cold—perhaps Mrs Harker has been suffering as a result of the change in air."

"Or perhaps she was inducing tears with a menthol balm, a common practice in the theatre."

"Her tears could genuinely have been the result of anguish."

"Your generosity of spirit knows no bounds, Watson. I shall endeavour to keep an open mind."

"As well you should, Holmes, by the doctrine of your own method. Besides, it is highly unlikely that a lady of Mrs Harker's years would have any involvement in the theatre—she simply cannot have pursued a successful teaching career and been an actress too."

"She would not have to be an actress to acquire a few tricks, Watson. Besides, I think it is clear that Mrs Harker knows at least one budding young thespian. Don't you see?"

At first, I did not, and to Holmes's amusement I pondered the question as we walked in the brisk sea air back to our lodgings.

When the fact came to me, I realised I had been a fool, and exclaimed, "Lady Godalming!"

CHAPTER TEN

THE FATE OF THE *DEMETER*

I woke next morning later than I would have liked, mouth dry and head fuzzy from one too many glasses of Tokay—the only acceptable tipple available in the bar of the Angel Hotel. I had ignored Holmes's advice to moderate my drinking, too obstinate and cross with him was I over his patronising nature earlier, and too heartsick with the memories of my late wife, which had come tumbling back into my mind following our visit to Mina Harker. Now, it was after nine o'clock, and Holmes was nowhere to be found. He had clearly been up long before me; our portmanteaus were gone, though Holmes had left a few essential items in the sitting room, including my revolver and my medical bag. I placed my gun in my overcoat pocket, and went down to breakfast alone. Almost an hour later, and at a loose end, I left the hotel, only to have Holmes bump into me on the street. He had a copy of the *Whitby Gazette* tucked under his arm, and a cheerful look about him.

"Excellent, you are up!" he said. "While you slumbered, I have been busy indeed. You recall I mentioned those fair-haired men following us yesterday? Well, they had this place under watch last night."

"They are here?"

"Not now. I struck out early, and made a feint of not noticing them. I led them a merry dance back towards Mrs Harker's residence, and ensured that I lost them. They would have to be well trained indeed to keep up with me. Since then I have sent a telegram to my old informant Langdale Pike, and should hope to find a reply waiting when we get home."

"How long have you been up?"

"Since before dawn. I was watching those men as they watched us… they were not terribly circumspect about it. Perhaps they underestimate us, or perhaps they are rank amateurs. Best keep our wits about us today in any case."

"I thought we were returning to London?"

"Not immediately, although I had our bags sent ahead so that we would not have to return here under observation—the more mobile we can remain, the less chance there is of our enemies catching up with us. Before we depart, we need to pay a visit to the docks. Come now, a walk along the harbour may do you good."

Holmes was right—the walk down to the West Pier did certainly blow away the grogginess from my head to some degree. Indeed, it was such a bright, fine morning, with a brisk, salt-spray breeze blowing in across the Esk, that it now seemed ridiculous to me that I held such fear over a supposed apparition the previous night. That fear, and the dreadful longing for that which was lost, now drifted away from me like the last snatches of a dream.

Holmes was in fine fettle—too much so considering he had not had a wink of sleep. Any suggestion that he should rest would be met, as always, with derision. I could only observe, therefore, and offer my services as a doctor should he require them.

As we strolled along the harbour wall, we pieced together from memory the mysterious events surrounding the stricken ship, *Demeter*. The vessel had sailed from Varna on 6 July the previous year; it was, according to the Dracula Papers, carrying boxes of earth from Dracula's homeland, without which the vampire was unable to rest. During a long and perilous voyage, the crew were slowly wiped out. At first, the captain believed the murderer to be a Roumanian crewman, but soon there came reports of a mysterious stranger aboard, believed to have stowed away. One by one the crew perished, until only the captain remained. Lashing himself to the ship's wheel, the captain steered the course alone to Whitby, where he had the great misfortune to perish in one of the worst storms to hit the town in many a year. Eye-witnesses saw an enormous dog leap from the ship as it was wrecked—Van Helsing later explained that this was Dracula himself, in the form of a wolf. The captain's log was found tucked in a bottle, and was translated for an unnamed newspaperman by the Russian consul.

"There are so many irregularities in this affair that it is hard to know where to begin," Holmes said. "Take, for instance, Count Dracula's motives. Van Helsing would have us believe that Dracula was behind every misfortune to befall the *Demeter*. He conjures a fog to throw it off course; he slays its crew; finally, he summons a great tempest to wreck the ship. This leaves the Count the onerous task of recovering his earth-boxes from the wreckage, and transporting them to London. The Dracula Papers tell us that the Count left instruction with a local solicitor to take charge of fifty boxes of earth from the wreck, an instruction that was carried out in defiance of all salvage laws and in advance of both the official inquest and the intervention of the Admiralty Board. I also put to you that Dracula is not normally described as utterly insatiable—indeed, the Count is generally depicted as a masterful tactician, with considerable control over his bloodlust. We know that Dracula does not even need to kill his victims—he could slip from his hiding place each night, drink from a victim, hypnotise him so that the man remembers nothing, and then slip away. He demonstrated this ability with poor Lucy Westenra, after all. So why endanger his only means of transport? If he can control the winds, why not assist the ship in reaching his destination swiftly and safely, rather than jeopardise his whole plan?"

"When you put it like that, Holmes, it does sound rather far-fetched."

"More so when you consider that, eventually, Dracula was forced to flee England on board another ship, the *Czarina Catherine*. Somehow, upon the return voyage, he managed to abstain from killing the crew. Are we to believe that the Count simply wished to make the most dramatic arrival possible? For whose benefit? Consider, too, the events in the Dracula Papers, the section where the 'Crew of Light' pursue Dracula from Varna to his home in the Carpathians. That journey, conducted at great speed, takes considerably longer than six days. According to Harker's journal, however, that is precisely how long the Count took between leaving his castle and boarding the *Demeter* at Varna. I put it to you that Count Dracula was never aboard the *Demeter* at all, and that some other misfortune befell the crew."

I confessed that these things had not occurred to me, so engrossing had the tale been, and told from the point of view of a neutral reporter.

"Neutral?" Holmes scoffed. "A sensationalist, perhaps. An agent of Van Helsing more likely. I was at the offices of the *Whitby Gazette* this morning." He waved the newspaper at me to illustrate his point. "This is a copy of the paper printed the day after the storm, 9 August. The fate of the *Demeter* is mentioned only as a footnote, and yet it was a lengthy story in the 'Dailygraph'. I presume this is meant to be the *Daily Telegraph*, a London paper. That is logical, as the 'Russian consul' that translated the *Demeter*'s log is in London. Verifying this fact will be devilishly hard—not only is the newspaper article retyped by Mrs Harker, but so too are the excerpts from the *Demeter*'s log reproduced therein. There are far too many possibilities for error within these transcriptions, and thus too much opportunity for plausible denial of any conclusions we may draw from them."

"So what do you propose, Holmes? That Van Helsing was the mysterious stranger, slaying the crew for who knows what awful purpose?"

"Unlikely. I certainly believe that Van Helsing was present in London much earlier than we are led to believe by the Dracula Papers, although it would be a stretch to place him on a ship sailing from Varna to Whitby. No, the *Demeter* was stricken by some mysterious misfortune at sea that we may never fully understand; one of those vagaries of naval misadventure that old sailors tell tales of for generations. However, I would guess that the story of the *Demeter* was so evocative that Van Helsing seized upon it, twisting the facts to make his story appear even more plausible. However, it is a fiction too far."

There was no time to press Holmes for his precise theories, for we at last reached the harbourmaster's office, and were forced to join a queue of new arrivals to the docks, all of whom had to be registered and have their goods accounted for by a despairingly small staff. My own huffs at the interminable wait were drowned out by the more colourful opinions of visiting seamen, who were only too willing to give loud voice to their complaints.

When at last we found someone to attend us, Holmes used all of his powers of persuasion and haughty manner to speak to the harbourmaster himself, and eventually we were admitted to the records office, whilst being told every step of the way that it was "most irreg'lar". In a dingy, windowless room crammed with thick ledgers, we were left to our own devices for some time. It was all

I could do not to nod off more than once as, poring over crinkled pages by the light of a paraffin lamp, we searched diligently for the log entries of the *Demeter*.

"Aha!" Holmes exclaimed after our interminable search had taken us well into the afternoon. "I have the very transcript here, of which some small fragments made their way to the Dracula Papers. The original pages, written in Russian, are enclosed also, although they are barely legible."

"Looks like there are large portions missing," I said. "Indeed, there are. Even if the log is complete, it appears that almost a quarter of the entries are smudged beyond recognition, or torn to pieces. They were recovered amongst the wreckage."

"If the papers were in such a state when the transcript was made…"

"Then we have no way of knowing what was a factual recording, and what was a complete fabrication," Holmes finished.

"And the transcript in English—it concurs with the Dracula Papers?" I asked.

"Remember that the Dracula Papers contain a reporter's rescript of these very notes. They are the same, though they omit many of the mundanities found here in this ledger. Weather readings, soundings, supply rationing, watch rotations and so on. The boring minutiae that have been included purely to throw an investigator off the trail."

"How can you be sure?"

"Without an expert witness to assist me, I cannot. I would need someone with a great deal of sailing knowledge to verify all of this technical information. However, that probably will not be necessary. I have ascertained all I really need from the study of the handwriting in this ledger."

Graphology was something of a specialty for Holmes, but here in the gloomy conditions, with a ledger so scruffily presented, I could not see how it could help us, and said as much.

"While much effort has been taken to disguise the style of writing," Holmes replied, "such copious amounts of text—undoubtedly written from dictation—could not have been quickly produced without some errors; that is, without incorporating just a few of the natural flourishes of the writer's true hand. See here," Holmes pointed to a line of sloped text that barely fit upon the lines of the page. "Note the capital 'S', and all of the lower-case 'd's. They are much more rounded than those found in the first paragraph on the page—the writer was evidently becoming tired. But the hand is confident, the control of the nib elegant. This is a woman, of strong will, and aged between twenty and thirty, in my humble opinion."

"Mina Harker?"

Holmes produced a letter from his pocket, unfolded the paper, and placed it next to the ledger. He took out his magnifier and studied the two pieces of writing, side by side.

"There can be no doubt, Watson," he said. "This is the letter from Mina Harker given to us by Miss Reed. The penmanship is identical in those places where she allowed her concentration to slip. And of course, this tells us something else about Mina Harker that ought to be invaluable in this case."

"Oh?"

"She is a skilled forger. Much of this work has been meticulously written in the same hand as the previous entries, probably that of a clerk of this office. It is only the tedious length of this ship's log that gives the true author away. On shorter texts—letters, signatures, and diary entries, for instance—I imagine Mrs Harker's skill would make her hand undetectable. With this log, however, we have our first piece of real evidence against her. I could have a world expert in the forensic science of handwriting testify on this sample in our favour, of that I am certain."

This was a true success, and I allowed myself a chuckle. I had not, until last night, truly considered Mrs Harker as our enemy; now I most certainly viewed her as such, and a devious one at that. Finally, however, we had an advantage.

Holmes put away the letter, took up the heavy ledger, and marched at once out into the adjoining corridor. There, the harbourmaster, who had apparently been about to join us, attempted to stop us from removing the log, quoting chapter and verse all manner of procedures and by-laws regarding the official status of the document. Holmes fixed the man with his most imperious glare, and said, "If you wish to protect the reputation of this office, you will explain to me at once why this ledger contains a forged ship's log, which falsifies the accounts of several mysterious deaths at sea. I assure you, sir, that charges of conspiracy will be brought upon every man in this office unless you cooperate."

There was a brief spell of defiance from the aging harbourmaster, who was clearly not used to being browbeaten by civilians; yet ultimately he was a public servant, and understood only too well the seriousness of the matter being put before him. All the bureaucracy in the world would not protect him should Holmes's accusations prove true. He explained that the head of the Harbour Board was one Robert Browning, who was responsible for all logs regarding wrecks and disasters at sea. He would have signed the documentation regarding the *Demeter*'s log personally.

With a tip of his hat, Holmes marched out, with me in his wake, and soon we were heading up the lane to the Harbour Board offices.

"I am a very busy man, Mr Holmes, can't we do this some other time?" Mr Browning was an uncommonly brusque gentleman, who did his best to give Holmes and me short shrift, but he had not counted on Holmes's tenacity.

"I am afraid not," Holmes replied. "We must return to London today, and this matter is one of utmost urgency. Now, will you talk to us, or should I take this to Scotland Yard and have them pay you a visit?"

Holmes dropped the ledger upon Browning's desk. The man had been glancing nervously at it for the whole time we had been arguing, and now he became very quiet. Browning's clerk had been standing behind us in the door of the office, trying to get us to leave; now, Browning waved him away, and the clerk removed himself from the room, closing the door behind him.

"Now then, Mr Holmes, what's all this about?" Browning offered an innocent smile, but beads of sweat had already formed upon his balding brow. Here was a man who carried great guilt.

"I think you know very well," Holmes said. "This ledger contains the supposed translation of a ship's log—the *Demeter*, a schooner wrecked off the coast of Whitby last year. The log, as added to the official archives by you, sir, is a work of fiction; a forgery, provided by a third party to obfuscate some terrible crime."

"Wh… where is your evidence?" Browning stammered.

"I can prove beyond doubt that the log is a forgery. I can prove who wrote it, for I am already investigating her part in another crime entirely."

"*Her?* Then you know—"

"Indeed I do. What I do not know is why you, a respected public servant—an elected official, no less—would allow this travesty to occur unchallenged."

"It… I… Look here, Mr Holmes, I took that record on good faith. It was translated from the ship's log by the Russian consul, and—"

"Translated," Holmes snapped. "From this?" He took out the pages of the original log and placed them on the desk beside the book. "Eight pages survive, and more than half their content smeared and illegible. And yet miraculously the ledger contains sixteen pages of precise, uninterrupted accounts of the *Demeter*'s fateful last voyage. Did you fail to notice this oversight when you received the pages 'in good faith'?"

"Pages… must be missing," Browning said, panic in his voice. "Misplaced. Yes, that's it, misplaced. There must have been more."

"I think not, Mr Browning. I think that when I take these scraps to the Russian embassy myself, I shall find little in common between the truth and the official account. Why would you do such a thing to those poor sailors?"

"As I said, I received those pages in—"

"So you claim incompetence? Or perhaps negligence? Both preferable, I suppose, to criminal conspiracy, although I am not sure how a judge will see it."

"Look, Mr Holmes, the *Demeter* is long gone. Her crew is gone. There was no funny business on the part of any man or woman in Whitby that contributed the wrecking of that schooner. No crime has been committed, beyond the alleged falsification of records. No harm has been done."

"No harm?" Holmes raised his voice now, and drew himself up to his full height. His aquiline nose and angular features took on the aspect of a buzzard ready to strike down at the gizzard of a startled rabbit. The effect was not lost on Browning. "All hands died aboard that ship. Families mourn the loss of brothers, sons and friends, with only lies and fairy stories to console them. And yet you say no harm was done? For shame, sir! Perhaps I should give your regards to the Russian embassy while I am there— perhaps they will share your sentiment."

"Enough, enough!" Browning held his palms out in a gesture of surrender. "What can I do to make amends, Mr Holmes? Please, I cannot let this thing come to light. I would be ruined."

"Then why strike a bargain with such a villainess? This

Wilhelmina Harker—yes, I know her name, do not look so surprised. You can begin with an explanation as to why a Harbour Board official would become a partner in crime to such a woman."

Browning's head sank into his hands, and finally he explained himself.

During the investigation into the mysterious wreck of the *Demeter*, Browning was approached by a young woman whom he had never seen before, and was suddenly and passionately thrust into a romantic affair with her. Browning described how he quite lost his head upon receiving the attentions of such a pretty, eloquent and confident woman, and in the heat of the moment reneged on his marriage vows to forsake all others. The very next day, however, Browning received a visit from the woman, who showed to him several photographs, taken by an accomplice, and threatened to show these photographs to his wife unless he helped her.

Under these conditions of blackmail, the log of the *Demeter* was handed to the woman—who he now knew to be Wilhelmina Harker—and later returned to the Harbour Board office by a London reporter, with a signed statement supposedly from the Russian consul regarding the log's translation. Browning, already too far embroiled in a plot he could not understand, presented this information as fact at the inquest, and no more was heard on the matter. The unnamed newspaper correspondent made sure to be indiscreet in his local enquiries, causing gossip to spread like wildfire amongst the fishwives, fortifying Mina Harker's version of events in the popular imagination.

"What do you suppose really happened to the *Demeter*?" I asked.

Browning shook his head. "I do not know for certain, and I doubt we will ever know the truth, for the original log is in too poor a condition to read. Perhaps one of the sailors carried some horrid disease, or perhaps the first mate really was a murderer as the captain first suspected. And then there was the dog…"

Holmes's eyes lit up. "Yes, the dog. It was later described in the Dracula Papers as a wolf, but the original statement makes no such claim. I would guess that the hound carried some foreign illness that beset the crew, and then itself escaped in the wreck. Several witnesses saw it run along the shore."

"I daresay you are right, Mr Holmes, although no dog was ever found."

"Back to these photographs, Mr Browning—are they still held over you?"

"They are, which is why I would not testify to anything I have told you unless my life depended on it. For the sake of my poor wife…"

Browning broke down in a fit of trembling, his eyes full of such remorse that it was hard not to feel for him, for all his foolishness. He asked Holmes to swear that his name would not be dragged into the case unnecessarily, so that he might at least attempt to make it up with his wife and, of course, keep his position on the Harbour Board, for which he had worked all his life.

"I can make no guarantee," Holmes said. "I will do what I can, on that you have my word, but your actions have allowed more than one murder to go undetected and unchallenged. Though I am sure you would have behaved differently had you known, the fact remains that the consequences were severe indeed."

At these words, Browning almost wept, and expressed his gratitude to Holmes. Here was a man of great seniority within his little world of sailors, fishermen, clerks, records and cargoes. And yet before Holmes he had become timid and humbled. I could only be glad that I was Holmes's friend, and not an enemy.

CHAPTER ELEVEN

SMOKE AND MIRRORS

When finally we returned to Baker Street, my head still aching dully from the previous night's trials, we found two letters waiting for us. The first came as some surprise to me—it was from Van Helsing himself! Due to our trip to Whitby this letter was not received until a delay of some two days had passed. Holmes bemoaned this as soon as we received the communication, but also found a silver lining: Van Helsing had not expected us to go north quite so suddenly, which led Holmes to believe the things we discovered there were of genuine interest, rather than any staged performance of Van Helsing's design.

Letter, Abraham Van Helsing to Sherlock Holmes,
10 April 1894

I have reviewed your cases, and see you have an impressive record of bringing to justice criminals most nefarious—or most careless. Though the police they celebrate you highly, Mr Holmes, it appear to me that without the mortal foe who to make mistake, the great Sherlock Holmes is no more than the bloodhound chasing the wounded fox, no? I tell you in words plain, Mr Holmes, there are some foes in this world that are beyond you. The greatest opponent that you ever face was the Professor Moriarty, who almost was the end of your life. Yet the creature Dracula, whom I pursue to the end of the earth, was worth ten of your Moriarty. I am the one who see to the end of his threat most terrible.

I am to think that you would fare not so well against the likes of Dracula, you with your mind so closed to possibilities beyond the five senses. Imagine therefore how poorly you would fare against one who could defeat even Dracula. I am to hope for your sake, Mr Holmes, that you never are to discover a foe so powerful, so ruthless, and so single-minded in his goals.

Van Helsing

The second letter was from Holmes's informant, Langdale Pike, who had indeed sent a reply via messenger. Holmes had asked Pike for any information he could find on Mina Harker and Genevieve Holmwood, notably regarding if either of them had any history in the theatre.

Letter, Langdale Pike to Sherlock Holmes, 13 April 1894

Holmes,

How interesting that Lady Godalming has come to your attention. You must surely know that I have been collecting snippets on her for some time, for she caused quite the stir last season, and who knows what marvellous scandal she will incite this time? We simply must exchange intelligence when next we meet.

Genevieve Holmwood was once simple Jennie Megginson of Scarborough, a lady's maid, of all things, who went on to play the seaside dancehalls. She had a particular talent for stage make-up and costumery, and worked her way up from assistant to actress. It seems she's always been quite the ambitious one. She spent some little time in London, where she auditioned more than once under the name Genevieve Kidd, for a certain theatre manager whom I know. She had some talent, it is said, and even portrayed Juliet at the Royal in '89, though not to any notable acclaim. He says her success was somewhat disproportionate to her talents, and she was a touch too self-absorbed to be a true artiste. Anyway, she disappeared from the limelight not too long after that, due to a poor temperament making her ill-dispositioned toward critique, and she has not been heard of again, until now, of course.

That is all I could find at such short notice, but I shall continue to make discreet enquiries. In exchange, I expect you to attend my next dinner party—you always make for the finest entertainment, Holmes, and yet you rarely put in an appearance. What are friends for, after all?

Your friend,
L.P.

Upon reading the letters, Holmes at once scribbled two messages—one a reply to Pike, and the other a short missive to Inspector Bradstreet. He then ran downstairs to find a messenger, and despite the late hour returned successful.

"I am afraid your hot bath and rest shall have to wait, Watson," he said. "We must work quickly if we are to tighten the net."

"Whatever now? What can you hope to achieve at this hour?"

"Why, night-time is the perfect time for our purpose."

"Which is?"

"To find a vampire, of course!"

CHAPTER TWELVE

THE BLOOFER LADY

We stood beneath the shadow of St Michael's, looking along a dark, cypress-lined avenue that led to the sombre Egyptian-style tombs of Highgate Cemetery. Inspector Bradstreet and I stamped our feet against the midnight chill, while Holmes seemed not to notice the cold at all. The weather in London had taken a turn for the worse, and even now a fog was dropping upon an already gloomy scene.

"Excellent," said Holmes. "The conditions are almost as they were on that fateful night when Lucy Westenra's corpse was seen walking abroad. What better time to recreate those ghastly events."

Bradstreet looked alarmed. "Recreate them? With all due respect, Holmes, I did not come all the way out here to cut the heads off any corpses."

"Nor will you have to, Inspector," Holmes said cheerfully. "The corpse in question has already been mutilated by Lord Godalming; I shouldn't imagine it will do any walking about on our watch."

Since receiving confirmation of Lady Godalming's theatrical

past, Holmes had become convinced that she had played another key role at the behest of Van Helsing—that of the mysterious "bloofer lady", or the "Hampstead Horror"—an Un-Dead of Dracula's making that had been seen haunting Highgate, and eventually revealed to be the restless body of Lucy Westenra. This "vampire" had snatched several children from the surrounding area before fleeing back to her tomb, whereupon she had been stopped once and for all by the Crew of Light. At Van Helsing's instruction, Arthur Holmwood had struck Lucy's head from her body, ending the new vampire's reign of terror.

Holmes now clutched several pages from the Dracula Papers, and scanned them once more. "We tread in the very footsteps of our notorious vampire hunters," he said. "Let us see if we can find out how the trick was performed."

Bradstreet was by now well in our confidence, and as certain as Holmes that some great conspiracy was underway. After seeing the fate of Frank Cotford, however, he was not inclined to take his suspicions to his superiors without hard evidence. Holmes had sent a messenger asking Bradstreet to meet us at Highgate, and to bring a set of tools with him. To his credit, Bradstreet had come equipped for some grim work, even though he did not have the support of Scotland Yard on the matter.

"I've never been one to believe in fairy stories," said Bradstreet, "though I tend not to tempt fate where I can help it. I hope you aren't planning to wake the dead tonight."

"Why, Inspector, what a peculiar thing for a man of the law to say. No, I do not presume to wake the dead, though perhaps they shall speak to me."

"This is a raw night for loitering around graveyards, Mr Holmes, especially if you're planning on opening up a tomb."

"Actually, Inspector, given the legalities of such a venture, I was going to insist that *you* open it."

The inspector grumbled at this, while Holmes set off briskly, taking the path through the graveyard, explaining to us his theory as he went.

"We are told by the Dracula Papers that this particular Un-Dead fiend preyed exclusively on young children. I'd guess that 'bloofer lady' is in fact a child's attempt at saying 'beautiful lady', recorded literally by the reporter. None of the children who encountered the bloofer lady were killed, but all had small, inexplicable puncture-marks on their throats, and were lethargic and weak. What restraint this fledgling vampire showed! Do you recall the descriptions of the women in Castle Dracula given us by Jonathan Harker? Do you remember how insatiable in his bloodlust Dracula himself was aboard the *Demeter*, according to the falsified log? But here we have an Un-Dead, newly made, hungering for blood, and yet able to drink but a token amount from so tempting a victim as a plump child?

"Genevieve Holmwood, in the guise of Lucy Westenra, walked about the cemetery at night, scaring the wits from anyone who saw her.

"Van Helsing hired Lady Godalming—then simply plain Miss Kidd, do not forget—based primarily on her appearance. An actress with her best days behind her, of notably similar looks to Miss Westenra… well, I imagine he thought Christmas had come early. Even though she must have known the immorality of what she was about to do, Miss Kidd entered Van Helsing's employ, probably for the first time in what would become quite the criminal partnership. She abducted children who played out late upon the neighbouring heath, luring them to her, and probably feeding them sweets laced with laudanum. When the children fell into a drug-induced sleep, during which they would feel nothing, Miss Kidd pricked at their throats, perhaps with a brooch-pin, and then left them to recover alone. The children would have remembered nothing during their fug, but for the mysterious woman, and certain nightmares induced by the drugs in ones so young. After several repetitions of this ruse, the local community would have become fearful for their children. Rumours would have spread, tales would have become taller. By the time word of the 'Hampstead Horror' reached the ears of our newspaperman, the story was so entrenched in the popular imagination that it almost wrote itself."

Inspector Bradstreet nodded, and unfolded his arms. "Well, Holmes, despite there being a great deal of conjecture in your theory, it is certainly a more plausible story than the alternative."

"Such a commendation from a man of the Yard is praise indeed," Holmes said, with a thin smile.

"What would possess Miss Kidd to embark upon such a terrible endeavour?" I asked.

"Money. More than anything," Holmes said with a wave of his hand. "Even now, I suppose Van Helsing pays her a handsome stipend, whilst draining her husband's estate. If he does not pay her, he surely threatens her. Of course, for an ambitious young actress, the social status alone would be worth the ignominy of becoming Van Helsing's puppet. She is seen on occasion at the best society balls, is she not? Even without her husband?"

"I believe so."

"There you have it. Now, if I may continue?"

"Of course."

"Let us look to Van Helsing, for it was he that claimed the bloofer lady was Lucy Westenra, and secured witnesses to verify her identity—first showing her to Dr Seward, alone, and then later to Seward, Morris and Lord Godalming together, the last of whom struck the stake through the heart of his deceased love, and has paid for that act with his sanity since.

"When Lucy Westenra was first interred, Van Helsing placed

upon her lips a crucifix. He gave no explanation for this wholly useless act, though Dr Seward believed it was to prevent Lucy from rising to become Un-Dead. Later, the crucifix was revealed to be in Van Helsing's possession once again. He claimed it was stolen by a woman—who goes unnamed—and that he recovered it. This incident spurred Van Helsing to return to the cemetery with Seward to see if Lucy had indeed become a vampire."

"All well and good," Bradstreet said.

"Not in the slightest, Inspector! Do you not see? It is highly unlikely that a low working woman would enter a tomb, and in later descriptions of Lucy's resting place there is no mention of any other thefts, despite the funerary trappings of Miss Westenra being somewhat opulent. The crucifix was retrieved by Van Helsing himself when he returned to the tomb to tamper with the body, and the story of the theft was used to cover this unsavoury fact and give a reason for Seward to accompany him to the cemetery to witness the vampire Lucy walking abroad."

"A difficult task for one old man acting alone," Bradstreet said.

"If he was acting alone, that is true enough. But Van Helsing had the key to the tomb, supposedly because he planned to give it to Arthur Holmwood later. This would have made his progress much simpler."

The Inspector frowned. "If he had a key all along, then you're right—his story about the robber-woman is unbelievable. Why, it is all smoke and mirrors, Mr Holmes. You are saying that Van Helsing staged a performance in order to bring the other men into his confidence."

"There you have it, Inspector. Seward was already a sycophant when it came to Van Helsing, and would believe anything the professor told him. But Arthur Holmwood and Quincey P. Morris? No, they had to see the Un-Dead with their own eyes to believe it, and with this great illusion, playing upon the hearts of men who loved Lucy Westenra, Van Helsing bought himself a confederacy of useful idiots, who would die for whatever cause the professor set them upon."

"And what exactly was his cause?" I asked.

"To hound Count Dracula unto death," Holmes replied. "I believe Van Helsing had some great reason for doing so, and was unlikely to have been working entirely on his own initiative—I rather suspect we are stumbling headlong into a greater plot of intrigue. However, the elaborate manner of Dracula's demise, and the subsequent demonising of the man... that suggests a more personal vendetta."

"Such as what?"

"That, my dear Watson, remains to be seen. Suffice it to say for now that I have my theories. One thing at a time, however. Shall we see how the great trick of bringing Lucy Westenra back to life was done?"

We came at last to the Westenra vault. The gravestones and undergrowth were mere black smudges in the quickly dropping fog, and Holmes led us about the immediate surrounds of the tomb as he painted a picture of events of the previous September.

"The first of our suspects to see the bloofer lady was Jack Seward. Let us assume, just for a moment, that he had no idea of what he was about to see—he was tricked by Van Helsing, quite masterfully.

"Having convinced Seward that Lucy's immortal soul was in danger, Van Helsing led the doctor down here in the middle of the night, and entered her tomb, just as we have done. He reminded Seward of his love for the girl, heightening his suggestibility to fever-pitch. By the time the professor opened the coffin, Seward was a bag of nerves. You may not recall it, but Seward was wary of any noxious gases emitting from the coffin as the seals were broken and the lid thrown back; Van Helsing did not flinch. Seward puts this down to the professor's absolute certainty that

Lucy was walking abroad as one of the Un-Dead. I think the professor knew the coffin would be empty for a different reason."

"He had already moved the body," I said.

Holmes nodded. "Once Seward had seen the empty coffin for himself, Van Helsing led him outside to show him the Un-Dead in action. This cemetery is vast, and yet Van Helsing directed Seward to one spot in particular, whilst he himself stood elsewhere, and between them they happened to sight 'Lucy' walking through the graveyard. Fortunate timing indeed. From the very spot that Seward stood—a spot that Van Helsing had directed him to, remember—he allegedly saw Lucy vanish through the locked door of the tomb—a feat that she would repeat in identical circumstances later, when Morris and Holmwood were also present. Of course, this is a simple trick. Van Helsing was careful to position his witnesses exactly where required so that a fractional opening of the door would not be noticed. He was also careful to position himself in their eye line, to partially block their view. Van Helsing had a key, and it is therefore safe to assume that Miss Kidd had a copy. She is a slight woman, and could slip through the door stealthily enough."

"And what then?" Bradstreet asked. "Did not Van Helsing, and several witnesses, follow her into the tomb? How did the woman escape?"

"They did not follow her, Inspector, that's just it. Twice was this trick repeated, and on each occasion Van Helsing stepped first to the door of the tomb, 'sealed' it with crumbled communion wafers, and persuaded all present—first Seward alone and then Holmwood and Morris—that they should leave the scene and return later. The alleged vampire was powerless to act against Van Helsing on each occasion, so why not simply destroy her on that second occasion? The other men present, although appalled, were ready to do so.

"I put it to you that, on the first occasion when Van Helsing brought Seward to the tomb, he had simply moved the body, so that Dr Seward would find an empty coffin. We already know from the papers that Van Helsing had spent much of the preceding day at the cemetery 'on watch'; thus he had ample time to perform the act, and indeed to learn the comings and goings of the watchman. After seeing the coffin empty, Van Helsing led his shocked guests outside, where they saw Miss Kidd appear as I have described. The men all then fled the scene. When they next returned, they found a body in the coffin, looking strangely alive and with the teeth of a vampire—again, Van Helsing had sufficient time to tamper with the body, and I expect Miss Kidd's expertise in theatrical make-up came into play."

"Would Lady Godalming—I mean, Miss Kidd—do such a gruesome thing?" I asked, recalling the slip of a young woman I had met only recently.

"I imagine the rewards for her services would have been ample, Watson. An actress, particularly one whose star has faded quickly, does not have the best of prospects, after all.

"Now, gentlemen, there is something that perturbs me about the events of those fateful nights—even more so than all of these other points. On each of those two occasions, a child was recovered. A victim of the bloofer lady. And on both occasions, Van Helsing persuaded the other men to leave the child on Hampstead Heath, where a policeman might walk by and find him. A child supposedly weak from loss of blood, disorientated, and perhaps— by the professor's own shaky logic—at risk of becoming a vampire themselves. Tell me, Inspector, what would you say to that, had you heard it at the time?"

"I... I would have been outraged, Mr Holmes, to tell the truth. It seems a callous act, for police patrols are not frequent. If the child was unconscious, and an officer failed to notice it, then what else may have befallen the unfortunate soul? If the men had nothing to hide, then they should also have nothing to fear from taking the child to the nearest police station."

"Aha! So you see they did have something to hide. Many things, in fact. Van Helsing would undoubtedly argue that drawing attention to his plans would jeopardise the destruction of the vampire Lucy, for the authorities would have put a watch on the tomb, and arrest anyone entering or leaving it. But surely a little white lie to the police would have served just as well? A midnight stroll across the heath perhaps? The word of Lord Godalming to assuage the questions of the constabulary. Or they could simply have deposited the child on the steps of the police station incognito, and been away in secret. No, leaving the child as they did suggests callousness indeed, and that detail alone would make me question the intentions of such men.

"Now, all that remains is to see if we can find some physical evidence to support these hypotheses, or else we have nothing more concrete than the Dracula Papers themselves. Inspector, if you would be so kind, it is time to see in what state the body has been left."

Bradstreet and I exchanged nervous glances; disturbing the dead was not a cheerful prospect at the best of times. Now, however, I could not help but wonder what the consequences might be if Holmes was wrong. What if some satanic, Un-Dead really had lain in the tomb beneath us, and we were about to disturb it again?

When finally the door creaked open, Holmes struck up a lantern and led the way inside. He stopped just inside the door, at the top of a flight of steps, and illuminated the lock. "As Seward kindly observed for us in his journal, there is the falling lock, allowing the door to be opened from the inside if necessary. An interesting feature, don't you think? One I suspect Van

Helsing stipulated—he was, after all, present during the funeral arrangements, and doubtless had a hand in them knowing he would have to enter the tomb to cut off the head of the corpse."

The tomb itself was not large—three steps dropped to a simple, rough chamber, with only enough room for perhaps six people to gather around the coffin, which sat in the centre of the space upon a carved plinth. Dead flowers hung in great clumps all around us. Upon the lid of the coffin sat a bunch of dry garlic flowers and a handful of holy wafers. I shuddered at the thought of the evil that those items were supposed to hold back.

Holmes set the lantern into a small niche in the brickwork and set about brushing aside the flowers and wafers.

"Holmes," I said, despite myself. My friend paused only to look up and smirk at me incredulously.

"Really, Watson. Do you suppose a vampire will burst forth from the coffin? Even if Lucy Westenra was one of the living dead, she is supposed to be at rest now, her head struck from her body."

Holmes felt about the lid of the coffin, and eventually his fingers found purchase. The coffin lid wobbled slightly as he pulled at it.

"Excellent," Holmes said, "the seal was not restored after Van Helsing's last foray down here. But the lid is heavy—won't one of you help me?"

Bradstreet made no effort to move, and I saw him swallow hard. I stepped forth and took hold of the other end of the lid.

"Wait, Holmes," I said. "What are we about to find?"

"That's the beauty of it, Watson," he replied with facetious cheerfulness. "For once I have absolutely no idea."

I braced myself for a horrible sight, and heaved away at the lid of the coffin with Holmes. I tried not to look inside the casket as we lowered the lid to the ground. The underlying, sickly sweet smell of the undertaker's unguents could not mask the noxious fume of decomposition, aided as it was by the stale air that had penetrated the coffin's broken seal.

"Well, I half expected it to be empty," Holmes said, nonchalant in the face of the grotesque.

I first looked across at Bradstreet, whose face had turned so pale that it was luminous in the lantern-light. I followed the inspector's gaze to the casket, and to the corpse within.

The body itself, that of a young woman, was clothed in white funerary robes. A tangle of golden hair framed a skull-like face, the flesh grey and shrunken. The head sat a couple of inches from the body, and at the neck was a terrible black wound. We could just see the very top of the stake that, as the Dracula Papers described, had been sawn off. The point of it was buried somewhere deep inside the corpse's breast, beneath a blackened stain. It was truly a sight to chill the blood, even for one who has treated soldiers upon the field of battle.

"We are in luck," Holmes said.

"Luck?" Bradstreet said, hoarsely.

"Everything is just as Van Helsing left it. The screws are still loose, and the seal is still broken. He could have sent someone to remove any evidence left behind. In his arrogance, I expect he thought no one would ever be brave enough to make a thorough inspection."

"What do you expect to find?"

"Hush now, let me work."

Holmes set about tapping at the stone pedestal, and pushing at the coffin, though it would not budge. He nodded to himself, deep in thought.

"Holmes," I said. "Did not the men describe how Lucy's face transformed in the moment they transfixed her with the stake? From monster to beauty."

"Wishful thinking and the power of suggestion make a heady mix. Or... perhaps not."

Holmes took out his magnifier, and began to make thorough scrutiny of the casket, outside and in, sweeping it slowly and meticulously along every inch of wood, stone, brass and, grotesquely, the corpse itself.

He stopped at the head of the casket, and ran his hand along the wood and satin within, his lips upturning into a smile as he did so.

"Hand me a turnscrew, would you, Inspector? The longest blade you have."

Bradstreet handed Holmes the tool; I saw that the inspector's hand was shaking slightly.

Holmes slid the end of the screwdriver between the wooden panels near the decapitated head with some relish. At first his workings appeared fruitless, until at last the base of the coffin wobbled, shaking some of the dust from the corpse's cerements. Both Bradstreet and I stepped back involuntarily.

"One of you, bring a jemmy and help me."

Bradstreet swallowed hard and stepped forward. Directed by Holmes, he placed the bar in the gap between the sides of the coffin and its base, and pulled. Lucy's head rolled away from him, wedging against her shoulder.

Holmes fished around beneath the base of the coffin, which lifted far too easily, I realised, bending upwards at the end as it was staked down in the centre. Holmes at last pulled out his dirt-encrusted hands, which held two items. In his left hand was a broad, flat coil of metal; in his right, something tiny and dirty, which he rubbed between his fingers before holding it up to the lamplight.

"A tooth!" I said.

"Indeed. Inspector, you may rest easy now, we are done."

Bradstreet looked relieved, and withdrew the jemmy, with but one last look of disgust as the head wobbled once more.

"So, Mr Holmes," Bradstreet said, "will you now reveal the trick of it?"

"I shall indeed. Take this." Holmes handed the coil to Bradstreet.

"What is it?"

"A metal spring. One of several that I felt under the coffin's false base. The only reason I can imagine for it being there is to cause the base to wobble when the stake was plunged through Miss Westenra's heart, thus lending the impression that the body moved one last time in its death throes. Having ensured that Holmwood witnessed this trick, Van Helsing then stepped forward to say a few words. What he actually did was remove this, and its twin of course, from Lucy's mouth, and secrete them down the side of the false panel, never to be found."

Holmes held out the tooth once more.

"A vampire's fang…" I said.

"No, the fang of an animal, perhaps a cat. When Van Helsing prepared the body for his charade, he—or possibly Miss Kidd had she the stomach for it—would have affixed these to Lucy's own teeth with stage glue. Like so."

To my dismay, Holmes pulled back Miss Westenra's blue lips, with no small difficulty, and held the tooth in place. It fitted almost perfectly, proving his point that someone had gone to great lengths to alter the appearance of the corpse.

"May we speak outside, Mr Holmes?" said Bradstreet impatiently, throwing a furtive glance at the headless corpse. "The air in here is… rather close."

Soon we were back outside in the cold air, though it offered us little relief, for the fog had thickened in the graveyard, clinging thick to trees and tombstones, yellowing in colour and taking on a tar-like quality. It seemed a London particular was coming upon us, which would make our investigations in the city a miserable affair if it did not pass quickly.

"Mr Holmes, it's a bad business that we have embarked upon

tonight," Bradstreet said. "You have convinced me that some evil plot is at hand, and that I owe my old friend Frank Cotford an apology for doubting him."

"Do not reproach yourself, Inspector," Holmes said. "Cotford did himself no favours. We may, however, find some use for him yet."

"Oh?"

"You said yourself that you are not here tonight in any official capacity. Given the way the assistant commissioner dismissed Cotford, I assume also that he would give you short shrift should you try to reopen the investigation."

Bradstreet looked uncomfortable—I guessed that he did not like to be reminded that his authority had limitations.

"You are right, Mr Holmes, although the evidence we have uncovered might be enough."

"Let us not risk it," said Holmes. "Van Helsing has both money and influence. Who knows how far that influence extends? Even if our findings tonight are taken seriously by your superiors, Van Helsing will deny any involvement—he might even claim to be the victim of trickery just like the rest of us."

"So what are we to do?"

"First of all, we must find people we can trust to keep an eye on the tomb. I can call upon a few agents, and perhaps you can persuade Cotford to take up the mantle of investigator once more. It would appeal to his pride to be involved in any case against Van Helsing. Not only that, but if you stress that we cannot trust even the chiefs of Scotland Yard, he will feel at last vindicated in his paranoia. Play it true, Inspector, and I think you will find Cotford a valuable ally."

"Very well, Mr Holmes; Dr Watson," Bradstreet said, and extended a hand, which Holmes and I shook in turn. "I rather think this Van Helsing bit off more than he can chew when he took on Sherlock Holmes."

"I do hope so, Inspector," Holmes smiled. "I do hope so."

CHAPTER THIRTEEN

A GRIEVOUS BLOW

We had barely reached the landing of 221B when Mrs Hudson appeared. It was not the kind of unsociable hour that our landlady would usually keep, and her presence set me at once on guard.

"Mr Holmes, Dr Watson, something terrible has happened!" she cried.

Holmes sprang to action before she could even explain, and barged into our rooms. I followed, alert to danger. The rooms—never the tidiest by any stretch of the imagination—were now in complete disarray. Whomever had come here had been thorough in their search, and utterly callous in their destruction of property. Every drawer of the desk was upturned on the floor. Every book was strewn from the shelves. Holmes's unopened correspondence had been taken from its place upon the mantelpiece, where it traditionally sat transfixed by a knife-point, and now only one lonely page remained behind. Our armchairs had been overturned and the fabric across the undersides ripped open to search for concealed items. Papers, broken crockery and even our clothing lay on the floor. The open doors to the bedrooms told us at once that we would find a similar situation there. 221B Baker Street, so long our headquarters and sanctuary, was compromised.

"I did not call a constable, Mr Holmes," sniffed Mrs Hudson, entering the room behind us. "I know how you always complain about the police stomping all over your evidence. I am only sorry I could not stop them."

Holmes spun around. "You saw them?"

"Yes. They... they..." she trembled, unable to say more.

I patted Mrs Hudson's hand. "There, there," I said. "Surely they did not threaten you?"

Our landlady, who always seemed so formidable, now shook like a leaf, and nodded, tears in her eyes. "They threw me down into the armchair and told me to say not a word, or they would... they would..." She could not finish.

Holmes's features contorted into a violent thunder for a second. He strode over to the Persian slipper by the hearth, and fumbled about in the toe for his tobacco. Only when he had filled his briar and lit it did he finally speak.

"Mrs Hudson, I am so terribly sorry you were involved in this unpleasantness. You have my word that it shall not happen again. As for the men who did this—were they two large, foreign gentlemen perchance?"

"They were, Mr Holmes."

"Fair of hair?"

"I could not tell. It was dark—they wore hats, and had scarves about their faces. I only knew they were foreign when they ordered me to be quiet."

"Was anyone else with them?"

"I saw no one else."

"What time did you discover them?"

"I heard a noise, just a few minutes before midnight. At first

I thought you had returned. Even when the banging and crashing began, I thought it might be you, if you'll pardon me, Mr Holmes. You have been known to keep strange hours and peculiar habits. But as time went on I thought better of it."

"Can you remember anything else that may assist us? Any detail, no matter how trifling?"

"I can do more than that, Mr Holmes. I remembered how much you value these things, and so I followed them downstairs."

"Mrs Hudson!" I exclaimed.

"Watson is right," Holmes said. "These are dangerous men. However, if you have learned anything that may be of use, it is possible that the risk was worth taking. What did you see?"

"They got into a carriage—a private one."

"Liveried?"

"No, plain black."

"But a driver?"

"Yes. I got close enough to hear their instruction to the driver, though they spoke foreign."

"They spoke to the driver in German?" Holmes mused. "Mrs Hudson, did you make out any part of what they said? Think! It is of the utmost importance."

"They said only three words, and I did my best to remember them for you. But... but it sounded so vulgar."

"That's German for you. Lean forward, Mrs Hudson, and whisper it, to spare Dr Watson's blushes."

Mrs Hudson whispered in Holmes's ear, and at once my friend stepped back and laughed.

Mrs Hudson turned beetroot red. Holmes apologised at once and adopted a more sober expression.

"Oh, Mr Holmes. Is... is this what comes of your line of work?" Mrs Hudson asked tearfully.

"Do not fear, Mrs Hudson, I shall have all of this made right.

Watson—perhaps Mrs Hudson requires one of your tonics, for the shock."

"Of course, Holmes," I said, and at once ushered Mrs Hudson away, seeing that Holmes needed some peace to make a thorough examination of our rooms, which were now a crime scene.

When I returned, I found Holmes writing a letter, creating an awful frowst while he was at it by puffing incessantly on his pipe.

"Have you found anything of use?" I asked.

"Nothing I did not already know. The letter that was left behind on the mantelpiece was the missive sent to me by Van Helsing. It was not there originally, because as you know only unopened post is kept there. The letter had been removed from the desk drawer and pinned to the mantelpiece—an obvious message from the good professor that he now has the upper hand. We are dealing with professionals here, Watson. They wore gloves to avoid leaving fingerprints. Their shoes were clean, and they were careful not to drop anything that might incriminate them. I found a small mound of ash from an imported German cigarillo on the carpet over there, but it is not of an uncommon type, and not the cigars smoked by Van Helsing. It tells us nothing new about the intruders."

"This is an outrage, Holmes," I said. I had contained my anger in Mrs Hudson's presence, but now it spilled forth. "Twice now these Germans have threatened a defenceless woman. I would like to see how they fare against men!"

"You may have your chance, Watson, but these men are not the immediate danger. They have what they came for, and I imagine they shall leave us be, for a while at least."

"And what have they taken?"

"The Dracula Papers, Watson," he said. "Every scrap of evidence we have gathered so far. They have it all—the log of the *Demeter*, Cotford's journal, Kate Reed's letters, even Pike's message… confound it all! I have inadvertently put lives at risk."

"Holmes, you weren't to know."

"I should have known. We must have been seen about Whitby carrying a ledger from the harbourmaster's office, which is now in the hands of our enemy."

"Will you at least tell me what Mrs Hudson said to you that so amused you?"

"Oh, yes," Holmes said. "The phrase that Mrs Hudson thought she overheard, and made a fairly bad fist of repeating, was '*Die Botschaft, schnell*'. That adds to my suspicions."

"My German is not what it once was, Holmes. What does it mean?"

"Among other things, it means 'the embassy, quickly'. Our German friends may not be mere ruffians—they could be spies of the German government. It is reasonable to imagine, therefore, that Van Helsing is a spy also."

"You are saying we now find ourselves embroiled in espionage? Against the German government, no less! Should we not call upon Mycroft at once?"

"Not yet. We have lost our evidence, and now only have the hearsay of our landlady. Mycroft would disavow us immediately, and Van Helsing would probably sue us for barratry."

"A fine state of affairs! Well, what are we to do now, Holmes?" I asked, weary and utterly downhearted over this latest setback.

"I need to make a further search of these rooms to see if our burglars left any other clues behind. While I do that, you must go out, Watson, at once."

"Holmes, it shall soon be dawn…" I groaned.

"Which is why I must send you—there will be no messengers about, but you may be able to persuade a cabbie."

I sighed. It was not merely the prospect of hard work and a night without rest—I felt deeply guilty about Mrs Hudson's predicament too.

"What am I to do?" I said, resigning myself.

"Take these letters. This one must be given in at Langdale Pike's club—for all his influence, Pike has made himself a target by assisting us, and it would be remiss not to warn him. These two letters must be sent to Exeter. One is a warning for Miss Reed, the other a note for the police inspector there, asking him to remain vigilant lest the woman receives any unwelcome visitors. Lastly, you must give this missive to Bradstreet."

"He won't be happy about that! We've only been apart this last two hours."

"We must be careful in whom we place our trust. Bradstreet is in our confidence, and only he will do for now."

There was little more to be said. Before long I was on my way, feet leaden and head fuzzy. The fog had by now reached the city, and would soon take on an ominous, orange glow when the dawn's light struck it. I sighed. There were no hansoms about, and so I began the walk to the nearest livery stable office at Regent Street, at least thankful that the lack of sleep would stave off nightmares about bloofer ladies and headless corpses.

CHAPTER FOURTEEN

THE MAID'S TALE

It was a surprise to me that Holmes allowed us some scant hours' sleep before embarking once more on the trail of our villains. Holmes himself appeared none the worse for yet another long night of toil, while I was beginning to feel like the Un-Dead myself. It was well after midday when we finally struck out, engaging a hansom to ferry us around for most of the afternoon, making enquiries about town.

The objects of our search were the former servants of the Westenra family at Hillingham. Holmes and I concurred that their role in Lucy Westenra's final days was one of the strangest and most inexplicable details in the whole narrative.

The version of events that the Dracula Papers gave was as follows:

A few days before the death of Lucy Westenra, on the night that her mother died, Lucy was left alone. Despite all of her ills, and the belief that Dracula was attacking her, Van Helsing was called away on some other business abroad. He sent a letter to Dr Seward, summoning him to Hillingham to look after Lucy, but incorrectly addressed the envelope, so that the letter was a day late in reaching the doctor. Meanwhile, in a conveniently timed assault, Dracula supposedly entered Hillingham by impelling a wolf—stolen from London Zoo—to smash through a bedroom window, thus destroying the safeguards placed upon the entry points of the house by Van Helsing. That would have been curious enough, but for the strange detail that followed.

The shock of the attack caused Lucy's mother to die of a sudden heart attack. Lucy was able to tend to the body with the help of her four maids, but then instructed them all to go to the dining room and take a glass of sherry from the decanter to calm their nerves. When later Dracula attempted to gain access to the house, Lucy called upon the maids, but found that they were all asleep—the wine had been drugged with laudanum.

The question Holmes posed was a simple one: who drugged the sherry? Van Helsing and Seward were not in the house. The implication was that Dracula was responsible, but why, given his great powers of hypnotic suggestion, would he even bother to steal into the house, drug the wine, and then return later in such theatrical fashion? The only way to answer the question conclusively would be to question the maids, but their names and eventual fates were not recorded in the Dracula Papers. Only Frank Cotford was likely to still have the maids' names in his personal library of notebooks, and Bradstreet had gone to call on him, as advised by Holmes in his letter of the previous night.

Holmes and I wondered if the inspector's house call would prove fruitless, but some hours later a telegram had arrived for us, providing the name of one of the maids, and her last known employer.

In the months following her dismissal, the maid had changed situations several times, and our wending route through London, which had begun in the leafy suburbs around Hampstead, took us to gradually poorer territory. Now, after three stops, we found ourselves back in the East End, looking out at a dark, squat building, which loomed out of the fog.

"You are awake at last," Holmes said. "Good; we are here."

"Where?"

"A poor laundry, where our former lady's maid now works for two shillings a day."

"So she has fallen on hard times?"

"Of course. Van Helsing had her dismissed and she received no reference. A girl with no reference will always struggle to find work in a respectable house, and if she manages it she will find herself out on her ear at the first sign of a mistake. I have spoken with two of her subsequent employers while you slept, Watson, and although they did not accuse her of any great fault, neither did they think her services remarkable enough to retain. And so here we are."

"If you think the young woman is innocent of any wrongdoing, then this is a terrible thing to befall her."

"I doubt Van Helsing has ever given those four maids a passing thought. They are merely collateral damage in the workings of his devious machinations. Come, let us interview the girl, and hope that she can shed some light on events."

Betty Hobbs was a meek woman of few words, whose lined face and rough hands made her look considerably older than her probable true age. I had seen her like many times—the product of a hard life, with sunken, dark eyes and a hacking cough brought on by poor working conditions. Persuading the manageress of the cramped workshop to let us speak with Miss Hobbs had been no easy task, and had required the production of enough coin to constitute her girl's entire day's wages, let alone the few minutes that we required. Persuading Miss Hobbs herself to speak with us privately was equally tricky; it took some cajoling for Holmes to win the woman's trust enough to question her, and even then he had to disavow Van Helsing several times before she would talk.

"Now, Miss Hobbs," Holmes said gently, "I have given you what assurances I can. All I require from you is that you tell us, in your own words, what really happened on the night of 17 September last year."

"It was more or less like people been sayin'," she replied.

"More or less?"

"Yes, sir. We was all woke up by a scream—Mrs Westenra had taken a funny turn, and was havin' a heart attack."

"A scream? Whose?"

"Miss Lucy's, I think."

"And no other noise woke you? It was definitely the scream?"

"I know what you're going to ask, sir, and I swear it now as I swore it to that copper at the time—I didn't hear no dogs, an' certainly no wolf."

Holmes exchanged a severe glance with me. I recalled that a note in the Dracula Papers for the evening in question had recorded that the entire household had been woken by the howling of the neighbourhood dogs, agitated by the appearance in the vicinity of a large wolf, named "Berserker", that had escaped from London Zoo that night.

"Which policeman did you speak to?"

"Dunno. Some fancy inspector."

I guessed she was referring to Cotford, whose subsequent disgrace would have seen to it that the maid's statement was never heard.

"Did you speak to any policemen at the scene?"

"The scene? The house, you mean? No, sir, that Dutchman arrived and dismissed us, just like that, after two years' service."

"Hmm. We shall come to him in good time. Think back again

to the moments leading up to Mrs Westenra's tragic death. Were you the first to wake?"

"I think Mary was first… I can't be sure. I remember waking Wendy and Alice, so I was one of the first up."

"I am sorry to repeat myself, but the official record states very clearly that there was a broken window, followed by the howling of many dogs, and that is what woke the household. Are you saying this was not the case?"

"That did not happen, sir, I swear on my life."

"That won't be necessary, Miss Hobbs; I believe you." Holmes attempted a charming smile. "What happened when you found Mrs Westenra?"

"We ran into the bedroom, and found Mrs Westenra dead, but in her last moments she had fallen upon poor Miss Lucy, and we had to lift her off, with Miss Lucy being so frail and all. Miss Lucy was beside 'erself, as you'd imagine. When we'd laid the body out, like, and Miss Lucy had calmed down, she sent us off to get the sherry, and told us all to have a glass first to steady our nerves. That's what we did, but it's the last thing we remembered before we woke up and the Dutch doctor was there."

"There was laudanum in the sherry."

"So they say."

"Yet you did not smell it at the time?"

"'Course not, sir, we were all at sixes and sevens. Besides, I for one wouldn't recognise the smell o' the stuff. Mrs Westenra used it sometimes, but I never saw to any of that."

"The official account states that the bottle of laudanum was on the sideboard, open and empty."

"It was not, sir. If it had a' been, we'd have seen it and not touched the stuff."

"Quite. Was the elder Mrs Westenra in the habit of putting her laudanum in her drink?"

"Oh no, sir, she drank it neat when she needed it."

"And no one else was in the house?"

"No." There was something curious about the woman's manner when she answered, and Holmes evidently saw it too, for his questioning became leading.

"Someone was expected, however?"

"I... I don't know what you mean, sir."

"Miss Lucy was expecting a visitor. Someone for whom you would all have to make yourselves scarce. A gentleman caller, perhaps?"

"Miss Lucy was engaged to be married... to Mr Holmwood."

"Now Lord Godalming, of course," Holmes said. "But that is not why she sent you from the room. That is not why she drugged the sherry and ordered you to drink it."

The girl's eyes darted about as she tried to piece together the puzzle.

"I offer you a chance to set the record straight," Holmes said. "If you are completely honest with me, I shall see to it your good name is restored, and the other three maids, too, if they can be found. I may even be able to find you a situation more... suitable." Holmes looked about the filthy room we had been shown to with a small measure of distaste.

"Wh—what is it you need to know?"

"I shall speak plainly with you, Miss Hobbs, as I hope you will with me. The only person who could have drugged you on that night was the person who instructed you to drink—Miss Lucy Westenra herself."

The woman gasped.

"I do not believe for one moment that she meant you any harm," Holmes said. "The arrangement had been made solely to get you out of the way, so that she could have some privacy. To go to such lengths, however, would mean that she intended to do something illegal, dangerous, or scandalous. As a lady's maid in a relatively small staff, I am certain you would have overheard something, or perhaps even been taken into the confidence of your young lady. So, which was it? Illegal, dangerous, or scandalous?"

The young woman cast her eyes downwards and fumbled with her pinafore. "Scandalous," she muttered.

"Ah. I was correct then when I mentioned a gentleman caller?"

She nodded.

"His name?"

"I... I don't know; not his full name. I only know that he was foreign, an' that Miss Lucy was sure her mother wouldn't approve."

"Was the man so disreputable that the knowledge of the liaison might bring on a sudden heart attack in Mrs Westenra?"

"Mrs Westenra had a bad heart, sir. The slightest shock could set her off, the doctors said. That's why Miss Lucy said her ma couldn't find out. She swore me—" The girl stopped speaking at once, and looked tremendously guilty.

"We agreed to speak plainly, Miss Hobbs," Holmes said. "So, Lucy confided in you about her gentleman. You said you did not know his full name, which means you must have known part of it. Correct?"

She nodded again, nervously. "An initial, upon a letter he signed. It was a 'D', although I don't know what it stood for."

Holmes's eyes sparkled. When he next spoke, I could tell that his mind was turning over the possibilities of the case even though he was still talking to the maid. "But I am certain you have guessed by now who he was, if you have followed the papers at all."

"Miss Lucy would never... not with... a *vampire*." She crossed herself.

"Count Dracula was no vampire, Miss Hobbs. He was a man, like any other, whose reputation has been besmirched even more than your own, for some transgression that we have not yet ascertained. I put it to you that Lucy Westenra had arranged to meet this man, regardless of what it might look like to the outside world. We cannot be certain that it was a romantic liaison, but let us assume, for now, that it was. She was as secretive as she could be, but somehow her mother suspected something, and forced her to confess the truth. Lucy told her, and Mrs Westenra flew into a rage so violent that she assaulted her own daughter and suffered a massive heart attack. You found her body on top of Lucy—this was no accident, but a product of a physical attack gone horribly wrong. Miss Westenra, devastated at her mother's reaction, and perhaps feeling less inclined towards the love that binds mother and daughter, dusted herself down and prepared to meet this man anyway. She had already arranged the drugged sherry, probably intended for her mother. However, seeing that you four maids were now awake and distressed at the death of your mistress, Lucy instructed you to partake of the sherry, so that she could still meet the man despite the tragic circumstances."

"She would not be so cold!"

"If that is so, then I wonder if perhaps the meeting was not a romantic one after all, but something else entirely. Maybe Lucy Westenra's honour need not yet be questioned."

"I wish that to be so, sir, more than anything. But…"

"But what? What more do you know that you have not told us?"

"I have a letter."

I could see from the twitching of Holmes's lips and the widening of his keen eyes that he had not anticipated this.

"Who is the letter from?"

"It is from this man, this 'D' to Miss Lucy."

"And what does it describe?"

"Not much, but it seems to me to be a note between lovers, sir."

"How did you come by it?"

"It was given to me with a bundle of others, to destroy. She trusted me, but I—I read it, sir. And what I saw was so shocking that I did not destroy it."

"It was not your intention to blackmail your mistress?"

"No! What d'you take me for? I was just interested, that's all, and then it just slipped my mind, until... well, after what happened, I thought I should keep hold of it, in case any of that Dutchman's friends ever came knocking at my door."

"We must see this letter."

"I... no. I cannot. I will not blacken Miss Lucy's name."

"I would not have it so either, and if there is any way around it, I give you my solemn promise that I shall avoid such an outcome. But Miss Hobbs, lives have been lost as a result of this tryst, and more lives may yet be lost. Would you have that on your conscience?"

She thought about this, and then exhaled a bitter laugh. "It will cost you, sir, to have that letter."

Holmes sighed, and I felt something of his frustration. It seemed that remuneration was ever a greater motivator than justice. He delved into his pockets and fetched out some coins.

"There are six shillings here," he said.

"Begging your pardon, sir, but I'm tryin' to feed my family on two shillings a day. It'll cost you six pound, not six shillings."

"Six pounds!" I interjected. Holmes at once held up a hand to stay me.

"I can have it for you later. When shall we meet?"

"You know the Vine Tavern at Mile End Gate?"

"No, but I shall find it."

"Seven o'clock. I'll meet you outside."

"You shall have your money. But for that princely sum I must stipulate something else."

"What?"

"When the time comes, you must testify in a court of law to what you have told me today."

"No. I ain't going to no court. I've kept my head down, sir, from that day to this, afraid that the Dutchman or one of his cronies would come find me, but they never has. Now you come here and ask me to stick my neck out? Not likely. This Dracula was a powerful fellow and the Dutch professor hunted him to the ends of the earth and killed him dead. I don't want to end up like that."

"If you will not testify, then we shall do without the letter. Unless…"

"'Less what?"

"Unless you will sign a sworn statement. It is as good as a testimony, but your whereabouts will remain a secret until Van Helsing is put behind bars for his crimes. I can guarantee you that much."

She pondered this, weighing up the advantages of six pounds in hand against a frisson of danger. Eventually, we saw from the gleam in her eyes and grudging nod that the scales had tipped in our favour.

"I'll sign your papers," she said. "But I trust you to keep your promise, as a gentleman."

"Depend upon it."

"So Dracula and Lucy Westenra were acquainted after all," I said when we had returned to our cab. "Does this mean Dracula was in Whitby?"

"No, Watson. It is quite possible that he wrote to Miss Westenra previously, and that the letters may have played upon her mind. But I do not believe he ever set foot in Whitby. Miss Westenra's hastily scribed memorandum, written on the night her mother died, must have been tampered with considerably, and some fantastic elements added after her death. The wolf that crashed through the window—a fiction! And one made all the more feasible by the discrediting of the maids. We must work out what Dracula and Lucy Westenra were about. Whatever it was, it was grave enough for Van Helsing to kill her over it."

"You sound more certain than ever."

"I am. Whatever is going on here, there is some great secret that Van Helsing is desperate remains hidden. It seems to me that Lucy found it out, or was on the cusp of doing so. After her death, when Van Helsing seized all of the papers from Hillingham, he was not doing so simply to hide evidence of his gross malpractice. He did it to hide something deeper. When we find out what that secret is, Watson, we shall have him!"

When we returned to Baker Street, we found a police constable at the front door, as Bradstreet had promised. Mrs Hudson met us on the stair outside our rooms, and handed Holmes a small parcel, and a message from Inspector Bradstreet. The package contained various papers, and Holmes beamed as he leafed through them, handing each of them to me in turn.

"The inspector has been industrious indeed," said Holmes. "I always thought he lacked imagination, but he has acted upon his initiative to very helpful effect. He has not only had some success with Cotford, but has been to the office of Leverson & Critchley, the undertakers who arranged the offices of Lucy Westenra and her mother. Well, well… it seems that Mrs Critchley, the undertaker's wife, remembers Van Helsing requisitioning all legal papers from the Westenra estate, and persuading Arthur Holmwood to give up his rights to them. It says here that the police coroner was refused access to Lucy's body, and that Van Helsing was seen bribing him! The woman has signed this statement and agreed to testify if called. Bradstreet has not yet found the coroner in question, for he appears to be no longer in the employ of the Metropolitan

Police. By the looks of things the good inspector has been turning the screws—we can only hope he has not attracted any undue attention in the process, for subtlety is not normally a byword of Scotland Yard. Look here also! What a fine fellow! He has found an original police report regarding the missing wolf from London Zoo. He has circled the date."

"By Jove, Holmes," I said. "The Dracula Papers tell us that the wolf went missing on the day of Mrs Westenra's death. This date would suggest it occurred on the following day."

"The only report in the Dracula Papers on the matter was a newspaper interview with the wolf-keeper. The erroneous date could easily be put down to an editorial error, but it proved most fortunate for Van Helsing's version of events. I believe that, once Van Helsing struck upon the queer idea that Dracula could transform himself into a wolf, he went to great lengths to make this fiction appear reality; but these dates do not tally. We shall have to find out more. I want to review our evidence before meeting Miss Hobbs again tonight. Can you feel it, Watson? Those rogues fancied they were dealing us a great blow, but instead they have galvanised us! We shall have them yet."

CHAPTER FIFTEEN

FROM BEYOND THE GRAVE

Holmes did indeed visit Mile End Gate that night, and returned with the promised letter. Added to the cache that Inspector Bradstreet provided us, we took some heart once more. The evidence was scant, but Van Helsing could not yet be aware of it, and so we were grateful for every scrap.

Undated letter, received by Lucy Westenra on 17 September 1894

My dear,

I cannot express the joy that your letter brought to me, and how happy I am that we are finally to meet. I shall call on you this Sunday, as you asked, at nine o'clock. I am ashamed to insist upon secrecy, but no one can know that I am in the country at present, or I am certain I would find stiff opposition to my plans. It is of especial importance that Arthur Holmwood not learn of our meeting, for we are neither of us yet ready to face his questions. I am counting the hours until our meeting; until then, you have my utmost admiration.

Your servant,
D.

Holmes pored over this short letter for some time, leaving me to sit in silence wondering just what he could find so interesting. Eventually, he passed the letter back to me and explained his thinking.

"It is genuine. The page has been kept in poor conditions, so the provenance of the paper and any scent that may once have suffused it has been lost. There is no envelope and no postmark. It would be unlikely for a court of law to look favourably upon this as evidence were it not for the signed statement that I procured from Miss Hobbs, with no small difficulty."

"So how can you be sure it's genuine?" I asked.

"Simple. From the lack of creasing or curling, we can assume that the letter has been kept sandwiched between the pages of a book. This allows us to ascertain with reasonable accuracy just how much wear and yellowing the page should have commensurate with its age. Seven months have passed since this letter was supposedly written, and I would say that is a fair approximation.

"Next, look at the writing. The ink is expensive; it has barely faded, has a uniform flow, and dries to a red-brown sheen that speaks to the inclusion of cochineal and hydrosols in its manufacture. I have studied only three letters produced in similar ink during my cases, all of which were written by titled gentlemen, two of whom were minor royalty from the continent.

"Finally, look at the distinctive flourishes—some of the lower-case letter 's's have the telltale *cedilla*. Yet even without those, note the odd, angular forms of the letters, and here they are coupled with Grecian capitals, written very ponderously... you can see where the ink is darker as he has deliberated over the letters. This is a man not used to writing in English, who is classically educated, and almost certainly of middle age. From the letter formations alone I would suggest the native language of the author to be one of those Eastern European tongues of the nation-states surrounding the Danube, the Balkans, or perhaps the Ottoman Empire. In short, Watson, all things considered I am confident that this letter was written by a Transylvanian nobleman whose name begins with the initial 'D', and there is only one such gentleman pertinent to our story. This is a breakthrough indeed, Watson, for it appears that the Count, so long the subject of our investigation, has finally revealed himself, speaking to us from beyond the grave."

"And what does he say to us?" I asked, thrilling at the very thought of it—a part of me still thought of Count Dracula as some Un-Dead fiend, despite Holmes's careful arguments to the contrary.

"Read the letter again, Watson. At first glance, it appears to be a suitor arranging a romantic tryst with another man's fiancée. But there are other interpretations."

I studied the missive once again.

"I suppose you're right, Holmes," I said. "Perhaps he wished to speak to Lucy about some secret regarding Arthur Holmwood... that would explain why he sought especial secrecy from him."

"Indeed. And look also at the phrase, 'I am certain I would find stiff opposition to my plans'. Note the use of 'my plans', not 'our plans'. If this was a romantic plot he would have included Lucy in the arrangement. No, I suspect the opposition he expected would not have come from Holmwood, but from Holmwood's associates—Van Helsing in particular."

"So why keep the meeting a secret from Lucy's mother, if it was innocent?"

"Perhaps because Mrs Westenra was already in the confidence of Van Helsing. More likely, however, because whatever Dracula had to say would cast uncertainty over Arthur Holmwood's eligibility to marry Lucy. Like all mothers of beautiful young ladies, Mrs Westenra was surely keen to marry her daughter into a wealthy family."

"As it happened," I said, "it was Holmwood who benefitted the most from the union."

"No one knew that at the time. I wonder, was Dracula about to inform Lucy that her betrothed's claim to his inheritance was not as strong as she believed? Or was he to inform her of some personal scandal that would ruin any hope of a wedding? That is something we cannot be certain of yet."

"But how do we find out?"

"I am certain all shall become clear with time. For now, I think it is safe to say Van Helsing believes he firmly has the upper hand. Soon, our intelligence-gathering will become telling, and finally we can begin to tighten the noose about this villain. Tomorrow we shall visit the final member of the Crew of Light—one I know you have been thirsting to speak to since we began."

"Dr Seward."

"Yes. I have held off on the alienist until now, for if the Dracula Papers are to be believed in his regard, his loyalty to Van Helsing is so powerful it is almost a mania. If he is as convinced of the professor's goodness as his diary entries suggest, then I doubt we shall convince him otherwise. When we give him a push, Watson, he shall run straight to Van Helsing and warn him. Then the professor shall know we have not given up the fight."

"What then, Holmes? Are we to play our hand?"

"Not all of it, no. But we are to set the cat amongst the pigeons. When that happens, I am sure we shall get the chance to visit justice upon two fair-haired German men, who have so far found only women to threaten."

CHAPTER SIXTEEN

THE ALIENIST

"Now, Watson, this is liable to be most interesting, and, I hope, will be for the betterment of our case rather than its hindrance."

Holmes took up a missive from the tray by the door, and flashed the envelope in my direction. The simple lettering read, "To S.H. from L.P."

"Pike?" I asked.

Holmes smiled as he tore it open, and sat in his favourite armchair by the fireplace to read it—an armchair that was somewhat tatty since the German intruders had paid a visit. I ate my breakfast distractedly, eagerly awaiting the news.

"Watson, I am afraid this matter requires my urgent attention. I must go to see Pike this very afternoon."

"If we must, Holmes," I sighed, not relishing a meeting with the languid fop.

"No, Watson, I must go alone, for we cannot diverge too far from the plan if we are to bring our case to a swift conclusion. You shall go to see Seward—you are the better candidate for the trip anyway, given your credentials. I'm sure I would only put

Seward on the defensive. All you need do is delve into the tragic case of Seward's notorious patient, Renfield. If that isn't enough to provoke agitation, throw in some insinuations about medical malpractice on the part of Van Helsing—that should do the trick."

"We want him to become angry?"

"Absolutely. He is no good to us if he's thinking straight. If you are able to pry into the affairs of the asylum further, pray do so—I am certain Seward keeps a good many records, and perhaps the rest of the staff recall the fate of Renfield."

"I am not averse to the idea, Holmes, but I believed this visit to Seward to be of singular importance. I would rather you were there to ensure the plan is executed smoothly."

"I trust you implicitly in this matter, Watson. Now, finish your breakfast and make a start. I shall meet you for a spot of luncheon at Jack Straw's Castle—shall we say one o'clock? I had better change if I'm to meet Pike—you know how he cannot abide slovenliness. I shall see you this afternoon."

I was thankful that the previous day's particular had not lingered overmuch, although the air still smelled smoky and stale, like a card room the morning after a lengthy session of whist. Upon our last visit to Purfleet Asylum, Holmes and I had entered the grounds by stealth. This time, I gained admittance at the gate, and strolled along a broad drive that wove through manicured grounds towards the large redbrick hospital. A few inmates pottered around the lawns, taking exercise, with white-coated orderlies close at hand. Caretakers, doctors and civilian visitors seemed free to mingle amongst the feeble-minded patients, affirming what Holmes and I had already discerned—that this establishment in no way catered for lunatics of a truly dangerous bent. Lunatics such as Renfield.

R. M. Renfield represented a conundrum in the Dracula Papers. A madman of great unpredictability and physical strength, he was supposedly under the psychical influence of the Count, although his past history with Dracula was not detailed in the papers. Categorised by Seward as a zoophagous lunatic, he had spent much of his time under Seward's care collecting flies, which he then fed to spiders, and then to sparrows, which he in turn ate. His great mania was the belief that all life was equal, and that by consuming life in ever-increasing quantity he would somehow gain power like his "master", Count Dracula. Dr Seward had made a morbid study of the man, encouraging his fixations to the point of irreconcilable lunacy, which had surely contributed to Renfield's death. A death that had occurred away from all witnesses, in a cell occupied only by Renfield and Van Helsing. The professor's sworn testimony was that Dracula had materialised in the cell and killed Renfield, but there was no other witness to support this account. To my mind, for the death of Renfield and the quackery that had surely sent Lucy Westenra to an early grave, Dr Jack Seward had much to answer for.

Arranging an audience with Seward was easier than I had anticipated. Once a duty nurse had established my credentials were in order, I was asked no difficult questions about my business at Purfleet. It seemed that the entire staff was used to impromptu visitors, from benefactors to professional men curious about the latest advances in alienism. The doctor himself was on his morning rounds, and in his absence I was extended every professional courtesy, being given a cup of tea and shown presently to Seward's office, where I was asked to wait.

The tremendous opportunity of sitting unaccompanied in Seward's office was not lost upon me, and I at once set about examining everything I could, employing the methods that Holmes had for so long tried to impress upon me.

The office was not over-large, and even in the morning an electric lamp was on, as only a small, barred window in the south wall provided natural light. I would have expected Seward, as the administrator of a private establishment, to choose a more comfortable office for himself.

Dominating the room was a large desk, scattered with many papers and books. I tried each of the six drawers in turn, finding only two unlocked. In one was a stack of papers too dauntingly large to sift through in the uncertain amount of time I had. In the other was a folio of hospital stationery, ink, pens and a blotter. More interesting to my eye was a small bottle tucked towards the back of the drawer, containing chloral hydrate. It was perfectly plausible that Seward kept it for use on his patients, but there were no other drugs about the office, as far as I could tell. I recalled that he had admitted in the Dracula Papers to using the drug.

I closed the case and the drawer, and looked around quickly. There was a large file-chest against the wall, and a side table next to it upon which sat Seward's prized phonograph. It occurred to me that the chest might contain Seward's wax cylinders, and so I opened a few of the drawers, and found my assumption confirmed. Each drawer contained rows of neatly arranged cylinders, each marked only with a small label, upon which was a date written in the nigh-illegible scrawl of a doctor—a good reason why he favoured dictation over a handwritten journal, perhaps. The cylinders were arranged only roughly in date order, as though they had been taken out and played multiple times. I cursed the fact that our copy of the Dracula Papers had been stolen, for I had not had the chance to memorise many of the key dates. However, there were two periods that I had committed to memory: 17 September—the night Lucy Westenra's mother died in such dramatic fashion—and 2 October, when the lunatic Renfield had been killed.

I searched as quickly as I could, trying not to disturb the cylinders such that Seward might tell they had been tampered with. To my frustration, it appeared that the entries for the dates I required were missing. I wondered if Mina Harker had ever returned them to Seward after transcribing their contents, or if they had been destroyed so that the only remaining evidence was Van Helsing's narrative. This begged the question of why so many cylinders for the year 1893 remained. Did they merely contain records of his patients, unrelated to the Dracula Papers? Or were they additional diary entries that Seward had deliberately withheld?

Spurred on by that thought, I continued searching even as I heard footfalls in the corridor outside, drawing steadily closer. I turned each cylinder towards me quickly and methodically, scanning each date and then turning it back as I'd found it. I heard a voice, and was sure my name was being spoken some short distance away. The footsteps resumed.

At last, I saw with small triumph the date "21 September '93". This was close enough—indeed, it was the date of Lucy Westenra's funeral, if my memory did not deceive me.

Shoes squeaked on the floor directly outside the office, and I acted purely on instinct. In a trice, I had taken the cylinder, and pushed the others back to close the gap. I shut the drawer as quietly as I could, slipped the cylinder into my bag, and bent over the phonograph machine as if in study of it, when a man entered the room and cleared his throat.

"A beauty, isn't she? Dr Watson? I am Dr Seward."

I straightened, and turned to shake the man's hand, conjuring my most congenial smile. "Pleased to make your acquaintance; I have heard so much about you."

"All of it good, I hope?"

"Thank you for making the time to see me," I said, side-stepping any insincere platitudes. "You must be a very busy man, with such a large establishment to run."

"Yes, but part of the task of overseeing a successful private hospital is entertaining visitors. We thrive on donations from patrons as well as payments from families of the sick. And, of course, the odd referral from respected physicians never goes amiss."

"It is interesting that you brought up the subject, Dr Seward. Was it a referral that brought the infamous zoophage, Renfield, into your care?"

"No, as a matter of fact it was chance alone. I imagine any number of hospitals could have admitted him, but it was strange happenstance that brought him to my door."

"Might I ask who it was that paid for his care? Family? An employer?"

"I cannot discuss the private affairs of patients with just anybody, Dr Watson—even those of deceased patients. And you should know better than to ask." He affected a scolding tone in an awkward jest. "Now, Doctor, I am sure you are not here to pick my brains about finances, and you have certainly not come to make a donation, though I hope I may persuade you of the value of our little enterprise all the same."

"It is true, I am here primarily on business of another kind; although, as a man of medicine, I am always ready to expand my knowledge of other disciplines."

"Excellent! An open-minded man is always welcome at Purfleet, I assure you. However, I must urge you to speak plainly about your other business here. I have heard, of course, that the famous Sherlock Holmes and the indomitable Watson have taken an interest in the Dracula Papers, but I would hear your side of the story first."

Seward said this with a grin and a conspiratorial wink, which I could not truly understand. If he had heard I was investigating him, then why would he appear so at ease? Holmes had said that

Seward might well be innocent of all but the adulation of his old teacher. I, on the other hand, harboured a deep suspicion of the man, both for his delusional medical procedures that doubtless saw Lucy Westenra into an early grave, and for the cruel and unusual way in which he nurtured the mania of his patient, Renfield.

"I would say that I have no 'story', Dr Seward. My friend Sherlock Holmes is investigating the precise circumstances around the death of Miss Lucy Westenra and—"

"Why?"

"Pardon me?"

"A court of law has already ruled that no wrongdoing occurred, which means that the legal system has admitted the existence of vampires. So why would Sherlock Holmes concern himself with any of the details of the case? Unless, of course, he has taken a turn for the mad and you really do wish to admit him. Wouldn't that be delicious? Imagine the study that could be made of such a brain."

Seward was quick of wit, certainly, though somewhat haunted about the eyes. His interruption had thrown me slightly from my rehearsed lie. I could not very well confess that Holmes had been set on this path by a brother in government.

"Information has been passed to Mr Holmes that raises questions of reasonable doubt over the veracity of the Dracula Papers," I said at last.

"Raised by whom?"

"I cannot say."

"I admire your integrity, Doctor. However, I stand by every word of the Dracula Papers, and would swear to its factuality on oath. There is an end to it." He folded his arms, and gave me a satisfied grin.

"Every word?" I asked. Seward's smile faded a little. His eyes shadowed.

"Yes." He sounded uncertain.

"It is just that—and please excuse my directness—there are some details within the papers that I had assumed to be honest mistakes, certainly on the parts of yourself and Professor Van Helsing."

"Professor Van Helsing does not make mistakes," Seward snapped, jerking forwards angrily, and then quickly resuming a more relaxed posture. He leaned back against the door, and smiled again, only this time there was a twitch to his lips. The light in the room was poor, but I believed there was a jaundiced cast to Seward's features and a puffiness around the eyes, that spoke to his reliance on chloral hydrate.

"Then the mistake must have been yours, Doctor, unless you can explain to me otherwise." I held his gaze firmly. Although I had been instructed to antagonise the man, I also had to extract some facts from him—it was a fine balancing act, and I was uncertain if I had the guile to succeed.

"I shall endeavour to assist if I can," Seward said.

"Miss Westenra's physical state—the symptoms described in the papers sound remarkably like anaemia, wouldn't you agree?"

"Yes."

"And yet she was not treated for the condition?"

"Lucy's many symptoms were enough to convince Professor Van Helsing of the real cause of her illness. He alone amongst us had seen such things before."

"Symptoms such as…?"

"Rapidly fluctuating levels of energy, occasional delirium and… and the marks upon her throat."

I nodded thoughtfully. All but the marks were plainly caused by conditions well known to science, though apparently not to Seward. The marks… after hearing Holmes describe the deliberate pricking of small children by the "bloofer lady", I imagined someone close to Lucy had made those puncture-marks. All of this went unspoken. Instead I prompted, "But you did analyse her blood?"

"And found it healthy. This is on record."

"But no such test exists that could rule out anaemia, Dr Seward. If she was drained of even a small amount of her blood, it would have been paler, and you would have surely seen a marked drop in blood pressure. By a similar token, if anaemia was to blame, a qualitative analysis would have overlooked—"

"Dr Watson, I was trained by Van Helsing himself. Perhaps his methods of diagnosing exotic blood disorders have not reached these shores yet."

"There is nothing exotic about anaemia."

"And there was nothing anaemic about Lucy!" Seward's eyes blazed. Seeming to realise that he had become angry, he thrust his hands into his pockets. "Besides, the Count was possessed of so many uncanny abilities, the professor has often postulated that he could control the very blood in his victim's body, like the moon pulling the tides. His influence would have made my tests quite inconclusive."

He sounded sincere enough, but his words could easily have been spoken by one of his patients.

"Which is why you initially thought Lucy's symptoms were mental, rather than physical?" I asked.

"I had much reason to suspect a mental cause for Lucy's problems at first, Dr Watson. She was suffering from terrible nightmares—what some might call 'night terrors'—and sometimes this led her to bouts of sleepwalking. This habit returned in Whitby, where once she walked out in the night along East Cliff, and was found by Mina in a terrible state."

Something about his tone set my mind working, and I interrupted his flow. "You sound familiar with Whitby, Dr Seward," I said. "I myself was there only recently, but for the first time. Did you visit often?"

He paused, his large eyes scanning my features. "Not often,

although I did pay a visit to Lucy and Mina at the start of the summer."

All at once I recalled reading a similar allusion in the Dracula Papers, but had put it down to an error in the telling. So, Seward had met Mina Harker before Lucy's death—I was not certain whether this fact was significant.

"Was it a casual visit, or were you already worried about Lucy's health?" I asked, trying my best to maintain a friendly tone.

"If you must know, Dr Watson, I received a telegram from Miss Murray—now Mrs Harker—expressing concern for Lucy's state of well-being. Of course, I travelled there as soon as I could."

"What about her own physician?"

"It was natural that she should call upon me. Lucy and I were... close... once upon a time. That's all."

"Well, if the Dracula Papers have taught us nothing else, it is that Lucy Westenra was an extraordinary young woman. I mean, she must have been, to have so many good men prepared to lay down their lives for her."

"She was the best of women, Dr Watson. The Dracula Papers give only the vaguest insight into Lucy's qualities. She was fickle in love, certainly, but she was not the empty-headed girl that some might think."

Seward sounded melancholic in the extreme. The Dracula Papers certainly had made Lucy Westenra sound somewhat woolly-headed, but Holmes and I had already seen evidence to the contrary in her correspondence with Miss Reed—correspondence that Seward presumably knew nothing about.

"I say this only reluctantly, given your obvious strength of feeling," I ventured, "but something has troubled me deeply since I read the Dracula Papers, and it has nothing to do with vampires."

Seward said nothing, only looked at me earnestly with his dark eyes. I found what I had to say unpalatable, but remembered Holmes's instructions, and so determined to be resolute.

"The blood transfusions given to Miss Westenra… the basis for their medical efficacy is thin indeed. It might be said, by those experienced in such matters, that such transfusions could only have served to expedite the patient's passing."

At those words, all colour drained from Seward's face. His expression became so grave, and his pallor so ghastly, that I felt wretched for my indelicacy.

"I would never have harmed Lucy. Never. My love for that fine girl forbade such a thing. The Hippocratic Oath forbade it."

"The Hippocratic Oath requires that one provides a regimen for healing the sick, based on one's ability and judgement. It does not preclude… errors." My stomach turned somersaults as I continued goading the man, but I did my best to set my features and steady my hands. I was determined to get the measure of him.

"Errors of judgement, or of ability?" This question was delivered almost with a snarl. Seward walked past me, and sat in his chair so that the desk was positioned between us. Either he felt vulnerable to my questioning and sought sanctuary in the familiar, or he looked deliberately for a way of projecting some form of authority over my challenge. What better way for a mind-doctor to do that than to take up the position of consultant, forcing me to assume that of the patient.

"We all make mistakes, Dr Seward, especially when the case is so personally affecting. Your duties here, as well as the great mental strain, must have left you exhausted." I did not want to mention the man's drug use unless I had to, though I suspected it had something to do with his lapses of judgement.

"Which is precisely why I called upon Professor Van Helsing to guide me. I would not risk the life of any of my patients for the sake of pride."

"I am sorry, Dr Seward, but one only has to look at the case of Mr Renfield to know that is not entirely true."

Seward leant forward across the desk, his fingertips pressed together. "You return to the topic of Renfield, Dr Watson. Perhaps I misjudged your visit—perhaps you are here to talk about him, after all."

"Among other things, Dr Seward. His story is a rather pathetic one. The treatment he received here appeared, at least to me, improper."

"Improper how?" Seward had now adopted a sardonic smile, as though he were toying with me. I could not fathom the man— he seemed inconstant and irrational in the extreme.

"You provoked Mr Renfield; you encouraged his mania."

"The better to understand his condition. One man's singular discomfort, put under the most intense experimentation, may derive a cure for similar cases of madness in the future."

"Is that also why you drugged him, in order to steal his pocket-book?"

"It is. And the contents of that book, which were jealously and violently guarded by Renfield, were invaluable to my research."

"What about the man's family?"

"He had none."

"Someone must have admitted him to your care. Was there nothing from his past you could glean that would have answered your questions, rather than feeding him spiders, and promising him a kitten for his depraved appetites?"

"Perhaps I did delve into the man's past, Dr Watson. Perhaps what I found was irrelevant."

"You described Renfield as an undeveloped homicidal maniac," said I. "Surely something must have triggered these tendencies?"

"Something did, Doctor. Count Dracula."

"Ah. And when Renfield broke free, on more than one occasion, he was somehow impelled to run to Carfax, the home of Dracula?"

"You see, Doctor, you have read the papers, and yet you feign ignorance."

"Not at all, Dr Seward. I only try to clarify those events not explicitly described by the Dracula Papers, and yet of singular interest to a detective. For instance, Renfield was supposedly a man of great physical strength, prone to violent outbursts, unpredictable in the extreme, and, you say, under the malign influence of a vampire. And yet you kept him here, in conditions not suitable for containing such a man. The other patients here do not appear dangerous. Why, many of them walk about the grounds perfectly harmlessly. The walls surrounding this property can be scaled quite easily by a determined man—hardly sufficient to hold back lunatics who might prove a danger to society."

"Are you quite finished, Dr Watson?" Seward said, with a raised eyebrow.

"That depends, Dr Seward, on whether you have any answers."

"I shall do better than provide answers. Come, Doctor, let me take you on a little tour of my establishment, and you will soon see for yourself the measures that were taken to contain Renfield, and how his death was a tragedy, albeit an unavoidable one."

He opened the door and held a hand out to indicate the corridor beyond. I stood, took up my hat and bag, and followed.

Our tour took us deeper into the hospital, which was more sprawling than it appeared from the south front. The primary block, containing staff quarters, consulting rooms and operating theatres, led to two long, narrow wings, which jutted northward either side of a paved quad. One wing was for female patients, and another for males, and it was into the latter that Seward led me. He droned a practised patter about the merits of his establishment, until finally we reached a small stairwell.

"And here, Dr Watson, we reach the part of the hospital that most visitors do not get to see. But if it will put your mind at rest, I shall give you the extended tour. I have nothing to hide."

I followed Seward down the narrow stairs, which led to a basement level where no natural light permeated. Electric lights were affixed to the walls, but they were dull and yellow compared to those upstairs. At the foot of the stairs was a heavy, reinforced door, which Seward opened by the means of three separate locks, using his ring of great iron keys. As the door swung open, we entered a dimly lit corridor, all stone floor and bare-brick walls, with a musty odour of damp pervading the air. A steward sat at a desk before us, with a paraffin lamp burning away so that he could better see his copy-books and charts.

The corridor was lined with metal doors, each of which had a grille inset at eye-level, which could be covered and uncovered to look in upon the patients. A hatch in the centre of the door was positioned so that the steward could push the inmates' meals into the cell. I hesitate to use the word "cell", but there is no better description for these chambers. Not all of them were occupied, but as we passed by the ones that were, Seward directed me to the grille, so that I could see the poor devil within while he gave a commentary of their condition. My presence at the door invariably encouraged a terrible wailing, or a physical protest as an inmate threw themselves against the door, while struggling within a strait-waistcoat.

"This poor devil has a morbid fear of his own flesh," Seward said. "He thinks there are invisible insects crawling under his skin. It is a fascinating mania. If his strait-waistcoat is removed for more than a few minutes, he begins to tear at his own face quite violently. The scars you can see are from a time when he was able to acquire a knife from the refectory, with quite gruesome results. Ah, this next one is a favourite of mine."

I peered through the grille to see a scrawny man, with a filthy glove-puppet on his hand. Though I could not hear what he was saying, he appeared to be in deep conversation with the puppet. When it "replied" to him, the man's lips did not move at all.

"Terrence is a talented ventriloquist," Seward explained with a chuckle. "He communicates mostly through the doll. It tells us that it is the heir to a fortune, trapped in a doll's body by a jealous family. I have no idea of the cause of this particular story, for the man himself is not rich at all. It is a queer tale indeed. Anyway, come, Dr Watson—Renfield's old cell is just up here."

We walked on, leaving the howls of the mad echoing behind us. We reached the end of the hallway, where a second steward was stationed, and the corridor took a left turn. Here there were two further cells, one of which Seward unlocked and opened. It was a small room, perhaps six feet by eight. A small window, grubby and barred on the inside, was sited near the ceiling, letting in scant light from the quad above. A cot-bed, latrine bucket and small locker were the only furnishings. It would be much like the berth of a merchant vessel were it not for the padded walls. "You see, the room is presently unoccupied, but I doubt it shall be so for long. I have several intriguing cases clamouring for my attention—the result of some small notoriety since the Dracula Papers became public knowledge. I can take my pick of the finest lunatics."

I stared at him aghast.

"Oh, don't be censorious, Dr Watson." He smiled. "The patients upstairs represent my primary income, and no expense is spared in either curing them or keeping them comfortable for the duration of their stay—whichever the family desires. I would do nothing whatsoever to cause them discomfort. Those down here, however, are lost causes. They represent my personal collection of acute mental disorders, which I study in the hopes of one day finding a cure for others like them. If that proves impossible, then at least I can say I had in my possession a truly unique specimen."

"Renfield… was he such a specimen, in your eyes?"

"Naturally. Renfield was the first—the one who showed me that only the close pursuit of madness would ever lead to the cure for madness. He was much disturbed, and his illness incredibly specific. Were it not for the influence of Count Dracula over his poor mind, I imagine he would have been a crowning glory in my catalogue of manias. As it was, his brain afforded me an interesting study, though alas I could find no physical signs of psychical manipulation within the grey matter."

"You dissected his brain after his death? To find what? Physical evidence of psychical phenomena?"

"Precisely!" Seward's eyes lit up. "And I shall do the same with all of these subjects when the time comes. Imagine if I could find the exact part of the brain that causes a man to think himself possessed, or the reincarnation of Napoleon, or infested with insects like our man back there. With a simple insertion of a needle into the affected area, the condition could be cured. Or perhaps even induced... now there's a prospect!"

"I remind you of that Hippocratic Oath again, Dr Seward. 'Into whatsoever houses I enter, I will enter to help the sick, and I will abstain from all intentional wrongdoing and harm, especially from abusing the bodies of man or woman, bond or free.'"

"Wonderful, you quote it verbatim. But of course, I did not enter Renfield's house. He entered mine."

"Hmph. *Melius anceps remedium quam nullum.*"

"Ah, you are from that school of thought. 'It is better to do something than nothing'. But I *am* doing something, Dr Watson. I am giving these wretches a greater purpose."

To my mind, the real Jack Seward had now materialised. For all of his fine manners and unctuous fawning, I now saw Seward as a reptilian fellow. For him, everything was a calculation, an experiment; ethics be damned. I wondered that he could display such depth of feeling for Lucy Westenra, or such fierce loyalty to

Van Helsing. Such erratic, almost compulsive behaviour would have made it easy for Miss Westenra to spurn him, and easier still for Van Helsing to use him. I saw now that this was a machine playing at being a man, without a true understanding of what that meant. He was Holmes without genius, without empathy.

"And what purpose did Renfield serve?" I asked. "Your study of his brain yielded no clues. Your literal feeding of his obsessive mania only prompted him to escape, more than once, and eventually sped him to his end."

"Dracula sped him to his end, not I."

"There were no witnesses to the terrible fate of Renfield... bar one."

"You are about to make a serious accusation, Dr Watson, against one of my oldest and dearest friends. Be careful what you say." Seward remained cool in his manner. There was no outburst as when I had questioned him about Van Helsing earlier. This was altogether more disconcerting, for I had no idea what the man was thinking.

"What other conclusion am I to draw? To the outsider, it would appear that Mr Renfield was driven beyond his endurance, his fragile grip on reality torn away. And it was you who allowed that to happen. In the end, utterly lost to madness, he could just as well have killed himself. He could have assaulted Professor Van Helsing, leaving your friend little choice but to act in self-defence. Or..."

"Or what?"

"Maybe Van Helsing was acting to protect you, so that none would learn just what a wretch you had made poor Mr Renfield."

"Protect me?" Seward got to his feet and looked down his nose at me. "No, Professor Van Helsing taught me self-sufficiency, resilience, and objectivity. He nurtures such qualities in all he meets. In fact, there is only one man he has ever coddled as long as I have known him."

"Oh?"

"You must surely know that the professor holds my good friend Arthur—that's Lord Godalming, of course—as dear as his own lost son." Seward's tone was noticeably bitter.

"I have met Lord Godalming recently, and it did not seem so to me. It was quite to the contrary, in fact, given his lordship's condition."

"Really?" Seward looked almost pleased at the news that his friend was suffering. "Then maybe Arthur will now learn to stand on his own two feet, lest he end up in my care."

"A fate I'm sure he would do well to avoid," I muttered. This drew a fierce glare from Seward.

"I can see, Dr Watson, that I am not going to convince you of the efficacy of my methods, the value of my establishment, nor of my innocence of whatever crime you imagine I have committed. As such, I'm afraid I must, with regret, ask you to leave."

"I apologise if you are insulted," I said, deliberately mealy-mouthed. "I would hate to outstay my welcome." We walked back along the corridor a little way, before I paused and said, "The cell in which Renfield dwelt has bars at the windows—they all do. How then did he come to escape through the window, as stated in the Dracula Papers?"

"When Mr Renfield first came to us, we did not know what a danger he could be. He was kept upstairs. After his second escape attempt, we made a home for him down here. There is a simple explanation for all of your suspicions, you see." Seward said nothing further to me, but instead spoke to one of the attendants. "See Dr Watson out, would you? I think I shall stay and have a chat with our puppet-man. Or, rather, with his puppet."

I was ushered from the dank cellar, the rattle of Seward's keys at a cell door behind me making me shudder as I thought of what might befall those poor lunatics in Seward's care.

I left the steward behind as we reached the entrance hall, and intended to depart straight away, but I was intercepted by another man, a stout fellow, with auburn moustaches. He held out a large, freckled hand in greeting.

"Dr Watson, is it? I'm Dr Hennessey. Pleased to make your acquaintance. I heard the friend of the famous Sherlock Holmes was here, and could not resist coming to meet you. I've read your reports in the *Strand*. Fine stuff, eh? Could I detain you for a few minutes?"

I remembered Dr Patrick Hennessey from the Dracula Papers, for his sworn statement appeared in the manuscript, detailing one of Renfield's escapes to Carfax whilst Dr Seward was away tending to Miss Westenra. The inclusion of his account in that collection of lies and elaboration led me to be suspicious of the man. However, his request upon my time was delivered earnestly, such that I was certain he had some pressing business that he could not state publicly. For that reason, I acquiesced and followed him to his office.

The room was on the first floor, next door to the hospital library. It was far more lavishly appointed than Seward's, and I remarked upon it.

"Ah, yes. Traditionally this is the administrator's office, but Dr Seward likes to lead a monastic existence downstairs, close to his patients. He is a man of singular habits."

"I had noticed," I said.

Hennessey offered me a cigar from the box on his desk, and I accepted gratefully. While we smoked, he came down to business.

"I will speak plainly, but quietly," he said, in an Irish lilt. "The walls have ears in this establishment, and no one is to be fully trusted. Not the nurses, not the orderlies, and certainly not the administrator."

I nodded my understanding.

"What do you make of this Dracula business, Dr Watson?"

"I… remain unconvinced," I ventured.

"As well you should. For sure, I saw some queer goings-on with regards to Renfield, but that's par for the course in a place like this. I had no reason to suspect any 'supernatural' cause for Renfield's mania until Dr Seward called Professor Van Helsing in for a second opinion. And what an opinion he gave!"

"Unbelievable, some might say."

"I do say," Hennessey scoffed. "Look, Dr Watson, I do not know you, save for what I have read. I do not know Sherlock Holmes. If either of you are not what your reputations suggest, then I am damning myself by what I am about to tell you. But if you have even half the integrity and decency that your stories suggest, then perhaps there is hope for me, and for the inmates of Purfleet Asylum."

"I can only endeavour to be the best that I can be," I said. "As can we all."

"It is harder for some than for others, trust me." Hennessey took a puff on his cigar. I saw now the worry lines upon his round face; the weariness of his expression. Something weighed greatly upon the man's mind. "What did you make of Dr Seward's collection?" he said.

"To be frank, Dr Hennessey, I found it troubling, and unethical."

"Then you are a man after my own heart."

"Begging your pardon, but why then do you work under him? I am not sure I could be party to such cruelty at any price."

Hennessey winced. "I have wrestled with my conscience for some time, Dr Watson, and in truth I feel the same way, but there is more here than meets the eye. I could say that I stay for the sake of the other patients—those who have not yet experienced the crueller side of Seward's treatment. I could say also that I stay out of loyalty to the friendship I once shared with Dr Seward, before he became… changed. Both of these things are true, but I know that they are not reason enough. In truth, Seward knows things about my history that, should they come to light, would see me out of work, probably for ever.

"I was not always an alienist, or 'mad-doctor', as some call us. I was once a physician, like yourself. I do not know you, Dr Watson, and will not confess all my sins; I only ask that you believe me when I say I once made a mistake, and one of my patients paid for that mistake gravely. When it seemed my career in medicine was over, Dr Seward offered me an opportunity here. Unfortunately, what I took for altruism was actually something more sinister.

"With the arrival of the lunatic, Renfield, Dr Seward's behaviour became steadily more erratic. The man who once swore never to perform any treatment that might agitate a patient's mental disorder, upon his oath, began to do exactly that, provoking violent turns and fuelling Renfield's dangerous delusional fantasies.

"It was only when Renfield escaped to the empty house next door—Carfax—that I realised the extent of Seward's cruelty. I apprehended the patient with no small difficulty, and once he was sedated I wrote my report for Dr Seward, who was away on some other business. I delivered my report to Seward's desk, and whilst there, something caught my eye. I saw his notes concerning Renfield, strewn across his desk. What I read there sickened me to the pit of my stomach.

"A few days later I confronted Seward, who was here with Professor Van Helsing, and we argued. I threatened to resign, and Seward played his trump card. He had kept records of my earlier misdemeanour, and had invented further embellishments besides—embellishments that might not only cause me to be struck off the medical register, but perhaps even put on trial. He is blackmailing me, Dr Watson. Oh, I don't believe he would have stooped so low when I first met him, but he is a changed man. His personal tragedies, his growing obsessions, and his… vices, have gone hand-in-hand to transform an idealistic young doctor into a megalomaniac."

"You speak of his feelings for Lucy Westenra," I suggested. "And his dependency upon a certain drug."

"You have seen the symptoms for yourself?"

"And the evidence, too."

"And there is more. I feel Seward has been manipulated."

"By Van Helsing?"

"Aye. But whatever the cause of his change of character, the damage is done. I have been warned quite explicitly to stay quiet, and not to contradict the version of events as told in those dratted Dracula Papers."

"I see. So why speak out now? And why to me?"

"As I said, I believe you to be a man of integrity. Besides, a gossiping nurse has already revealed to me that Seward appeared quite agitated in your company. That alone tells me that you are not in his pocket. The same cannot be said of the police—I hear Van Helsing dines regularly with the assistant commissioner of Scotland Yard."

"Really?" That was interesting news indeed, for it in some way explained the rapid decline of Cotford's career.

"How else would such a cock-and-bull story as that contained in the Dracula Papers gain such traction? Van Helsing has friends in high places, which has so far left me nowhere to turn. But then here you are, Dr Watson. I confess I have selfish reasons for putting my trust in you. If Dr Seward should receive his just desserts, I would be free to start afresh. He could make his accusations about me all he liked, but if his own reputation were in tatters, I would be more likely to weather the storm of scandal that would follow. Who would listen to a man who drove his own patient to madness and death, and whose shocking neglect contributed to the death of an innocent young woman?"

"You know something of the case of Miss Westenra?"

"Enough to know that the treatment that Seward and Van Helsing administered to the girl was quackery."

"Dr Hennessey, I believe you and Sherlock Holmes would get along famously."

"Perhaps, if he is the forgiving sort." Hennessey looked sad, and quickly changed the subject. "We don't have much time, Dr Watson. Here, be so good as to sign this for me. It is a copy of *A Study in Scarlet*. If Dr Seward asks me why I spent time with you this afternoon, I shall tell him that I enjoy your stories of the great detective."

I took the book and signed it for him.

"Now take these, Dr Watson, and tell no one here that you have them." Hennessey passed me two large, tattered notebooks. "They belonged to Renfield. Seward ordered them to be destroyed shortly after the man's death."

This was an unexpected boon, and I took the notebooks eagerly. Flipping through the pages, it appeared that one was written in a neat hand, including many pages of shorthand. A packet of letters was stuffed untidily inside the front cover. The other journal was written in a scrawl, and contained page after page of tally charts and childlike scrawlings.

"There were others, but these were the only two I could save from the incinerator. The one you hold there was written during his time here, and is a cruel account of a man's descent into utter madness. The other was admitted with him when his legal firm brought him to us."

"Legal firm?"

"Oh, didn't you know?"

"Please, Dr Hennessey, what legal firm? Who admitted this

man Renfield to the care of Dr Seward?"

"A man who is no longer with us," the doctor said. "One Peter Hawkins, of Exeter."

The information given me by Dr Hennessey had set my head in a spin, and I left as quickly as I could thereafter, the better to take this vital new evidence to Holmes. The Irishman had explained that R. M. Renfield had been a junior solicitor in the Exeter legal firm owned by Peter Hawkins, and now administered by Jonathan Harker. The journals he had given me not only cast doubt upon how much Seward and Van Helsing had known about the Harkers before the start of their tale, but also just how much of their insane story had come from a true madman, from Renfield himself, rather their own imaginations. It was Renfield who had first been sent to Transylvania to meet Count Dracula; it was Renfield who had contracted brain fever and been driven mad by his experiences in the Carpathians. It was Renfield, not Jonathan Harker, who had been Dracula's guest.

I made my way next to Jack Straw's Castle. On the journey, I immersed myself in Renfield's journals, which instilled within me a sense of fearful dread. We had since the beginning discounted the possibility that Jonathan Harker and Dr Seward had been among the knowing conspirators. Now, I had to consider that Van Helsing and Mina Harker were not the only villains in this thickening mystery, but were only part of a conspiracy to murder.

CHAPTER SEVENTEEN

DRACULA'S GUEST

The papers that I read on the way to Jack Straw's Castle were all too familiar, for they were, in places, identical to the journal entries supposedly written by Jonathan Harker and published as part of the Dracula Papers, though they pre-dated his accounts by nearly a year.

Renfield had travelled a similar path to the one described by Harker, stopping for a time in Munich before travelling onward on to Transylvania. It seemed that Renfield met with some misfortune in the wilds while in Germany, resulting in his experiencing vivid, waking dreams, in which he was assailed by gigantic wolves, and feelings of inexplicable dread. When he awoke from his nightmare, he was in the castle of Count Dracula, whereupon he discovered that his host had sent a party to look for him and carry him to safety.

Renfield's writings trod a hazy line between fact and fiction. It seemed clear to me that he had taken a turn after an ill-advised trek through the snow, becoming feverish and confused as a result. Though Dracula had taken him in and nourished him, Renfield had not received the medical attention that he so badly required, and thus a bout of brain fever slowly drove him mad.

Entry after entry detailed the poor man's downward spiral into insanity. I wondered what the Count had made of it all—seeing his guest become increasingly delusional and raving, until there was no choice but to lock Renfield in his room and arrange for him to return to England and the care of Peter Hawkins.

The version of events penned by Jonathan Harker was so rational in comparison—so believable—that the discovery of these papers now appeared a great betrayal. The obvious lunacy had been eradicated from the accounts; times and places had been altered. Jonathan Harker's journal, which formed the bedrock of what would later become the Dracula Papers, was a lie.

Letter, R. M. Renfield to Peter Hawkins, 15 April 1892

Mr Hawkins,

I regret to inform you that, although I have reached Castle Dracula, it is after some delay and not without toil. I experienced an accident on the road some distance east of Munich, and although my injuries are not severe, I am quite unwell. I feel it worsen, in my blood.

Count Dracula was pivotal in assisting me, for despite the great distance he was able to direct a party to find me and bring me safely to Transylvania. The Count is proving an amiable and attentive host. He expresses regret that you were not able to take the trip personally, but hopes that he shall meet you when he visits London to further discuss his investments.

I expect to be detained for several weeks, though I shall endeavour to conduct our business as agreed.

R.M.R.

Extract from R. M. Renfield's Diary, 2 May 1892

Every night the same. Every night the Count tests me. He summons me to dine with him, long after the others have gone to bed. He never eats. He never drinks. He merely watches me. Studies me. He says he has my best interests at heart, that he wishes only to keep me away from the bustle of his household, that I am weak and should be resting, but I see what he is doing.

He is a strange one, or so I first thought. Now I see that there is more to the Count than meets the eye. When we do not speak of business, we speak of Transylvania; of his ancestry; of ancient battles and ancient kings, united by blood.

I understand the test. The Count is powerful, and ancient. All this talk of tradition, of war, of Magyars and Boyars—he tempts me. He shows me glimpses of power that he himself has surely wielded, of victories he has tasted. How can it be? How can a man so youthful have endured down the long years? What powerful blood must throb in his veins for him to stand before me each night, a man and yet not a man?

Tonight, I looked out of the small window of my room, and I saw a shadow in the courtyard; a great wolf had entered the gates of the castle, and stole across the flagstones like one of the Count's hounds. A faithful creature of the night, summoned to its master.

I hear it now: it calls. And I wait.

Extract from R. M. Renfield's Diary, 20 May 1892

One fly. Two flies. Three flies. Four.

No, no, no. It did not work last time. I felt nothing. The flies alone are not valuable enough. Their essence is too weak.

Five flies!

Yes, five flies might do it. Five flies might be equal to a big fat spider.

I shall feed five flies to a spider, and that should make the spider worth twice its value in the eyes of the Lord. One spider eats five flies, and the spider becomes two spiders. That's how he does it. That's how his kind have always done it. He told me. The blood is the life.

Are spiders enough to nourish me the way the master's prey nourishes him? Perhaps I need something more valuable still.

They have little birds here in the mountains. Wagtails, with yellow breasts. They come to my window sometimes during the day. What must a wagtail be worth?

Ten spiders.

Yes, a wagtail is worth ten spiders. So for each wagtail I must catch five spiders, and feed each spider five flies. That will make the approximate worth of ten spiders. It is easier to catch flies than spiders, and wagtails are noble little birds. They would surely not stoop to eating flies. They are not as wretched as me.

A wagtail that eats ten spiders is two wagtails. Are two wagtails worth a human soul? If I eat two wagtails will I feel the strength of the old country flow through my veins, like it flows through the master's? It is a great effort to catch a wagtail. I cannot waste it once it is caught. I may need several. I may need something larger first, like a cat. Yes, a cat! If a cat ate ten wagtails and became two cats, would that be enough?

Two cats? Can I get a cat, from up here in my solitary room?

And if I could get one cat, why not five?

CHAPTER EIGHTEEN

A DEADLY ENCOUNTER

My journey was interrupted by an unusually turgid slog of traffic along Spaniards Road, caused by an upturned ox-cart. I was forced to alight the omnibus and continue up the hill to the pub on foot, running the gauntlet of the bicyclists who seemed intent on riding the lanes regardless of the congestion and drizzly weather.

Seeing the obstruction up ahead, and an unpleasant-smelling load spread across both road and pavement, I took a winding path through the heath, leaving the cries of annoyance and frustration of cabbies and draymen behind me as I passed beneath the aged boughs of oaks and sycamores. The park was surprisingly quiet, with only a few walkers braving their Sunday constitutional after the previous night's particular, which still left the taint of smokiness upon the air and a yellowish haze upon the horizon.

I had walked for perhaps ten minutes, and was not far from my destination when I heard the crunch of a boot upon the gravel behind me. I thought nothing of it, until I heard it again, immediately close, and followed by the laying of a hand upon my shoulder. I turned at once, and found myself staring into a pair of steel-blue eyes, set into a broad, angular face shaded by a homburg.

"Doctor Watson. You will come with us."

At once I recognised the man's accent as German, and saw tufts of fair hair protruding above a collar that sat upon rather broad shoulders. The man's grip upon my shoulder tightened as he spoke.

"What's all this about?" I snapped. Did he know of the evidence I carried in my bag? Where did he plan to take me? These questions and more flashed through my mind.

"Please, *mein Herr*, we wish only to speak with you. Privately."

As he said this, I saw movement directly ahead, and another man stepped onto the path—the twin of the German who stood beside me.

I attempted to shrug the man away. "Unhand me, sir," I said, raising my voice in the hope of attracting the attention of passers-by; there were none immediately at hand, however, and though I felt panic rise in my breast, I would not show obvious distress while I could perhaps glean something from my opponents.

I studied them as perhaps Holmes would, scanning them quickly. They were identical, save that the one in front of me wore spectacles. They were large—taller than me, and as broad, both with fair hair and pale blue eyes. Their chins were square and lightly stubbled. They wore smart grey suits, grey overcoats and matching hats. Their shoes looked expensive, but were spattered with mud, as were their trouser-legs. All of this I discerned in an instant, though I knew not what good it would do me if I were to be captured.

"Come now, Doctor. We have a carriage beyond those trees there. We shall talk, and that will be all. There is no cause for alarm."

The grip tightened again, and I felt a shove in the small of my back, forcing me towards the other man, who grinned as he took hold of my other arm.

"Actually, gentlemen, I think there is every cause for alarm. Unhand the doctor, if you please."

All three of us turned at this interruption, and standing on the path behind us was Sherlock Holmes! His eyes were narrowed. I had rarely been so happy to see my friend, and I noted a whisper of a smile upon his aquiline features as he recognised my expression of relief.

"Ah, Mr Holmes," said my first captor. "You save us the trouble of finding you, no? Why don't you come along, too, and we shall work this out like gentlemen."

"Whatever you have to say, you may say it here," Holmes said.

"I think not," said the second man, and marched over to Holmes, great hands outstretched to seize my friend.

In a flash, Holmes had stepped sideways, his lithe limbs strong and nimble; he swept aside the German's grasping hands, and his right leg hooked the man's ankle, sending him sprawling onto wet gravel before he knew what was happening.

I took my cue, for if Holmes had come to fight, I knew our predicament must be serious. These were, after all, the men who had threatened dear Mrs Hudson, and it was this thought that lent strength to my elbow as I struck my captor's midriff.

His hand released me at once, and I spun about to strike him a left hook. The larger man was fast, however, and even as I turned I felt his fist connect with my jaw. I staggered at the force of the blow, my vision blurring. I heard Holmes scuffling with his man, and shouts in English and German. Great arms were around me again, hauling me backwards. My medical bag dropped now from my grasp, and I saw the wax cylinder roll across the path. I could not lose it!

I threw my weight against the man, pushing him against a tree with all the force I could muster. This time I was able to pull free and duck his counter-attack. I swung a left hook, connecting with the man's jaw satisfyingly.

"That is for Miss Reed!" I snarled, and then gave him my most powerful right, striking him on the bridge of the nose and sending him crumpling to the ground. "And that is for Mrs Hudson!"

I turned to see how Holmes had fared. His man was similarly prostrate, and Holmes gave me a familiar smile and a wink.

"Holmes!" I gasped.

"Don't stand there gawping, Watson," he said. "Take hold of that man."

From further along the path came a hue and cry, as someone had evidently been alerted to a scuffle on the heath, and a crowd of people was rushing to see what was going on.

I hoisted my man from the ground, and was about to question him, when I saw Holmes spring backwards. A dozen or so passers-by had arrived, and let out a collective gasp as they saw Holmes's opponent pull out a gun. Bicyclists, ramblers and park vagrants alike ducked for cover as the German aimed his revolver.

"Your last chance, Mr Holmes," the gunman snarled.

Before I knew it, Holmes also had a revolver in his hand.

"I think not, sir. The game is up," Holmes said.

"You would risk firing into the crowd, Herr Holmes? I think not. Believe me, I have no such scruples. Now, drop the pistol."

Holmes paused for just a second, and then dashed quickly, making for the trees behind me. The German fired. People screamed.

Everything to that point had happened so fast that I had not had time to think. Even now, I acted purely out of instinct, for my blood was up. A moment before the gunman pulled the trigger a second time, I gave his associate a sharp shove in the back, sending him stumbling towards the shooter, and directly into the path of the bullet. I could not have timed it better if I'd had all day to plan the manoeuvre, for the bullet struck the German's breast just beneath the heart.

A look of relief flickered over Holmes's features, before his sharp mind and rapid reflexes took control of the situation. He turned back and darted at the gunman, who appeared much disturbed by the felling of his partner in crime, and had lost all heart for the fight. He fled from Holmes, waving the gun about to part the gathering crowd like the Red Sea before Moses. Holmes took after him for only a short time, but gave up quickly as the press of bodies before him began to close in on him. Angry shouts came from the crowd; voices of shock and confusion rang out, challenging our authority, and demanding justice for a wounded man they did not even know.

Holmes stepped forwards imperiously. "Someone fetch a constable at once!" he commanded. "My colleague here is a doctor, and he shall attend to this man."

As if to illustrate the point, Holmes went to retrieve my bag, sweeping up the wax cylinder as he did so and placed it back in the bag. As he handed it to me, Holmes muttered: "It appears this bag is full of evidence, Watson. Guard it with your life. Of secondary note is this wretch—it would be well if you could save him, if only so that we may question him."

I nodded and set to work, as Holmes stood again to placate the crowd. Minutes later, the trilling of police-whistles cut through the rumblings of discontent from the assembled onlookers, and two red-faced policemen pushed their way towards us. Holmes directed them to secure a Black Maria for the wounded man, call a hansom for ourselves, and send word to Inspector Bradstreet to expect us at B Division headquarters presently.

By the time more policemen arrived, I was certain that the German could not be saved, and he had not confided in us any last words. His breaths came in stertorous rasps, his face was a deathly pallor. Holmes was careful not to allow this grave assessment to reach the ears of the crowd until enough officers arrived to keep them at bay, for some of them still held us with a great deal of suspicion.

I was more than thankful when we received word that the Maria had arrived—I had exhausted almost every medical procedure imaginable to make it appear that I was saving the lost cause before me. Two constables came down the path carrying a stretcher, and I helped load the patient onto it. Holmes and I in turn were escorted back to the road where a cab awaited us.

I stood gravely over the dead-room slab as the police surgeon carried out his examination of the body.

"What do you make of it, Holmes?" Inspector Bradstreet asked.

"It is curious," Holmes said. "The man is dressed well, in a suit with German tailoring, wearing German spectacles, and has false papers about his person. His revolver is German and I imagine that, when your surgeon has extracted the bullet, it will not be traced to any maker here in England. I have a witness who has once before seen these men, and heard them declare some association with the German embassy. I would, therefore, conclude that they are indeed spies."

"Yet you sound uncertain?"

"Spies, Inspector, are by their nature inconspicuous fellows. These men are not. They are large and distinctive in feature. Twins, no less, who have been seen together more than once. This man bears tattoos upon his body that would suggest some time spent in the navy—see here the obligatory anchor motifs, and the names of several *Frauleins*, probably waiting in various ports. Their shaving regimen is lax, their shoes caked in mud from not one but several days traipsing about. Something does not sit well with me here."

"Ex-navy, you say. Hired guns, then? Assassins, Mr Holmes."

"That had also crossed my mind, Inspector. However, I don't believe they actually wanted to kill me."

"But he fired…"

"Yes. However, I rather suspect I forced his hand by drawing a gun of my own and refusing to come quietly. From his prostrate position, he may have been firing a warning shot, which only struck home when his brother hove into his sights. I feel perhaps I am responsible for an unnecessary death, and one that will only serve to make this man's brother ill-disposed toward me should we meet again. I fear it was a misstep—I wonder now if we should just have gone along with them and heard what they had to say. However, at the time there was no way to know if they simply planned to do away with us."

"About that, Mr Holmes. Waving a revolver about in broad daylight… it makes it very hard to defend you."

"Yet I am sure you will do your best, Inspector. Now, to your office?"

I took a sip of the police station tea, which was weak, and a poor substitute for a small ale at Jack Straw's.

"What happens now, Mr Holmes?" Bradstreet asked.

"We go on, Inspector. Watson has had a most successful morning, perhaps better than I could have hoped for. I myself was not idle before I was forced to go to his assistance."

"Yes, Holmes," I said, "how did you know to be there? It's almost like you were using me as bait."

"Come now, old boy, I wouldn't do such a thing."

"You jolly well would," I grumbled.

"We were both followed from the moment we set out this morning, Watson. I lost my man early, of course, but I had no way of warning you. Instead, once my business was concluded I set about watching the roads for you. When the wagon overturned on Spaniards Road, it was most fortunate for my purposes, for it meant there was only one way by which you would come to meet me. Of course, if you were delayed unduly, I would have assumed the worst and come looking for you at the asylum; as it was, I had no reason to suspect the Germans would do anything more than watch our movements." Holmes turned to Bradstreet and changed the subject, perhaps hoping I wouldn't question just how much he had left to chance with regards to my safety. "Inspector, is there a phonograph in the station?"

"Yes, Mr Holmes. The police surgeon uses it from time to time."

"Excellent. Have it brought up, there's a good fellow. Watson came by a wax cylinder from Dr Seward's collection, and I wonder just what it contains."

Bradstreet sent a constable down for the phonograph at once, and in the meantime Holmes lit a cigarette and asked me many questions regarding my interview with Seward, and the subsequent conversation with Hennessey. As was his way, he interrupted often, in order to clarify some detail or other, and he seemed to devour the information with great interest.

"I am intrigued in particular about Seward's continued feelings for Miss Westenra," Holmes said.

"He carries a torch for the late Miss Westenra," I said, "even after all this time. I believe this melancholy accounts for much of his erratic behaviour."

"Seward appears to me a fellow of weak mind, which would make him of great use to Van Helsing. When Seward was led into the crypt by Van Helsing, for instance, he saw what he wanted to see, because his feelings for Lucy were so strong. From all else you have told us, I would say Seward is a trifle unbalanced, perhaps as a result of his great loss. Overall, Watson, what did you make of Dr Seward?"

"It would appear," I began, "that Seward was once a perfectly fine doctor; well-regarded, idealistic and diligent. I would suppose that there were some notable gaps in his medical knowledge, which given his specialism in illnesses of the mind is hardly surprising, and this would account for him abrogating his responsibilities while in the presence of Van Helsing. However, it is with some confidence that I can say that Seward is not simply a man out of his depth. I found him to be a man of low ethical fibre, and prone to sycophantic outbursts where Van Helsing is concerned. Furthermore, his lack of compassion for his patients was, frankly, disturbing. Add to that his complicity in Dr Hennessey's blackmail, and I think we have a man who is not so much in the thrall of Van Helsing, as a willing accomplice."

"Very good, Watson. If what you discovered about Renfield is true, then we need to widen our net."

"Would someone mind telling me what's going on?" Bradstreet interjected. Holmes and I had spoken at length about Renfield on the way to the station, and we had rather kept the inspector in the dark.

"Which part, Inspector?" Holmes asked. "The bit about Renfield having been a solicitor sent to Transylvania, or the part where Van Helsing murdered him?"

Bradstreet's face was a picture, and he barely managed to compose himself when the door opened and two constables entered with the phonograph. It was older and larger than the machine owned by Seward, and took both men to carry it. When they had gone, Bradstreet sat down behind his desk and puffed out his cheeks.

"You'd better start from the beginning," he said at last.

I apprised Bradstreet of all I had been told by Hennessey with regards to Renfield, presenting to him the journal as evidence.

"The implication is clear," said Holmes. "Either Jonathan

Harker was extremely unfortunate to have encountered almost the same maddening experience as Mr R. M. Renfield, or the entire account was a fabrication, based on Renfield's diaries and letters to Hawkins."

"You think Mr Harker also complicit in a crime?" Bradstreet said.

"It is not only Watson's findings that led to this conclusion, but my own investigation this morning, during which I uncovered similar incriminating facts. I shall come to that in good time. Taken together, Harker's part in this sorry affair becomes all the clearer. At first I had thought him one of Van Helsing's useful idiots, manipulated by a cunning wife whilst in a state of ill health," Holmes explained. "While Harker does indeed seem frail of mind, it is likely not through brain fever contracted in Transylvania, but through guilt and worry. It was a grave error on my part not to realise this sooner, for if I had known I might have been able to glean more in Exeter when I had the chance.

"Harker's employer, Mr Hawkins, was undoubtedly murdered by the Harkers for the purposes of inheritance fraud—a remarkably transparent fraud, at that—but now it is clear there was another reason, too. If Hawkins had lived to see the Dracula Papers published, he would have recognised Harker's diaries as being the experiences of his former clerk, Renfield. He was likely the only man alive to know the extent of Renfield's delusions and, being a kind man who felt responsible for his employee's circumstances, paid for his treatment at Purfleet Asylum. What Mr Hawkins did not know was that Renfield would meet a rather ignominious end there."

"The murder you spoke of?"

"Indeed. I think Watson has pieced this together well enough. Watson, would you explain to the inspector how Van Helsing managed to do away with poor Mr Renfield?"

"If memory serves," I began, "the events as described in the Dracula Papers run thusly. Van Helsing first asked to examine Renfield on the evening of 1 October, and found the man inexplicably raving, with no clue as to what might be afflicting his mental faculty. It is certain that Van Helsing learned of Renfield's obsession with Count Dracula, and of the Count's connection to the house, Carfax, after this encounter."

"Assuming he did not already know of it from his conversations with Jonathan Harker," Holmes interjected. "Exactly when Van Helsing began to concoct the finer points of his elaborate character assassination of Dracula has not yet been ascertained—given the arrangement of the Dracula Papers, and the fact that they have been clearly doctored more than once, we may never know."

"Quite. Seward's account in the papers tells us he saw the patient sleeping—his chest 'rising and falling' at least—shortly before midnight, and placed a man on watch at Renfield's cell. The next morning, 2 October, Seward found that the man on watch had fallen asleep at his post, and therefore could not be relied upon to report on Renfield's state. Indeed, before dragging this confession from the orderly, Seward said he found the man's manner to be 'suspicious.'"

"Suggesting that there was more to his lapse of diligence than mere dozing, and that even Seward was in the dark about what had transpired in Renfield's cell," Holmes said.

"I was coming to that. There was no mention of whether or not Seward checked on Renfield again that day. In fact, he was much distracted first by Harker and Holmwood, then by Van Helsing, who apparently struck out from the asylum to visit the British Museum, where he hoped to find books that might help him conquer the curse of vampirism."

"Books that he could have consulted at any time up to that point," Holmes interrupted again, "and yet instead chose to return to Amsterdam on more than once occasion for the purposes of similar research."

"Holmes..."

"I am sorry, Watson. The floor is yours."

I cleared my throat. "So we know that Van Helsing stayed in guest quarters at Purfleet Asylum overnight, and then made a show of leaving. For the rest of the day, Seward noted that Renfield was strangely quiet—what he meant, of course, was that he had received no reports to the contrary, for he did not personally visit the patient.

"Late on the evening of 2 October, an attendant burst into Seward's room and told him that Renfield had met with an accident. The man had cried out in his cell, and when the staff had entered, they found Renfield lying face down on the floor in a pool of blood. Seward rushed to check on the man, and quickly ascertained that his face had been beaten against the floor of the cell, his back, an arm and a leg all broken. Seward's first response was to move Renfield to a bed, which undoubtedly caused great pain and would have hindered any chance of recovery for the broken back.

"Professor Van Helsing was called for at once, and arrived at the cell within minutes. Van Helsing, for the benefit of the watching attendants, loudly confirmed Seward's assessment that Renfield's state was due to a 'terrible accident'—that the man had beaten his own head against the floor in a fit of crazed temper, inducing a violent fit that had led to the breaking of his bones.

"Van Helsing went to fetch a medical bag, and decided immediately to operate on the man with the apparatus he had conveniently brought along, even though he'd had no time to fully examine the patient. The attendants were dismissed, and instead Arthur Holmwood and Quincey Morris were sent for to assist in the surgery—I would suggest that an honest and upstanding man like Morris was required in order to witness what followed, and more to the good that he had no knowledge of surgical procedures. Harker was asleep upstairs, yet no one sent for him.

Within minutes of looking at the patient, Van Helsing decided that the best course of action was to administer an emergency trephination, by which a depressed bone could be removed from Renfield's skull, and any blood clot cleared. This method has been known to have an instantaneous effect, providing relief from pain and allowing the patient some lucidity—this is precisely what happened here, and Renfield was able to answer questions put to him by Van Helsing. However, it would have been impossible for any physician, regardless of skill, to gauge accurately where the hole should be bored after such a cursory examination. If the trephine was administered to the wrong location, that moment of lucidity—or, in Renfield's case, insane insight—could only have foreshadowed death. Remember that I was an army doctor, and studied the work of George Macleod, who determined that 'preventative trephining' on the battlefield was an archaic practice that could do more harm than good. Macleod was writing more than thirty years ago, and yet we are to accept that Van Helsing's knowledge is so up-to-date that he teaches medicine to this day."

That drew a smile from Holmes, which I took as approval. Bradstreet looked very grave.

"In my opinion," I concluded, "this entire passage of events was engineered by Van Helsing. Most likely, the professor paid the attendants to turn a blind eye to Renfield for the entire day, and then to beat him viciously. Van Helsing himself was ready to answer the call, and made sure that Renfield would never recover from his injuries by performing slipshod surgery."

"But you said that Van Helsing questioned Renfield, in front of an honest witness," Bradstreet said. "Why would he do that, Doctor? And what did Renfield say?"

"I am sure Holmes has an opinion as to why," I said. "As for what was said—"

"Renfield told Van Helsing of a terrible dream he'd had," Holmes said. "A dream in which his 'master' had entered his cell, in the form of mist, and attacked him without mercy. He also told the assembled 'Crew of Light' that Mina Harker was his master's next target, at which point everyone rushed upstairs and forced their way into Mina's room, just in time to find her stupefied and covered in blood, with the Count bent over her. The dark figure escaped in a puff of smoke, and all in attendance were finally convinced of the evil that they faced."

"You do not sound convinced, Mr Holmes," Bradstreet said.

"Because it is the most obvious case of misdirection I have ever heard of! Consider the evidence contained within the Dracula Papers themselves, Inspector. Abraham Van Helsing is noted for his skill at hypnotism. It would have been a small matter for him to hypnotise someone like Renfield—a highly vulnerable and suggestible individual, already prone to fantastical delusions. Using drugs and hypnotic suggestion, Van Helsing implanted the entire false memory of this 'waking dream', and then ensured it would become violently embedded in the man's consciousness by having the attendants viciously beat him. After the slipshod surgical procedure was conducted, Van Helsing questioned Renfield, doubtless using some kind of verbal trigger to ensure the man relayed the concocted story verbatim. The story included some nonsense about Mina Harker being in mortal peril, and we are to accept that at that very moment—completely by coincidence—the Count was upstairs, drinking Mina's blood.

"Everyone in attendance rushed upstairs, leaving poor Mr Renfield alone to die from his injuries. Right on cue, they saw the Count attacking Mina Harker, but were unable to stop him escaping. Now, all of the actors in our little story were accounted for, bar one. A man who, up until now, we have believed to be innocent of any real crime, and too addled by brain fever to be part of Van Helsing's deception."

"Jonathan Harker," Bradstreet muttered.

"Harker can't have been playing the part of the Count, Holmes," I interjected. "In the account given, he was present in the room, swept aside by Dracula and reduced to a stupor while his wife was bitten."

"There are three distinct possibilities, Watson, all of them equally likely," Holmes replied. "Firstly, let us say that the entire episode is a fabrication. Of the witnesses, since Quincey Morris is dead, and Lord Godalming is indisposed, Van Helsing has been free to make up whatever story he likes. However, I still do not believe Lord Godalming to be fully complicit in these crimes. There remains a risk, therefore, that his conscience could get the better of him, and he could denounce the truth of these events if he ever recovers his wits. Let us then consider the second possibility—that Van Helsing recruited a man to play the part of Dracula, and the whole scene was staged for the benefit of Morris and Holmwood. We know Van Helsing has associates of strong physicality, whom he could call upon if needed—one of them lies in the morgue below us.

"But there is a third possibility, and although it sounds incredible, it is my preferred theory. That the intruder was Count Dracula himself."

Bradstreet caught his breath. "You mean to say, after everything, you now believe in vampires?"

"Don't be absurd," Holmes sniped. "Vampires are not real, but Count Dracula is—or, rather, was. His existence has never been in question, only his nature. I believe he was lured to the asylum that night by some clever ruse on Van Helsing's part. It is easy to think that he may have been directed to Mina Harker's room unwittingly, to find her and her husband in a terrible state. He would have assumed—as would anyone upon seeing Jonathan and Mina Harker covered in blood—that a fight had taken place between man and wife, and perhaps a murder committed. Harker then attacked him—we know that Dracula's clothes were in disarray. Dracula was a large and powerful man, and fought Harker off, as no doubt he was meant to. Harker crumpled to the floor and acted as though in a stupor. Dracula then stooped over Mrs Harker to inspect the body, and she at once grabbed him, as though in her death throes perhaps, covering him in her blood."

"But why was she bleeding?" Bradstreet asked.

Holmes suppressed a flicker of annoyance at the interruption.

"The Harkers would have made a good scene of this before Dracula arrived, especially knowing that Mina would be examined later. I first thought they would use animal blood—or even the blood of an asylum patient—in order to complete the ruse. But they needed Mina Harker to be weak and pallid for the benefit of Holmwood and Morris. Therefore, I imagine Mina's blood was extracted using Van Helsing's instruments, and then dashed upon her clothes and around the bed. Puncture-marks would have been made in her neck, just as the bloofer lady inflicted them upon those poor babes on Hampstead Heath.

"At this point, Dracula would surely have understood what was happening, and that he was falling into a trap—doubly so if he recognised Harker, for the solicitor's presence there would have been too much of a coincidence.

"At that moment, the door opened, and there was the professor, along with the rest of the Crew of Light. Dracula must have believed that he had been framed for assault, if not murder— he had no way of knowing if Mina Harker was simply wounded or dying. He was like a trapped animal, caught in two minds of which way to escape. He first ran at his foes, and then checked himself, deciding instead to make for the window and climb out onto the quad. At this moment the Harkers' plan was completed. Whilst all eyes were on Dracula, Jonathan Harker set off a small smoke-bomb, of the type used for a sudden flash and puff of smoke in the theatre, and threw it under the bed so it would not be found later. Already making for the window, and deciding not to look a gift-horse in the mouth, Dracula dove from the window, climbing down the dense ivy that clings to the old part of the asylum."

"Too far-fetched, Mr Holmes," Bradstreet said. "Why not kill the man there and then, and have done with it?"

"Because Van Helsing needed to convince his followers that Dracula was an Un-Dead. Any enquiry would have found that Mrs Harker's injuries had not been inflicted in a struggle with the Count. Even if Van Helsing could have come up with a suitable story, there were at least two members of his own group who would have opposed him. No, he needed to have Morris and Holmwood on side, body and soul, and this charade was the way he did it. When Dracula eventually died, it was after being hunted by the Crew of Light, for everyone in that group either believed wholeheartedly that they pursued a vampire, or else were part of the conspiracy."

Holmes grinned triumphantly at his own cleverness. Bradstreet lit another cigarette.

"Now," Holmes said, after his summation had sunk in, "shall we finally see what's on this cylinder?"

Dr Seward's Diary, 21 September 1893

Something has been troubling me—a good many things, actually—but in particular something that transpired today.

Professor Van Helsing has been in the strangest of moods, which initially I put down to his great sorrow at failing to save Lucy. He speaks in riddles, and has several times taken me aside and impressed upon me in the most guarded terms a need for secrecy, for a great evil, he says, pits itself against us.

After the funeral, we were overheard talking by Quincey Morris, whose noble bearing dissipated in an instant, to be replaced by a fierce presence. The American is a fellow as strong in moral fortitude as he is in body, and his eyes blazed as if with the righteous fire of the peculiar preachers they have in the Americas. As he towered over the professor, I saw in his eyes the determination that has led to the United States fulfilling its "manifest destiny", and knew at once that Quincey P. Morris was not a man with whom to trifle.

"I see you, Professor," he said. "I see you takin' all these papers, and wrappin' up that little girl's affairs in your legal bindings and double-talk. I see that it benefits Art, and that's the only reason I keep my peace, be assured of that. Be equally assured that, should this arrangement change, and Art is made to suffer by your dealin's, I shall rain down holy hell upon whatever dark confederacy the two of you have going on here. Do I speak plain enough for you, Professor?"

The professor, though small of stature compared to the American, stared back at him with an utterly fearless resolve. I had seen Van Helsing rattled these past days, by mysterious illnesses and talk of the supernatural, but I had never once seen him cowed by a mortal man, and that clearly was not about to change.

"You speak plain enough, friend Morris," Van Helsing said. "I see you are a man most cautious, and not a trusting one, eh? That may stand you well in the days and weeks to follow. But you are misplace in your suspicion; I am not your enemy."

"No?"

"I see the way you look at me, friend Morris, and at John here, also. You give me that same look when first we meet. But was it not you who spoke of the terrible things you saw out on the Pampas—those things that remind you so well of Lucy's suffering. Was it not you who alone understood the signs of the vampire?"

Van Helsing referred to the conversation we had had on the night of Lucy's passing, when Morris had told us of his experience of gigantic vampire bats out on the great plains of Argentina, and how the animals upon which they preyed bore symptoms strikingly similar to Lucy's.

"It was me who said it, and I saw your eyes fair light up when I did. But I don't suppose for one minute that you suspected a damn vampire at work up to that point. I think I gave you the idea, Professor. I saw a change come over you in that moment. You remember how that night I patrolled the house the whole evening through, with my six-shooter ready? Do you think I was lookin' out for vampire bats, here in England? No, sir. I was makin' certain that none of you fellas called in on Lucy during the night. Maybe if I'd been here earlier, and done the same for these last few weeks, there'd be less garlic hangin' in that girl's bedroom window, and life yet in her sweet body."

At this, I became indignant. I had known Morris, on and off, for some considerable time, though I fancy he had never truly liked me the way he had Arthur. But to accuse me of having any hand in the death of Lucy, whom we both loved, was beyond the pale.

"Look here, Quincey," I said. "Lucy's ailment is beyond anything I have ever encountered in my years as a doctor, and Professor Van Helsing here is one of the foremost specialists in these matters. If he could not save her, then no one could have, and that is the truth of it. If the professor seeks to keep the details of this terrible incident from the public eye, or even from the hands of the authorities, then I am certain it is with good reason."

"And what reason might that be?"

The professor spoke again, his words full of authority and steel. "The world, friend Morris, it is not ready for the knowledge that I could bestow. It is not ready to know that true evil walk amongst us. You know it; you have seen it—I see that in your eyes. And before our time is done, you will come to understand that I was right, and I did everything in my power to help that so-dear girl. You loved her, yes? We all did, to me she was like a daughter, and you three men loved her as truly as any men ever loved a woman. It is grief that drives you now to anger. But what we need, friend Morris, is for that anger to change its direction. I swear to you by God that we give you an enemy soon enough, who will be the true and righteous target for your rage. We give to you the enemy who take dear Lucy from you, for it was not sickness that took her. You think you give to me the idea of 'vampire'? No, you merely were the first to give voice to that which other men think impossible. If you have vengeance in your heart, I ask only that you stay it for now. Go with Arthur, be a good friend to him in his time of need, and if when all this is done you still doubt the word of Professor Van Helsing, then you may take up your 'six-shooter' as you say, or that big knife you carry always, and strike me down. *Gott im Himmel* is my witness."

"Upon my oath, Professor Abraham Van Helsing, I shall hold you to that," Morris said. "If you can back up your claims, and show me Lucy's killer, then faith, you'll find no truer ally than me. I will leave you be for now, and as you rightly say it's because Arthur has need of me, and he seems to trust you. But woe betide you—both o' you—if it turns out that trust is misplaced."

"I take that as fair warning," the professor answered, with a wry smile. "For my sake, we hope I give you no cause to mistrust."

With that the American took his leave. That in itself would have been enough to trouble me, but the professor's reaction after Quincey had gone was peculiar indeed. He turned to me and said:

"This could be a business most unfortunate, yes, if we do not provide the proof that Mr Morris so seeks. He is a man of principle, John—the kind of man who cannot be bargained with if he feel wronged. If we cannot satisfy him, we shall have to take other means to keep him quiet."

"What do you mean?" I asked, worried at once by the ominous tone the professor had taken.

"Oh, mind me not, John. It is just a turning of the phrase. We shall show Morris the truth he seek, but first I still must convince you, eh?"

The professor would be drawn no further, and moved on to other matters. Foremost in his mind seemed to be the subject of Mr and Mrs Harker. Professor Van Helsing has mentioned them several times today, and has made a great show of sending a telegram to them, to inform Mrs Harker of Lucy's death. It is strange that of the great pile of correspondence that the professor has confiscated, only the Harkers have been selected for a personal missive, and an invitation to come and join us in London. He speaks of the woman, Mina, most highly, although he insists that they have never met, and he only knows what a fine woman she is from Lucy's own journals. He will not let me read those journals, though he himself has pored over every word several times. I cannot help but wonder if she wrote of me; if she wrote of why she passed me over for Arthur.

But I have again let melancholy and sleeplessness bring me to a bitter state. Best I end this recording now.

I make this recording on a separate cylinder. The professor has already intimated that my phonograph diary may be required in the near future, as a record of the grim business upon which we have embarked. These strange misgivings are not for his ears, for I would hate him to think less of me for any dark thoughts that cross my mind as a consequence of my unutterable sorrow.

Bradstreet leaned back in his chair so far I thought he might topple over, and once again blew out his cheeks.

"There's your man's motive for killing Morris," he said.

"It's almost like you already knew what would be on that recording," I said, slightly disgruntled that the evidence I had procured at great risk had not provided a new avenue of thought for Holmes.

"Not for certain, Watson, although the problem of Quincey P. Morris has occurred to me frequently. It stood to reason that the funeral would be the one time that tempers would boil over between men who all claimed to love Lucy Westenra. Do not fear, Watson—your efforts have not been in vain. You were clever to select this cylinder in particular, for it confirms my suspicions."

"It's a fine thing we have here," Bradstreet said. "Yet I must caution both of you not to get ahead of yourselves. This cylinder was stolen by the good doctor here, after all. Oh, do not look at me so, I do not plan on arresting you, Dr Watson. Only know that if we mount any case that relies heavily on this evidence, either Van Helsing or Jonathan Harker will see that it is never heard in court. They will have the judge's ear, I am certain, and this recording will be inadmissible because of the dubious means by which it was acquired."

"Then we shall have to ensure our case is watertight," Holmes said. "A pity, though, for the cylinder also quite clearly points the finger at Morris's killer."

"You mean Van Helsing did the deed himself?" Bradstreet asked.

"Preposterous," Holmes said, and Bradstreet cast his eyes downwards at the rebuke. "No, when Watson and I visited Jonathan Harker in Exeter, he had Mr Morris's bowie knife hanging on his office wall, alongside the kukri knife with which he murdered Dracula. At that time, I thought that Harker truly believed Dracula was a vampire, and was thus innocent of premeditated murder. I assumed that he displayed the bowie knife as a sentimental reminder of his great friend, honouring the man who laid down his life for his wife. As things now stand, there is another reason that he would keep that weapon in so prominent a place. And it is the more probable reason. He is displaying the weapons as trophies."

"What could Harker possibly have against Quincey Morris?" I asked.

"Nothing at all, at first," Holmes said. "But consider the recording we just heard. Immediately after being threatened by Morris, Van Helsing brings up the subject of the Harkers. At that time I believe he was already blackmailing Mina Harker, and it suddenly became forefront in his mind just how he would use the murderous, ambitious young couple. He knew perhaps that Seward would not kill for him—this is why he dealt with Renfield himself. Holmwood certainly would not have the fortitude for the task, being a bosom friend of Morris. Van Helsing, as we can tell from the recording, was physically outmatched by Morris, and was already under suspicion—it would be tricky to get the drop on such a man. So who better than the newcomer to the group, an unassuming solicitor—in fact a smiling assassin, who would purport to come as a friend, but who would kill if so commanded?"

"It is feasible, but it is all conjecture, Mr Holmes."

"It is, but it is the best theory I have for now. I shall either prove or disprove it as we go on."

"Well, if it's true, then this is a dark business, Mr Holmes, and it draws darker with each revelation." Bradstreet rubbed his hand across his shadowed face.

"And yet I cannot help but think that there is still more to the story of Quincey P. Morris. Perhaps the forgotten hunters will be able to shed some light on the matter." Holmes's mouth twitched as he forced down the semblance of a knowing smile. It was his most infuriating habit—I knew immediately that he had been holding back some knowledge until such time as he could dazzle us with it.

"Forgotten hunters?" Bradstreet took the bait.

"We have so far believed that the Crew of Light consisted of five men and one woman," Holmes said. "This is what we learned from the Dracula Papers. But once there were two other men in this loose confederacy, and I believe their stories—their suppressed narratives—are central to the resolution of this case."

CHAPTER NINETEEN

THE FORGOTTEN HUNTERS

"Langdale Pike is not suited to hiding," Holmes began. He took a sip of his tea, which was now cold, and winced at its awfulness. He set down the cup, put out his cigarette in the foul brew, and lit another at once. "His short exile has seen him exert his considerable network of gossips and social spies upon the subject of one Abraham Van Helsing, and those who assist him. Pike, it seems, has taken a dim view of the professor, to our benefit.

"He arranged for me to meet an old acquaintance this morning, who shall remain nameless, at least for now. He is a theatre manager by trade—Pike wrote of him in his earlier correspondence, the man who knew of the actress, Jenny Kidd. By a quirk of fate, this man is further connected to the players in our little game, for when Genevieve Holmwood auditioned for him years ago, she also introduced him to another man by the name of William Young, who now works as an accountant on the theatre staff. Mr Young, however, was once in the employ of Peter Hawkins of Exeter, as a junior clerk. He was passed over for promotion in favour of Jonathan Harker. When Harker took control of the firm, Mr Young was dismissed.

"Now, William Young has little part to play in our tale, save for the intelligence he provided me during our short interview. He did, however, know both Mina Harker and Lucy Westenra. I at first thought that Harker may have perceived Mr Young as a threat to his courtship of Mina Murray, but I quickly ascertained that this was impossible. Mr Young is certainly not the kind of man to have romantic interests in another man's sweetheart.

"Mr Young knew another friend of Lucy's—an artist, by the name of Francis Aytown. This gentleman is the real person of interest in this tale, for he was close to Miss Westenra, and by association knew Arthur Holmwood. Indeed, both of them sat for Mr Aytown at one time or another. At Ring, I studied several family portraits of the Godalmings, and the painting of Arthur was signed by one 'F. W. Aytown' if I recall correctly. I have yet to speak to Mr Aytown, but I believe he will be of singular importance to our investigation."

"You said there were two additional members of the Crew of Light—Aytown and Young?" I asked.

"No, Watson. Mr Young was well acquainted with our principal players, but he was not among the cast of characters (forgive my theatrical metaphor). As it transpires, Mr Aytown now works occasionally as a set-painter for several theatres, for he has fallen on lean times of late, and no longer has dashing young earls and society women sitting for him, by all accounts. It was Young who introduced Aytown to Pike's associate originally, and so you see how the theatre provides a link between our forgotten hunters. Mr Young intimated that Aytown fell afoul of a wayward business scheme, into which he had been cajoled by Arthur Holmwood and Quincey P. Morris."

"Why, if that's the case, we start to see a strong motive forming," said Bradstreet. "If only we could link this enterprise to Van Helsing."

"Oh, I am quite sure we shall," said Holmes, taking a long draw on his cigarette.

"So who is the second man?" I asked, rather impatiently.

"A man named Singleton. He spends his time researching the supernatural, exposing fraudulent Spiritualist mediums, or endorsing them, should they pass his tests. Aytown called him in when Lucy's ailments grew worse. Seward had openly speculated that her condition was beyond his skill to heal, and that a more… 'metaphysical' explanation might be needed. Of course, Van Helsing's arrival rather made Singleton's involvement redundant, and the professor saw to it that the man was thrown out on his ear."

"Why have neither of these men spoken out?" I asked.

"I imagine for the same reason that Miss Reed and Dr Hennessey did not speak out, Watson: fear of reprisal. However, something has evidently happened recently to change their minds. I give you Exhibit A." Holmes passed a letter to me. "I acquired this from Mr Young this morning. He has no wish to be dragged into the case any further than necessary, as he has some cause to expect retaliation, but he gave me this purely because of my reputation. Be so good as to read it out for Inspector Bradstreet's benefit."

Letter, Francis Aytown to William Young, 27 February 1894

Dear William,

It has been too long, Will, and I only wish I could write to you under better circumstances. As it stands, I am to leave the country for a time, and am not sure when I can return. I had to tell someone, in case anything terrible should befall us, and there is no one else I can think of who might half understand, save you.

Singleton and I have struck on something regarding

this awful Dracula business. He thinks we have been deceived, and that Art might be deceived still by that old crank Van Helsing. Being a singular sort of chap, Singleton has done some investigating of his own, and says the only way we'll find the truth is to strike out for Transylvania ourselves. I know it's rash, but what can I do? That business with the railway practically ruined me—the inheritance is all but gone, and it appears I must now live the part of the poor artist, rather than simply romanticise about it. I dare not speak a word of what happened, for Van Helsing has taken an interest in Art's financial affairs, and has warned me away from Ring for all time. I am *persona non grata* in the home of my dearest friend.

So we go to Roumania, to visit this railway venture for ourselves, and then on to Castle Dracula to find whatever is left of the man who Van Helsing claims was a vampire. If anything should happen, or if we are not heard from again, then do with this letter as your conscience dictates, but do not let it fall into the hands of Van Helsing, or Harker especially. In such dire circumstance, it is like that we have met some ill fate at the hands of those mysterious thugs whom Van Helsing has set in opposition to us. Singleton will not be cowed. He has secured us tickets on a steamer, and we leave in the morning.

Adieu, my dear boy, adieu.
Your friend, Francis

"There, you see," Holmes said when I had finished reading the letter. "Singleton and Aytown did not have all the facts, but they must have had enough to piece together a little of the mystery that we have been investigating. Their researches have taken them back to the root of this story—to Transylvania. That in itself is rather telling."

"What's all this about a railway?" I asked. "It must be some pretty venture to have ruined several men, and Lord Godalming amongst them. Didn't Harker have a picture in his office of him and the others upon the site of a railway construction?"

"Watson, your memory is improving with every case. As soon as I first heard of this railway business, I thought the very same thing. If it is more than mere coincidence—and I fancy it is—then Harker must have been involved in this venture somehow, too."

"What does all this mean, Mr Holmes?" Bradstreet said, rubbing his head confusedly.

"I have not yet formed a complete picture, but Mr Young confided some details to me. All of our principal players, with the exception of Van Helsing, are linked at least tenuously by a foreign railway venture, which Mr Young said his firm worked on at the behest of Lord Godalming. That is, the elder Lord Godalming, not Arthur Holmwood. Part of Jonathan Harker's trip abroad had something to do with the scheme, although Young knows little of the details, for it was all done in the strictest confidence, and the case was given to Harker rather than himself.

"We now know that Quincey Morris and Arthur Holmwood invested heavily in the building of this railway—we can assume it runs through Transylvania, given the involvement of Count Dracula in our tale. Van Helsing appears to have taken a marked interest in the venture for reasons unknown—enough to use his men to warn off Aytown, at any rate. Perhaps financial gain was a motive for Morris's death, but Van Helsing already had motive enough. None of this makes complete sense—why would such an intricate plot be concocted to cover a railway investment in faraway lands? Why would Van Helsing dirty his hands to such an extent on behalf of Lord Godalming? Why would Lucy Westenra have to be killed for it? And Renfield? Jonathan Harker appears to have been dragged into the scheme later, judging by the photograph… it doesn't yet make complete sense to me. I feel we are missing several pieces of a very intricate puzzle."

"Maybe the railway was particularly lucrative," Bradstreet offered. "Maybe they killed Morris for his share, and then brought Harker in later."

"To what end? You don't kill a friend for his money only to give that money to a stranger. Harker has a law practice, a house in Whitby, the Hillingham estate… he has profited well from this whole scheme without resorting to business deals and assassination. No, I maintain that the stakes were higher still. How the other pieces of this puzzle fit together remains to be seen. But we will find them."

"What do we do now, Mr Holmes? I mean, I still need to take a statement regarding the altercation in the park, and the dead German. I can smooth things over for now, I'm sure. But then what? Singleton and Aytown are in Transylvania, our suspects are spread across England… I confess, this is a deal too thick for me."

"Which is precisely why you should remain here and ensure the police leave me to my work, insofar as possible. Besides, Inspector, if you stir up a hornet's nest, you might find yourself like Cotford."

"I wouldn't want that. Mind you, there are a fair few of the men here who would not hinder your business, sir, regardless of orders. You've garnered too much goodwill from the force over the years, and put too many villains behind bars."

Holmes smiled gratefully, but changed the subject at once. "Speaking of Cotford, he is on side now?"

"Yes, Mr Holmes. He fancies himself some sort of enquiry agent. The investigation has put new life in his old bones. He's talking about taking it up professional, once his 'Dutch devil' is brought to justice. Last I saw him he'd eased off on the drink, too. Perhaps he'll give you a run for your money in the future."

"Good. I want you to tell him everything I told you today: the German thugs, Seward's blackmail, Renfield's trip to Transylvania, William Young, Aytown, Singleton… everything. Leave out no detail."

"To what end?"

"Why, so he can make a deuced nuisance of himself of course! If Frank Cotford is anything, it's belligerent and tenacious. He'll not let go of a lead, no matter what confronts him. He might stumble upon something we have yet to think of. More likely, however, he'll provide a distraction."

"A distraction for…?"

"I'm afraid I cannot tell you, Inspector," Holmes said, his second cigarette stub hissing as he flicked it into his cold tea. "If you wish to remain on the side of the angels, you will ask no questions about my next move in this great game."

CHAPTER TWENTY

RETURN TO CARFAX

Our cab drew up on a quiet, tree-lined avenue, a short distance from Carfax. Holmes instructed the cabbie to drive slowly about in a circuit until we returned, and paid him a handsome retainer. As the cab drove away, we walked briskly along the darkening street, the last light of a blood-red dusk throwing portentous shadows across our path. I sighed as it started to rain.

We did not enter the property via the main drive as before, but instead clambered over an ivy-covered wall on the western boundary, and trekked through the overgrown grounds. We crossed a small natural stream that ran alongside a crumbling chapel, long abandoned. Groves of oak and beech trees provided ample cover for our approach, though the going was heavy as night fell upon us, and Holmes would not allow the lighting of lanterns until we could be certain that there was no one at the house who might observe us.

When finally we emerged from the dark grove, the rain had grown heavier, and our boots were caked in mud. The house lay before us. We had previously seen it from a more pleasant aspect nearer the road, but how different it appeared now. It was a straggling manor, clearly extended many times over the centuries. We were presented with a castellated, medieval tower, with thick stone walls and barred windows. Beside that, a half-timbered gallery joined the ancient part of the house to the smooth stone of the Georgian remodelling, its once-pristine face pockmarked from exposure to the elements, or else covered with ivy.

The house was entirely dark.

Holmes led the way, carrying with him his small bag in which he had packed a cracksman's kit. It was to the gallery that we strode, to the tradesman's entrance, which Holmes presumed would be easier to crack and more secluded than the grand front door.

"This is a fine thing," I whispered, as Holmes worked the lock with a set of tools acquired through less-than-honest channels. "Is this not what the Crew of Light did when hounding Dracula?"

"Stop clucking, Watson," Holmes chided. "The Crew of Light were hounding an innocent man. We are hounding an entirely guilty one. Almost there…"

The lock clicked, altogether too loudly for my liking, and the door swung open into a dark passageway. Holmes ducked inside, stopped to listen intently and, apparently satisfied, struck a match to light his dark-lantern. He left it cowled, shining its light in a tight beam like an expert burglar. He crept along the corridor, his feet making not a sound, and beckoned me to stay close as he entered a large kitchen. I considered, not for the first time, just what an excellent criminal Sherlock Holmes would make were he of a mind for it.

We crept through the great house, room by room, only now realising its extent. It was a warren of corridors and chambers all in various states of decoration. Furniture lay under dustsheets; the smell of paint hung in the air. Some rooms had not been finished, but rather were stripped back to bare brick, leaving exposed winding creepers of newly installed electrical cables—Van Helsing was transforming Carfax into a modern estate that would surely be the envy of London society.

Holmes had instructed me before we entered to be on the lookout for a study, library or office. We were most interested in Van Helsing's business affairs—anything that might link his activities to the railway venture Aytown had written of.

On the first floor we began to see those signs of life that one would expect from someone's home, suggesting that Van Helsing had indeed begun to live at Carfax, at least occasionally. We discovered a series of rooms that had been converted into a sumptuous living apartment, with lounge, dining room, games room and, finally, a library.

Though each chamber that we found was smaller than its counterpart downstairs, and had probably been sleeping apartments until recently, the library was the clear exception. It was the largest room on the first floor, and looked to have served the same purpose for some considerable time. Every inch of wall was lined with bookcases, and every inch of shelf filled with books. On the far side was a large desk, which I made for at once, stopping only when I realised that Holmes was not following, and thus I had no light. I turned to see my friend shining the lantern along the rows of books, moving rapidly, before coming to a stop.

"What is it, Holmes?" I whispered.

"I'm searching for Van Helsing's books, Watson," he said. "Most of those here were doubtless acquired with the property, as library collections often are. They represent myriad subjects that I doubt the professor would care for, and the poor state of them is not befitting of an academic. These ones, on the other hand, are like new."

Holmes ran his fingers along the spines of several leather-bound tomes, before appearing to find what he was looking for.

He began to chuckle, and the chuckle grew into a laugh.

"Shush, Holmes," I hissed.

"Oh, Watson, what a fool I've been. Several times during this case I have made errors, but none so fundamental as this."

"What is it?"

"These books—a goodly number are by Arminius Vambery. This one here, *On the Origin of the Magyars*... interesting."

Holmes pulled the book from the shelf and flicked through the first few pages, noting a handwritten dedication on the flyleaf.

"'To Abraham, my friend, with devotion,'" Holmes read. He squinted thoughtfully, and then took up his search along the shelf. "I knew I had seen it," he said, as he withdrew a hefty volume from its nook. It was entitled *A Treatise on the Customs and Beliefs of the Magyars, and those Peoples Indigenous to the Lands around the Austro-Hungarian Empire.*

"Long-winded title," I said.

"Look, Watson. The authors' names."

I looked. "Arminius Vambery and Abraham Van Helsing. So our man wrote a book about Transylvania—we already knew he was an authority on the matter. What's the significance?"

Holmes sighed impatiently. "There's no time to explain now; let us find what we came for and leave."

Frustrated as ever by Holmes's enigmatic methods, I followed as he began to rifle through the papers on the desk. He found nothing that interested him, and so set about picking the locks on the desk drawers. He went through each one systematically, finally pulling out a bundle of letters. Holmes shuffled through them like playing cards, setting aside four on the desk, before replacing the rest of the pile.

"What is it, Holmes?"

"I had not expected to find any truly incriminating documents here, for the professor has been using this house only on a temporary basis. But he has written correspondence at this very desk. Most of the letters are not pertinent to our case. These four, however, are coming with us. Three of them are indeed mine, taken from the mantelpiece at Baker Street—you can still see the knife-marks in the pages. I had not yet opened them, and it vexes me beyond words that confidential missives from potential clients reached the eyes of Van Helsing before mine. There were seven letters in that pile—the other four must have been of little or no interest to the professor, and have been discarded. These, on the other hand… I cannot see how they relate to the case, so I can only assume that they contain information that would allow Van Helsing to discredit or blackmail me, or the senders. I shall have to see to this once Van Helsing is brought to justice."

"And the other?"

"It is a note from Mina Harker."

Professor,

I have done all I can at Whitby, and am therefore joining Jonathan at Hillingham. I trust the preparations are made for your trip. If you require anything from us in your absence, be sure to send word.

You might find it interesting that our man at the asylum overheard Hennessey discussing delicate matters with W. We shall have to remind him that such actions have consequences. Trust me to take care of it, as always. However, you must speak with Jack upon your return—his behaviour becomes ever more erratic. I believe the pressure of this affair is too much for him.

Your obd. servant, &c.,

Mina

"Good Lord, Holmes," I said. "We need to find her and get the truth out of her!"

"I think you're right, Watson, for other lives now depend on our swift action."

"How rude!"

The room was dragged abruptly into bright light, and I squinted against the suddenness of it. There, by the door, stood the Harkers.

"We honour Lucy's memory by taking up residence," Mina Harker said. "We shall fill Hillingham with light, and laughter, and perhaps even children. We certainly shall not leave it unattended, like Carfax, so that any Tom, Dick or Harry can enter of his own free will."

"You shall, I trust, leave behind you some of the happiness you brought tonight." Jonathan Harker echoed the alleged words of Dracula, from his own account, and smirked at his own joke.

My eyes adjusted finally to the stark electric chandelier. Both of the Harkers wore jackets, and were damp from the rain—they could not have been here long. I saw now that Harker held the kukri knife in his hand—this was, I presumed, his preferred murder weapon.

"What brings the two of you to Carfax?" Holmes asked, his voice betraying not a hint of unease.

"Oh, a fine thing," said Mrs Harker, "to be asked that by a couple of thieves. The professor requested that we look in on the house while he is away. We came by to make sure that no disreputables had broken in and… well, here we all are."

As she spoke, I felt my anger rising. I saw what a fool I'd been in Whitby. I saw, too, how the lines of Mina Harker's youthful face could easily have been mistaken for my Mary's, but in a cruel reflection of her. The thought of my mistake still stung.

"You said the professor is away?" Holmes said, acting as though nothing at all was amiss—as though Harker was not brandishing a knife, and harbouring a dark look in his eyes. "Might I ask where he's gone? We had hoped to catch him tonight."

"Certainly. He's gone to look up some old friends—Aytown and Singleton, I think they're called. He was lucky to get a place on the last steamer. I'm rather afraid that you'll never catch him."

"Interesting," said Holmes, absently. "But tell me, why on earth would the professor think to find Aytown and Singleton in Transylvania?"

"Because we saw a most indiscreet former police inspector meet with a particularly foolish former solicitor's clerk, and they said one or two things they really oughtn't to have."

"But what of the former police inspector and the foolish clerk? Might I enquire what has become of them?"

Jonathan Harker took a step forwards. "I'm afraid they met with a terrible accident this afternoon," he said. "A fire. I saw the whole thing; dreadful business—I shall miss William. Still, it's not your concern."

"I see I have been rather played for the fool," Holmes said.

"More than once, Mr Holmes," mocked Mrs Harker. "Your reputation flatters you."

"You are not the first to have commented so these past days, madam—it is almost as though several personages have joined forces in mocking my humble efforts. I take it from this show of matrimonial unity I was entirely mistaken when I said you regretted your wedding vows?"

"You were, Mr Holmes. My husband is twice the man with me behind him, and I twice as rich with him by my side. A match made in heaven."

Jonathan Harker sniggered at that, though the remark did not flatter him.

"It is gratifying to think that Sherlock Holmes was fooled by mere feminine wiles," Mrs Harker said. "I had heard it was only your companion who was so soft-headed."

"I shall not make that mistake again, good lady, I assure you." Holmes bowed curtly.

"You shall not have the opportunity."

The charade was over. Jonathan Harker stalked forwards steadily, brandishing the knife. I reached into my pocket for my gun.

"Don't, Doctor," Mrs Harker snapped, and I saw that she had in her hand a small pistol, aimed right at me. "You see, we were asked to inspect the property, for the professor was concerned that intruders might be about. When we arrived, on a dark and rainy night, we found that his suspicions were in fact well founded. An altercation ensued, in which my husband overcame the intruders and slew them both with a blade. He was shot in the leg for the efforts. It was only after the terrible ordeal was over that we realised the men whom we had mistaken for burglars were in fact the famous Sherlock Holmes and the redoubtable Dr Watson. A tragedy."

"Shot in the leg?" Harker said, casting his wife a glance rather nervously.

"Yes, love, by Dr Watson's gun. In such fear for your life, and for mine, you showed the intruders no mercy. It's the only way."

Harker sighed. "Very well, but let's get the slaying part over with first."

A crash sounded downstairs, which caused all of us to freeze. Loud voices could be heard, drawing closer, and then heavy footfalls pounded on the stairs. I could see from the uncertain look upon the Harkers' faces that they were not expecting more visitors. Mrs Harker's finger tightened on the trigger of her pistol; I tensed, expecting her to shoot. I glanced furtively at Holmes, who alone was composed, back straight, his features impassive.

A police constable, breathless and red in the face, threw open the door behind Mrs Harker, so suddenly that she turned and I thought she might fire. The constable let out a gasp when he saw the barrel pointed his way, and then shouted gruffly for assistance. More footsteps drew near, and another constable entered, followed finally by Inspector Bradstreet.

"Well, well, well—isn't this a pretty situation?" Bradstreet said. "Put that gun away, madam, you shan't be needing it now. Would someone care to explain what's going on?"

"These men have broken into our friend's home, and are robbing him!" Mrs Harker cried, her voice full of affected breathy panic. "My husband and I apprehended them."

"Did you indeed? And you are…?"

"Wilhelmina Harker. This is my husband, Jonathan. We are friends of the owner of this house, Professor Van Helsing. You may have heard of us."

"I have heard of you, madam. And I've heard of the men that you have apprehended also—for they are none other than Sherlock Holmes and his associate, Dr Watson. I was summoned here by a neighbour who saw some suspicious characters lurking about, but I find it hard to believe that Sherlock Holmes would steal anything."

"You can believe it," Mrs Harker protested. "You will find several papers upon Mr Holmes's person that belong to the professor. And you might be interested to see what's inside that bag he's carrying."

Bradstreet strode over to Holmes, and took a glowering look at Harker's knife as he passed by, which Harker sheepishly pocketed.

"Well, let's see it, Mr Holmes."

"Of course, Inspector. It would appear that you have me 'dead to rights', as the criminal classes say." Holmes handed over the letters. "Strange though, is it not, that some of the letters there are addressed to me? And yet I found them here. Why might that be?"

Bradstreet leafed through the pages, and tutted.

"You're right, Mr Holmes, and it is strange. But I'm afraid

that doesn't excuse your presence here. A complaint has been made, and we must execute our duty as police officers. Perkins, Bryant—take these letters, and Mr Holmes's bag. They're evidence now. Mr Holmes; Dr Watson—I'm afraid you'll have to come down to the station."

"As you wish, Inspector."

"Mr Harker—I'll need to speak with you and your wife further. May I take your address and call upon you tomorrow?"

"Hillingham, near Hampstead," Mrs Harker said, even though Bradstreet had been addressing her husband. "But we are very busy at present—you shall have to arrange an appointment."

"I'll do that," the inspector said. "Now then, let's get these gentlemen to the carriage."

On the street, once we were certain the Harkers could not see us, Holmes shook Bradstreet's hand. "Very well played, Inspector," he said. "For a moment I wondered if I would have to resort to my alternative plan, but you arrived in the nick of time."

"Holmes," I said, "you mean to say that you expected this?"

"Not entirely. If the Harkers had not appeared, we would have been gone before the inspector arrived. What I did not tell you was that I noticed the police carriage following us earlier, and slipped our cabbie an extra half crown to let it do so. After our exchange earlier, I knew it would be too much for the inspector to resist seeing what we were up to. I also knew that, as an ally, he would not foil our little robbery immediately, but would doubtless intervene if he saw anyone else approach the house. Am I right, Inspector?"

"You are, Mr Holmes. When I saw those two arrive, I guessed they were the Harkers, and came running in case there was trouble."

"It's lucky you didn't come alone," Holmes said. "I think the sight of your man's uniform stayed Mrs Harker's hand."

"I told you there were men in the station who would see you succeed, Mr Holmes. And these are two such men."

"Mrs Harker mentioned Cotford, and Young…"

Bradstreet shook his head ruefully. "There was a fire, Mr Holmes, at a small theatre in Hampstead. Young is dead. Cotford is in a bad way—I doubt very much he'll survive."

A look of anger crossed Holmes's face.

"I was not careful enough. I underestimated the Harkers yet again. Inspector, keep a close eye on the two of them, for I guarantee Jonathan Harker was personally involved in the arson. He all but admitted it in there."

"If he was, Mr Holmes, I'll see him swing, be sure of it."

As we spoke, our cab came slowly along the street, having been circling the area as promised. Holmes hailed it, and shook Bradstreet's hand once more.

"Inspector, I promise that I shall share all evidence with you at the first opportunity. For now, it is imperative that the Harkers believe we are in your custody. We will by necessity be taking a short trip, after which I am sure this whole case will be resolved to your satisfaction."

"I will help as best I can, but I'm out of my jurisdiction here already. If the Harkers press the matter further, a warrant may be issued."

"Understood perfectly," said Holmes, already stepping onto the cab's foot-board. "When next I see you, it shall be either in triumph or manacles. Farewell!"

"Are you going to explain what's going on?" I asked, once the cab was well underway.

"Haven't you puzzled it out yet?"

"It's those books you found that confuse me most," I said.

"What's Arminius Vambery got to do with anything?"

"Vambery is one of the world's foremost experts on the folklore, languages and politics of the countries that now make up the Austro-Hungarian Empire. I've read several of his works—his grasp of linguistics is really first-rate. His involvement with Van Helsing is intriguing. The fact that Vambery is a spy for the British government suggests something more."

"A spy?"

"Yes. Disraeli did not think terribly highly of him, but he still works for our government. If he is intimately acquainted with Professor Van Helsing then I would suggest the good professor might have access to more secret intelligence than he ought."

"This is too much to take in, Holmes…"

"Let me simplify it for you, Watson. You may have heard of the Baghdad Railway, which the German government hopes will provide a direct link from Buda-Pesth to India, and thus encroach on trade that has traditionally been the sole province of the British Crown. As I'm sure you can imagine, the Crown does not want Germany to exert any influence over our interests in India, and is therefore opposed to the further extension of the railway, lobbying secretly to ensure the project never begins. However, as a pre-emptive measure, the British government has been surveying a similar line, taking a different route that would avoid Buda-Pesth altogether. Can you guess where the proposed route would take it?"

"Transylvania?" I offered.

"Precisely. This ambitious line will cross the Carpathians, making our colonial operations all the more simple, and bringing great wealth both to the Crown and to those who assist the British—the Hungarians and the Turks, primarily. There are several European powers who would seek to weaken this project, and it is safe to say that Germany is foremost amongst them."

"But why all the financial wrangling? What were Holmwood, Morris and Aytown doing investing in a government project? And why did it cost them so dear?"

"I need to research this more thoroughly before I can provide an answer, Watson. It is quite possible that the British line has been licensed to a private engineering company, in order to avoid outright diplomatic hostilities. If that's the case, then I would guess that Holmwood gave his backing to the project, and brought in a few choice friends to make easy money. Van Helsing must have had some link to Holmwood before he was called to help with Lucy's illness, and decided to upset the apple cart with regards to the railway investment. He tried to destroy all of the men involved in the scheme save for Holmwood."

"I don't know about that, Holmes. Lord Godalming did not seem in such fine fettle when we met him."

"No, but I'm not entirely convinced that was all Van Helsing's doing. Keeping Lord Godalming in an addled mental state until all of this is over may be the professor's idea of a kindness."

"I'm sure I don't know what you're driving at now."

"I'm sure you don't. Anyhow, think also of Jonathan Harker. The connection to the railway now makes perfect sense of his involvement, and explains how he seemed to know the others even before his part in the tale became manifest. As Mr Young told us, Jonathan Harker did take a trip abroad, as his firm represented Lord Godalming's interests in the railway. More likely he was retained by Holmwood as a solicitor to inspect the investment in the railway. I had thought the relationship between the Harkers and Van Helsing was a result of blackmail, but Harker must have proven more useful to Van Helsing than he ever would have thought. It appears they have become almost equal partners in the conspiracy."

"So this elaborate tale is little more than cover for espionage and illicit financial swindling?"

"Something like that."

"Holmes, I can't believe it. All of this… all of these fanciful tales of vampires, the Un-Dead; the erasure and rewriting of history… for what? Some financial scheme? For something as crass as monetary gain?" I knew I sounded disappointed, and how could I not? We had untangled such a web of intrigue, of lies and deceit, that I wanted the motive to be something greater, and the consequences to be vast, truly befitting of the case so far.

"In all of our time together, Watson, when have you ever known a crime to be committed for a reason beyond the three primary motives: money, passion and revenge? Yet do not think the Dracula Papers were written purely for Van Helsing's financial gain. I am pleased to inform you that there is more to it than that. This case has all three of those motives at work, and they combine in a white heat of criminal ingenuity, in which we find forged a criminal mind truly worthy of my attentions—Professor Abraham Van Helsing."

"But why Dracula? Why condemn this Transylvanian nobleman to such an ignominious end?"

"For two reasons. The first, I would guess, is that Dracula was a supporter of the secret British railway, and perhaps even sold land on which to build the track. If he was lending his support to a project secretly sponsored by the British government, it would explain why Mycroft set us on this path in the first instance— we can investigate Van Helsing where the government cannot, for fear of causing further diplomatic incident. Secondly, I still maintain that Van Helsing pursued a personal vendetta against the Count; there were other ways he could have ruined the man without resorting to reviling his name and then murdering him. The depravity of the whole plot suggests deeper emotions at work."

"Again, I suppose you aren't going to tell me your theory yet?"

"Right again, Watson; but I will show you."

"Show me? How?"

"In Transylvania. There won't be another steamer until tomorrow, but we have no avenue left to us. We must confront Van Helsing, and get the truth from him once and for all."

CHAPTER TWENTY-ONE

SECRETS AND LIES

Early next morning, we struck out from Baker Street. Holmes took every measure to ensure that we were not followed. His informants, "irregulars", and other paid servants I knew little about had already brought a steady stream of messages to our door, and set up a network of eagle-eyed guards for half a mile around.

We went first to Cockspur Street, to organise our tickets. We secured a compartment on a train from Charing Cross to Dover, thence the channel crossing on a steamer, followed by a night aboard the Orient Express. After another day's travelling we would reach Vienna in the small hours, and would sleep there, before setting out for Bucharest when the sun rose. From there, it would be a no doubt onerous task to find our way to Transylvania. I recalled vaguely how Harker had done it, but everything after his arrival in Buda-Pesth—where he had supposedly stayed only a few hours—was quite possibly a fabrication. Holmes and I would have to forge our own path.

From the office of the International Sleeping Car Company, we took a cab to Somerset House, where Holmes used his great familiarity with the somewhat impenetrable regulations there to secure access to many folios of records. Ledger after ledger, file after file, were brought to our table by a diligent clerk, until Holmes finally found what he was looking for. I had almost nodded off when he nudged me and slid a great ledger under my nose, waving a finger triumphantly at a block of tiny, neat writing. I leaned forward and squinted.

"The Atlas, Broadbent & Co. Engineering Company, principal shareholders. You see?"

I looked to where Holmes pointed. "Lord Godalming," I said.

"The size of this company is quite remarkable—it would surely be large enough to carry out the engineering work on our little railway venture. Given the late Lord Godalming's position, any licence granted to this company should be a matter of public record. I may have to ask Mycroft about that.

"Now, this is interesting too, in late of what we now know," Holmes said, placing another book before me. "The transfer of ownership of a London property, one which has lain oddly uninhabited for some time. Carfax."

"Much as I dislike what I see, Holmes, it all appears perfectly legal."

"Legal, yes. Honest, no." Holmes took the ledger back. "Purchased by Peter Hawkins on behalf of his client, listed only as D—, in August 1892. 1892, Watson! Hawkins completed the purchase even without Renfield's assistance, before he ever sent Harker to Transylvania. Which suggests that Harker's business in Transylvania was not the sale of Carfax, but something else."

"The railway?" I asked.

"Very good. Proof of this, if it still exists, most probably rests in the hands of Jonathan Harker. Now listen, the final purchase price of Carfax was little shy of fifty thousand pounds."

"Good heavens!" I said. "For a ruin?"

"This is why even the very wealthy tend to rent in London, Watson. When it changed hands again, the agent is listed as one Mr Harker, now the owner of the law firm formerly run by Hawkins. Ownership is transferred to Abraham Van Helsing for the cost of five thousand pounds."

"That is outrageous," I said. "How could they get away with it?"

"We have yet to find out. The date of the transfer, however, is 14 November."

"Dracula would scarcely have been cold in his grave."

"If he was buried. Are we not led to believe he crumbled to dust where he lay?"

I shuddered at that. I no longer believed Dracula was a monster, but it made my blood run cold to think of the ignominious death he had been dealt.

"But that's not all I have found." Holmes set the book to one side and showed me yet another, larger and fatter than all the others on the table.

"This is the history of the Godalmings," said I. "Births, deaths, marriages... what has this to do with anything?"

"Lord Godalming—Arthur Holmwood's father—was a very influential man. Far more so than his son. It was that influence which kept this information out of the gossip columns, and even away from the eyes and ears of our friend, Langdale Pike. Look here."

I followed Holmes's finger as it tracked across a particular paragraph. I had to read it twice before the meaning struck me like a thunderbolt.

"Arthur Holmwood is adopted," I gasped.

"I suspected as much from the moment I saw his portrait— you know how I pride myself on my study of portraits. A certain Henry Baskerville would not be amongst the living now had I not perfected that particular skill. Due to the lack of a natural heir, Arthur Holmwood inherited Ring, and is for all legal purposes

Lord Godalming. But I believe his true parentage lies at the very heart of our case."

"Come, Holmes, now you must lay bare this theory that you've been taunting me with."

"Certainly not! You have almost all the facts now, Watson—I'll leave you to work it out. You have until we reach Bistritz, so there's plenty of time."

Holmes made use of the Somerset House stationery that had been laid at his disposal, and began to scribble a letter rapidly, using shorthand symbols such that I could not tell what he wrote.

"Who are you writing to, Holmes?" I asked, as he addressed the envelope. "If it's time to get Scotland Yard involved it would be quicker to go there in person."

"No, Watson, this is for Mycroft. We are about to travel far from home, and perhaps cause a major diplomatic incident in the process. I need to give my brother fair warning, otherwise it might never be safe for us to return."

"If you know he's at the club, perhaps we should just go and see him."

"I find it better not to call on Mycroft unannounced, or at all. I have outlined my intentions, and given a cursory sketch of yesterday's events. He will do what is necessary."

Holmes sealed his cryptic letter, and took it to the clerk, with instructions to send a trusted messenger to the Diogenes Club to deliver the note.

"Mycroft may send a reply, or he may not," Holmes said when he returned. "There is nothing more for us to do here. We should return to Baker Street and pack our things."

When we entered our rooms, Holmes froze at once, and I did likewise out of sheer reliance upon his remarkable instincts. I looked around his angular shoulders and saw someone sitting in Holmes's armchair by the fireplace, identifiable only by a pair of legs, a nonchalant hand holding a fat cigar, and a plume of exhaled smoke.

"Heard you'd been burgled," a gruff voice intoned. "Not that one can really tell. This place is a mess."

Holmes propped his hat upon the stand and walked rather guardedly towards the fireplace.

"Mycroft. It is unlike you to make house calls."

"If you will insist on trotting about the globe to solve your problems, when more sedentary reasoning will do, then you leave me little choice." Mycroft leaned around the wing of the chair to acknowledge me, his round, lined face framed by tufty, greying hair, flinty eyes studying me, as they studied everything they beheld. "Hello, Watson. Stand at ease, soldier!" His laugh sounded like the bark of a fox, and tailed off into a rumbling cough.

"Logically, brother, if you would show your hand for once rather than leave me a trail of breadcrumbs, I would not have to travel far from Baker Street. As it stands, more people are dead, and our suspect is presently beyond our reach."

"Beyond your reach, maybe. And the fact that people are dead is precisely why I am here, Sherlock. My sources tell me that a certain Cotford, formerly of the Metropolitan Police, won't last the day. The man he was interviewing—who you also spoke to—is dead. The killers are unknown, although I'm sure you've worked out that those dreadful Harker characters are behind it."

"I have. Measures are in place to curtail their activities."

"Pretty poor measures, if you ask me. Never mind, I've seen to it. I have also sent a chap over to Exeter. The protection of Miss Kate Reed cannot be entrusted to provincial bobbies. They'll get a shock when Special Branch knock on their doors, eh?" He chuckled at the thought.

"Better have someone check on Dr Hennessey at the Purfleet

Asylum while you're about it," Holmes said.

"Hennessey?"

"If the Harkers have not reached him already, then he will be of great use in testifying against Van Helsing and Seward both."

"Why, Sherlock, you have managed to provide a fact that is news to me. Well done."

"Why exactly are you here?" Holmes said. His patience for Mycroft had always been short-lived.

"Very well. First of all, I have received word from a German intelligence agent here in London, one Adolph Mayer, that Van Helsing is not working with the German government, nor does he have any associates at the embassy."

"You have spoken with a German spy?" Holmes asked.

"He contacted us, as it happens. It seems a few recent escapades have not gone unnoticed by other powers."

"And you believe this man?"

"We have a certain… gentlemen's agreement."

"That means very little to a man of espionage when national interests are in conflict." Holmes frowned.

"True, but I can see from your thoughtful aspect that the information is useful."

"Perhaps. Those German twins who have been up to no good of late… they made a fine show of being spies, with their shadowing of Watson and me, and their threatening of witnesses. They even shouted some words in Mrs Hudson's earshot that suggested an association with the German embassy… I rather think it was too convenient that those words were so clear and loud from men of espionage."

"Yet they fooled you at the time, eh? Ha!"

"Nothing is proven yet, one way or another." Holmes was visibly irked. No one could get a rise out of him quite like old Mycroft. "I presume there is a more tangible reason for your visit beyond the denials of a professional dealer in untruths?"

"I have found a piece of evidence that you may find of interest—if you're intent on following Van Helsing to Transylvania, you'd better have it."

Mycroft handed a letter to Holmes, who took one look at it and frowned.

"If you'd given me this at the start, we would not be in this predicament."

"If I'd known it existed, I wouldn't have needed you in the first place," Mycroft countered. "It was taken from Van Helsing's hotel room by one of my best men. It was kept in a safe, along with a collection of other fragments, which you do not need to see, and which we are keeping as evidence."

"Might I enquire as to the nature of the other 'fragments' you discovered?"

"Let's just say you are finally on the right track, Sherlock. The small matter of Peter Hawkins's death will soon be put to bed. It seems Van Helsing visited Exeter himself early last year, and secured certain papers that prove the Harkers' involvement in the death of Hawkins."

"The blackmail folder. I knew it!" Holmes cried.

"Yes, but you guessed, brother. It seems you've been doing a lot of that of late."

"Well, if you will insist on withholding facts from me, Mycroft, I am shamed to the practice of educated guesswork. Luckily, my guesswork is more educated than most."

"You paved the way for the acquisition of this letter, I'll grant you that."

"The death of the German?"

"Quite. The other one—his twin—was posted at the hotel, but was so shaken by the loss of his sibling that his mind was not on his duties."

"He should rather have counted his blessings," Holmes muttered.

"Ha! I knew you had a bit of wit in you, Sherlock. Anyway, the living twin was last seen boarding a steamer, presumably to follow Van Helsing, or to abandon him. His absence probably explains why it was left to that Harker fellow to deal with Young and Cotford."

"When you say 'last seen', Mycroft, you mean you've lost him. Most careless."

Mycroft scowled. "You should treat me kindly, brother, especially as I've brought you yet another gift." He took a well-stuffed envelope from his breast pocket and passed it to Holmes.

"Hotel reservations?"

"In false names, with a little credit attached, using those papers. I know you have not had the foresight to have new documents forged since this case began. These will allow you to travel from Vienna safely."

Holmes handed an envelope to me. "Watson, you can be Chester Creak; I shall be Garnett Pym." Holmes looked to Mycroft again. "Garnett Pym?"

"No one would ever think those names were made up." Mycroft snorted. "They have the unfortunate ring of truth about them. Now, the rooms are at the Hotel Klomser. I know you'd prefer the Imperial, but I don't believe Garnett Pym and Chester Creak could afford it. If I were you I'd send your luggage in those names, too, just to be on the safe side. Take this. It is a coded message. Now, look here." He hoisted himself up and out of the armchair, struggling to free his stout frame of the chair's confines. Mycroft seemed to grow more portly each time I saw him. He took up a rolled map from beside the chair.

Holmes swept a pile of books and papers from the table and helped his brother unfurl the map.

"This is top secret," Mycroft said, "but of course you know

that already. This is the proposed route of the Carpathian Railway—you can see for yourself the number of revisions they've had to make, which should explain why it's been the ruin of so many investors. Here you can see the parts of the line that were actually built, before the plans were thrown into disarray and a new survey carried out. The construction was plagued from the first day—beset by adverse weather, insufficient funding, and even raids by hill-bandits. Anyway, look here. This bit was Dracula's. The construction rights were sold to Godalming's company, but they've rather lost heart of late due to raids by the Szgany—the local gypsies. The success of the railway depended on Dracula's involvement—not just his land, but also his influence. As such, we've had to take charge and send in some Royal Engineers, but with Dracula gone, our boys are on thin ice."

"Those rights," Holmes interrupted. "Brokered by Harker?"

"They were, and counter-signed by Hawkins at a later date."

"So he did go to Transylvania," Holmes mused.

"Of course he did. Why else would he be so useful to Van Helsing? Now, pay close attention. When you go on from Bistritz, you will need to find those Royal Engineers—I don't know exactly where; but they'll be near the Count's castle, somewhere along this line. When you find them, show them this, and they shall know you are on the side of the angels." He handed over one last document, which Holmes pocketed at once.

"So the government is showing its hand?"

"No other choice, old boy. Lord Godalming's company have made a poor fist of this project from the start. With the Germans sniffing about, we might as well send in our boys to do it properly, eh?"

"A little late for Morris, not to mention those men who have lost their fortunes on the venture."

"We are all of us responsible for the risks we take, Sherlock.

You should know that more than most. Now, I must be away."

"So soon?" Holmes asked sardonically.

"I've taken enough risks of my own today simply coming here."

"Of course. Leaving one's club is a risky business."

Mycroft shot Holmes a glare, and then laughed aloud again. He put on his hat, patted it down upon his head, and made past me for the door. He paused, turning back to Holmes. "You know by now that Arthur Holmwood was adopted?"

"I suspected as much all along, though it is now confirmed."

"Who do you think the father is? Van Helsing or Dracula?"

From Mycroft's grin, I discerned that he had his own theory, or else knew for certain, but he wished to test Holmes.

"I know, as do you. But I am letting Watson work it out; don't spoil the surprise."

Mycroft turned to me with a broad, raffish grin. "Well, I've narrowed it down to two for you, Watson old boy. If you can't work it out, just toss a coin, eh? That's what works for Sherlock. Farewell!"

CHAPTER TWENTY-TWO

THE WORDS OF THE COUNT

Letter, Count Dracula to Abraham Van Helsing, 2 June 1892

Old friend,

Word has reached my ears that Elisabet ails for something, that some terrible affliction has beset her. I have heard that she is committed to an asylum, at your word. At first I could not believe this to be true, but now I think it is, and it brings great sorrow to my heart.

You know that I loved her, and it must hurt you to admit that. Yet she chose you, Abraham, and left me alone to live out my time in this castle, which has been a prison for me since that day. I wish for nothing but her happiness, and that perhaps you can forgive me for the transgression all those years ago. Yet it seems, if recent reports be true, forgiveness is not a quality you possess. I fancy that you never forgave Elisabet, either—for how long have you made her suffer? Was it not enough that she should give up her only child for you? Was it not enough that she was forced to live an existence almost as wretched as mine for more than twenty years? And have you not suffered also? If this anger that you bear us has never left you, then can you not see what a bitter, twilit existence you have led? I wonder if your petty revenge was worth the destruction of three lives.

If there is truth to these latest rumours, then have the courage to make it plain. That Elisabet rots in a madhouse, while you carouse with the women of Amsterdam is bad enough. But I have heard tell of something more troubling still—that Elisabet's son is alive. That he did not die, as you told me. And that can mean only one thing, can it not?

Now, an Englishman has come to my home, and he comes to secure me passage to England, where I can see for myself if you truly have done this terrible thing. I go because we are far beyond honest questions and truthful answers, you and I. I hope my intelligence is false. If it is, then I hope beyond hope that we may still reconcile. But what if it is true? What if Count Dracula, alone in his crumbling palace, should discover that he has a mortal enemy still, set in opposition to his every desire? What then could Count Dracula do?

Believe me, old friend, when I say that there is nothing I would not do! I am an exile from the world because I choose to be. I attempt to atone for the wrongs I did you. But if Elisabet is hurt because of you, I swear there will be nowhere on this earth you can hide from me. You think me without influence? This is your greatest mistake. For twenty-three years you have harboured me ill will. It is you who forces me to re-join the world—you who drags me from my solitude. Remember, old friend, that the blood of conquerors flows in these veins, and such blood can boil with passions that your German line may never understand. Here in Transylvania we have a saying: the blood is the life! It does not translate well, perhaps, but I am sure you take the meaning well enough.

But again I say it; these rumours cannot be true. And when you tell me that they are not—when you look me in the eye and tell me that you still honour the last vestige of friendship that ever was between us—then I shall put back the sword of my ancestors, and perhaps, at long last, we shall have peace.

Whether you believe it or no, I am ever your friend,

D.

CHAPTER TWENTY-THREE

TO TRANSYLVANIA

It was well past 1 a.m. on the morning of 18 April, when Holmes and I arrived in Vienna and trod wearily to our rooms at the Klomser. The journey had been long, by boat, rail, and coach, and we were far from done.

"Get as much sleep as you can," Holmes instructed. "We don't have long if we wish to catch the early train to Bucharest."

"I still don't see why we can't catch the later train, Holmes," I said wearily.

"Call me 'Pym' from here on," Holmes said. "You never know who's listening.

"Van Helsing has a day's head start on us, and I wager he is not alone. He has travelled with murderous intent, for Aytown and Singleton must be in Transylvania already. The best hope for the two of them is that they stumble across the British Royal Engineers—they may then be afforded some protection. If Van Helsing finds them first, however, they are surely doomed.

"We must be relentless, my dear Mr Creak. Every hour we can gain on the professor is a chance of preventing the deaths of two men. Every hour we delay is a chance that Van Helsing will succeed in his plan, and our best chance of securing vital witnesses is gone for ever."

When Holmes put it so bluntly, I felt ashamed of my complaints, which were born of tiredness. We were strangers in a foreign land now, and doubtless had more enemies than friends to hand. I thought of Aytown and Singleton—Holmes and I were surely more prepared for the machinations of dangerous foes than they were, and it fell to us then, as a solemn duty, to assist them.

With this in mind, I took no brandy that night, and went straight to bed, only to lie awake for some considerable time thinking of what dangers lay ahead.

The station was quiet when we arrived, for the queues had not yet begun to form for the day's travel. Only those fortunate souls who had secured places on the Constantinople-bound Orient Express now made their way to the chilly platform outside. We noted duly that time was on our side at last—the Bucharest-bound train did not run on Tuesdays. If Van Helsing were only a day ahead of us, he would have had to arrange his travel using local lines, and even if his knowledge of the region were superior to our own, that would surely have presented him with several delays.

We had few opportunities to stretch our legs at the various stops along the way, and did not spend any substantial time off the train until Buda-Pesth the following morning.

From Buda-Pesth, our tickets afforded us travel first to Klausenburgh, and then to Bistritz upon a local service. Had I known just how basic the train to Bistritz would be, and how long the journey, I would have taken the time to drink in the comforts of the hostelries of Klausenburgh. As it was, I spent what seemed like an eternity on a small, uncomfortable seat, with an old woman bundled up next to me, snoring in my ear the entire way.

We had not seen hide nor hair of civilisation for the duration of the day. Forests, hills, and snow-capped mountains rolled past the train in an endless procession, with only the occasional fortified church, ruin or tiny medieval village in the distance providing evidence that men had ever trod these environs.

When finally we reached Bistritz, the sun had almost set, and the tiny train station had about it a lonely, eerie aspect. I was so relieved to walk in the fresh air that I did not care at all that it was freezing cold, or that the local people stared at us suspiciously. We walked a short distance along the main street, ignoring the occasional beggar-boy or the enticements of innkeepers touting for custom, and instead followed the directions that had been given us in Vienna. The concierge at the Klomser had sent our bags onwards to the Hotel Sahlings, though he could not guarantee it would reach our accommodation before us. The rest of our luggage had remained in Vienna—we would have to live pretty rough if we decided to stay on for more than one or two nights. Of our exact plans beyond Bistritz, Holmes had shared little; I wondered just how much of a plan he even had.

To describe Sahlings as "modest" would be to do an injustice to all those modest but comfortable hotels that populate the market towns of England. Situated just off the town square, the building itself was fine enough, if a little gloomy, but it was clearly running with a skeleton crew, and was in dire need of attention. We managed to communicate well enough with the weary-looking manager, who, I was thankful to find, had received a wire from Vienna and had our room prepared. I was most relieved to find our bags waiting for us, somewhat battered from what I presumed to be its time aboard a freight car, but otherwise a welcome sight.

Once we had washed and eaten a stodgy local stew, Holmes set about outlining our next moves. He sent me to see the manager again, to find any literature I could on the local area, and to engage the man in conversation regarding any recent English guests.

"You're the more personable, Watson," Holmes said. "Take a drink with the chap and see if you can find anything out."

"And what will you be doing?"

"I shall be about town, surveying the lay of the land."

"Holmes! We are in a strange country, and perhaps a hostile one. We should stay together."

"Nonsense. There is too much to arrange, and too much at stake. Need I remind you that Aytown and Singleton could be dead already, and if they are not, their lives depend on our quick action."

"How on earth shall we find them?" I asked.

"If they made it as far as Bistritz, I imagine it will be easy enough. Two Englishmen asking foolish questions will surely stand out. Of course, we will soon be in much the same position, so best have your wits about you. Now, run along, dear fellow—play your part, and I shall play mine, and I'll see you back here in a couple of hours."

It was closer to three hours later when Holmes returned, rubbing his arms against the cold.

"I was worried sick," I said. "It's past midnight."

"So it is. I ended up in a tavern, and I am afraid I drank rather too much of the local *tsuika*."

"Really, Holmes! How does this help our plans?"

"Simply because the local rowdies are amongst the most superstitious lot I have ever encountered. A few careful questions followed by several drinks loosened their tongues such that they lined up to frighten a stranger to their town with tales of vampires and werewolves."

"Did they tell you about Count Dracula?"

"After prompting, yes. Perhaps our mysterious Count is something of a phantom after all, Watson, for he certainly haunts our path through this elaborate tale. I maintain that Count Dracula was not a vampire. The locals, however, are not so sure. Here we have mean whispers of a strange, eccentric nobleman, living in his crumbling castle up in the mountains. He comes from an ancient family that fought the Turks in the time of Vlad the Impaler—a family with a reputation for hot tempers and bloodthirsty conquest. Some say he's immortal, others that the family has long been in league with Satan. No two stories were the same… It seems to me that this lonely 'exile', as he calls himself, has been the subject of malicious gossip for a long time indeed."

"I still don't understand how this helps us."

"Because when I brought the conversation around to Transylvania's proud heritage, and the pride of the ancient Magyars, one old man called Dracula a traitor to his kind. He said that foreigners had been trekking back and forth from the mountains on and off for well over a year, carting wagon-loads of goods to some secret location near the castle. I asked if they were German, and the man said no—they were English, like me. He also said that Dracula sat on a hoard of gold, which he never used to help the poor people of his domain, but instead used to line the pockets of foreign investors. A narrative has started to form in my mind, Watson."

"How is this narrative any more reliable than stories of vampires?"

"Because the old man was genuinely angry—he was not merely trying to scare a foreigner with childish tales. And he said something else, too."

"Oh?"

"He said that Dracula was so disliked by those hereabouts, that he could only find servants from amongst the Szgany."

"His gypsies," I said. These fearless horsemen had been well detailed in the Dracula Papers, as Dracula's faithful servants in the fight against the Crew of Light.

"Not his, apparently. The Szgany are ill thought of around here. They are said to be inconstant—mercenaries who sell their blades to the highest bidder. That led to Dracula's downfall: they turned upon him for a better offer."

"And did you learn who made this offer?" I asked.

Holmes shook his head. "But I'm sure you can hazard a guess. Now, Watson, that is all I discovered. I trust you had a quieter evening, but no less informative."

"As a matter of fact, I did," I said. "I have a map of the region about the Borgo Pass, and the hotel manager was kind enough to mark on it the road to Castle Dracula. He will also arrange a carriage for our journey tomorrow."

"Excellent. And what of Aytown and Singleton? Any mention of other Englishmen passing this way?"

"He claimed he did not know."

"Claimed? You suspect he was lying?"

"It could have been the difficulty he had in speaking English, but I would say he was reluctant to discuss it."

"Let us hope it was the former. If our host is in league with the enemy, we may well have a tough time ahead. But don't let me worry you, Watson—I am merely thinking aloud. We must get some sleep. Tomorrow will be another long day, and I fear there will be much danger to face before the end."

CHAPTER TWENTY-FOUR

CASTLE DRACULA

The coach-and-four set a fine pace along roads that had seen better days, and eventually on a bumpy trail that wended its way through gloomy pine forests. The strange calls of unfamiliar creatures sounded dully beyond the shadows that whipped past our ill-fitted windows, through which cold air gusted uncomfortably.

The driver, swaddled against the cold in such a heap of ragged blankets that he barely resembled a man, spoke very little English, and not much more German. He had managed to inform us that the journey to the Borgo Pass would take perhaps five hours, stopping only a few times at lonely inns and isolated villages along the way to water the horses and stretch our legs. By securing a private carriage at the hotel, rather than the public diligence, we were able to make good time. When asked if he would take us on directly to Castle Dracula, the coachman was strangely reticent, and pretended not to understand. If he refused us later, we would be stranded. I remembered Harker's diary—he had been likewise abandoned in a harsh wilderness, only to be picked up by a strange black carriage driven by a demonic coachman, who Harker had suggested was Count Dracula himself. Knowing that his account was a fiction proved little comfort now that we were here, looking out onto the mournful, desolate beauty of haunted Transylvania.

When we did pass by villages and farmsteads, groups of peasants, dressed in their sheepskins and gaily coloured *gatya*, stared at us impassively. One old woman, upon seeing foreigners taking the road to the Borgo Pass, made the sign of the cross; whether for our benefit, or her own, we could not tell.

We moved up and down great ranges of hills, until finally we crested a high ridge, and the landscape changed dramatically. Ahead stretched an interminable forest, painted upon the vista in daubs of green, blue and black, reaching all the way to the base of the purple mountain range with its snow-capped peaks lost to enveloping clouds. I considered myself well travelled, but had never seen a land so untamed, so starkly beautiful, and yet somehow so forbidding.

We passed a sign for Piatra, which we had noted on our map as the nearest large settlement to our destination. The coach forked away from it, however, following an easterly trail that led into a steep valley. The road seemed to be swallowed by the carpet of rocks and trees ahead, only to reappear on the upper slopes of the foothills beyond. We were forced to slow for the inequalities in the road, and had not travelled far when we saw that we were no longer alone.

From all sides came the shouts of men. From behind us came hoofbeats upon hard ground.

Upon hearing these sounds, something spurred our driver to action, and he at once took his long whip to the team. The sudden burst of speed along such an uneven road forced Holmes and me to brace ourselves so as not to tumble from our seats. When finally we regained our balance, we were able to look through the grimy windows to see just who approached.

A dozen or so horsemen trailed behind us, and more rode from narrow paths on either side, gaining rapidly. Although we were strangers in this land, we knew at once from the descriptions we had read in the Dracula Papers, and the things we had heard in Bistritz.

Szgany.

Dressed in silks and furs, with large moustaches and carrying long knives, the fierce gypsies of this region now hounded our advance. And behind the horses came a small carriage, which must have approached from the Piatra road, for it could not otherwise have caught us so easily.

The gypsies called to each other in their strange language, and shouted to our driver, who cracked his whip and quickened his horses to a breakneck speed, like the very devil were on our heels.

We thundered into a deep forest basin, and jolted up the other side, the snorting of our horses and clattering of the carriage wheels almost drowning out the whooping of the Szgany behind us. Gunfire cracked. We looked back, our teeth rattling in our skulls from the bumpy ride, and we saw that several gypsies had ridden to the fore, firing rifles in the air. If they wanted us to stop, their actions had the reverse effect.

Holmes reached into his coat pocket and pulled out a revolver. He gave me a nod, and I took up my own gun, which I had hoped I would not need.

Each of us leaned out of our respective windows, immediately assailed by the freezing mountain air. Holmes fired first—his shot was deliberately high, and caused the gypsies to flinch upon their steeds. One of them now lowered his rifle, holding it in one hand in a most ungainly fashion as he wrestled with the reins in the other. I could see that their warning shots had ceased, and the man intended to fire at us directly. With self-preservation foremost in my mind, I squeezed a round from my revolver, which must have nicked him, for he almost dropped his rifle and ducked low to the neck of his horse.

Another shot rang out from our pursuers, this time cracking against the rear of the coach. Splinters of wood erupted inside.

Holmes fired again, missing his mark. The coach now crested a hill; sunlight streamed into the cab, and illuminated the Szgany to our advantage.

One of the gypsies fell as a bullet struck him in the shoulder— but it had not been fired by me or Holmes. Our coachman cried out in his own tongue, and for a second I wondered if he was the gunman, or perhaps whether he himself had been hit. But then I realised his tone was one of surprise, and turned to look at the road before us.

The trees thinned out ahead, giving way to rocky, scree-covered slopes. And upon those slopes stood armed men. They were not Szgany, nor even Transylvanian by the look of them, but had the disciplined look of soldiers.

Our coachman slowed to avoid running into them, and the men at once fanned out, opening fire with their rifles—British, Martini-Henry rifles, if I were any judge—stopping the advance of the Szgany at once.

There was a short exchange of fire as some resistance was offered, but soon the gypsies had turned their horses about and were racing back down the trail. We thought for a moment that our driver would not stop, but Holmes leaned out and shouted to him in English and German until finally he reined in the horses. Before I could say a word, Holmes sprang out, and made his way back down the road towards our saviours. By the time I caught up with him, he was shaking hands with a tall, thin fellow who looked rather out of place amongst the military men at his side.

"Alfred Singleton, I presume," Holmes said.

The man looked surprised. "Why… yes. We learned just hours

ago that two Englishmen were leaving Bistritz after asking about Castle Dracula, and that the Szgany had taken a particular interest in them. But I would wager that our intelligence is at least partly wrong, and that you are neither Garnett Pym nor Chester Creak."

"You are correct. My name is Sherlock Holmes, and this is my associate Dr Watson."

"Bless my soul!" Singleton gasped, a look of unimaginable relief upon his pale, lined face. "I've heard of you. You're both the last person I'd expect to see out here, and the most welcome. What brings you to Transylvania, Mr Holmes?"

"You do, sir. I learned that a villain by the name of Van Helsing was on his way here personally, doubtless to finish off his dark business by murdering the last two true witnesses to his crimes: yourself and a certain Mr Aytown. Where is your companion?"

Sadness crossed Singleton's face. "You're too late, Mr Holmes. Francis met his end at the hands of the Szgany just a week ago. Indeed, he's buried on the ridge up there. It was sheer luck that I managed to find these men, and they have offered me protection while I continue my research at Castle Dracula."

"And these are Royal Engineers?"

Singleton nodded, and at last introduced us to our saviours. Holmes handed the message from Mycroft over to the leader of the group, Captain Brownsworth, who studied it carefully, before shaking Holmes by the hand also.

Before further pleasantries could be exchanged, two more Engineers rode up the trail towards us on horseback, one of them with the wounded gypsy thrown over his saddle, hog-tied and cursing.

"Put a gag on that man, and see to his wound," Brownsworth ordered. "We'll find out what he knows later." The captain turned to us again. "You are welcome to billet with us, gentlemen. We lodge at Castle Dracula."

Holmes turned to Singleton. "Did you find what you were looking for?"

"Oh yes, Mr Holmes. If it were not so dangerous, I would have returned home with my findings days ago. But the Szgany patrols have increased in frequency."

"They are receiving orders to stop you at any cost," Holmes said. "And I imagine those orders shall be extended to us now. They were accompanied by a small coach just now. Is that normal?"

"No," said Brownsworth. "It's a deuced impractical vehicle for these trails, too."

"Then they have a leader now. A man too old and out of condition to travel with the Szgany by horse. A man whose sense of retribution has led him here, to see personally what you have found in the castle, and to ensure it is destroyed."

"You mean to say that was Van Helsing in the coach?" Singleton asked.

"It had to be. He left England before us, though I had hoped he was delayed sufficiently so as not to plan for our arrival. It seems he had time enough. He will not let us leave here alive."

"That's grave news," said Brownsworth. "We don't have enough men to repulse a sustained attack. Just these, plus a handful more back at the castle. We are not provisioned for a siege."

Holmes smiled. "Perhaps a siege is exactly what we need…"

The road to Castle Dracula was winding and perilous, twisting its way up the south-east face of a tall mountain, and eventually looping beneath the curtain-walls of ancient fortifications. Many times our coach's wheels scraped so close to the edge of the great precipice that I was able to look out of the window to stare directly down into a yawning drop, the full extent of which was obscured by billowing cloud.

By the time we came to a halt, and I was able to step out onto the cobblestones of the courtyard, my legs were like jelly. If Holmes had experienced any anxiety over the hair-raising journey up the mountain, he showed no sign.

Before us, the castle loomed, black and jagged. It appeared solid enough—featureless grey walls grew upwards from a courtyard strewn with detritus, while parapets and crenellations towered precariously above. The outer walls were in a poor state of repair; ancient battlements stood proud, and even now were patrolled by the small garrison of Royal Engineers, who peered occasionally down the mountain-path through their binoculars. This was a castle that had seen hardship over the long centuries— whatever wealth the reclusive Count Dracula had possessed, he had clearly not used it to keep his house in order.

Once the detail had all gathered in the courtyard, Holmes at once asked to be shown the evidence that Singleton had discovered. Singleton agreed at once, and showed us and Brownsworth into the desolate castle, and down into the lower levels.

"Most of this part of the castle is carved into the very rock of the mountain," Captain Brownsworth explained. "It's really remarkable engineering, given its age. The walls above are four feet thick in places, and the ceilings vaulted stonework, reinforced by thick pillars. If it comes to it, this is where we shall hold out— even modern howitzers wouldn't be able to break through here—a true testament to the old masons."

The cellars were extensive—a warren of rooms, large and small, linked by wide passages or tight corridors here and there, with stairways leading to even further depths. Singleton lit torches as we went, which sat in rusting iron sconces, and now cast their primitive orange light about us. Eventually we reached a locked room, which Singleton opened up for us. Once torches and candles were lit inside, Holmes at once began to inspect the room, his keen eyes scanning every detail.

Several large, empty crates were scattered about the room. At one end, a large safe of fairly modern appearance sat open. Along one wall were shelves, mostly bare save for a few books and various detritus. A table was set up in the middle of the room, scattered with papers and trinkets.

"A treasury," Holmes said.

"You are right, Mr Holmes. Although it was pretty much like this when I found it."

"There are drag-marks across the floor, and leading out into the passage beyond. Is there another way into these cellars?"

"Yes," Brownsworth answered. "There is a fortified door on the south face, which provides another path down to the road. It is now blocked by rubble from the bombardment."

"But previously it would have been used to transport goods in and out of Castle Dracula?"

"Yes."

The boxes that Dracula sent to England probably started their journey in this very chamber," said Holmes. "I very much doubt that they contained dirt, as the Dracula Papers claim. Are those gold coins I see on the table there?"

"A handful remained when we got here," Singleton said. "There are smaller chests in an antechamber below us, stuffed full of gold. In his haste, he must have forgotten them—or perhaps the Count intended to return. These boxes, however, contained the bulk of Count Dracula's material wealth, which he sought to smuggle away. I have a letter from the harbourmaster at Varna, who swears that Dracula paid for the loading with gold from one of the boxes."

Holmes's eyes lit up. "The action of a man most assured that his wealth would buy him safety and loyalty, and also of someone so long in solitude that he had become naïve about the ill intentions of his fellow men."

"That was my opinion too. I rather wonder how smoothly his passage to England would have gone if any ship's crew knew the value of their cargo. Over on the table there are a few scattered remnants that must have been dropped in the Count's haste to leave. Some of the papers document the more valuable treasures. There are some letters, also, which I imagine will be of particular interest to you, Mr Holmes. And a gold locket, which I found in the rubble upstairs. I shall let you be the judge of its significance."

Holmes gave a look of surprised approval at Singleton's cleverness. I recalled that the man was a psychical investigator by trade, and in order to catch clever tricksters and charlatans had doubtless perfected some of the techniques upon which Holmes prided himself.

Holmes went to the table and examined the artefacts, his smile broadening with each paper he looked at. Finally, he picked up the gold locket that Singleton had mentioned, and opened it. He stared for some time at the contents. He removed the small oval portraits, and inspected the backs of each, before carefully replacing them. Finally, he handed the locket to me.

"Here is the final clue to a little mystery you've been dying to solve," he said wryly. "The portraits are labelled only 'D' and 'Elisabet' on the backs. What do you make of them, Watson?"

I studied the portraits. I did not recognise the woman at all. She was pretty enough, and fair, though the portrait was not particularly flattering. The man on the left-hand side of the locket, however, was strangely familiar. I knew it must be Dracula himself, but I had never seen an image of the man. He was dark-haired and pale-skinned; his lips were thin, his nose sharp, and his jaw angular and severe. His eyes were dark and penetrating, located beneath thick eyebrows. Though his features were harsh, he was still a handsome fellow. I stared at it for some seconds more, aware that Holmes was waiting for my epiphany; then it came.

"Arthur Holmwood," I said.

"You see the resemblance?"

"Very much. Lord Godalming has his mother's eyes, it seems, but for the rest he is the spitting image of Count Dracula."

"When we visited Ring, I studied the family portraits for some time. And the reason was simple—every portrait of every male heir above that grand staircase bore certain physical similarities. Sometimes these were pronounced, sometimes not, but every Godalming had some trait that would identify them as blood relatives."

"Except Arthur Holmwood," I said.

"He did not resemble his father, his uncle or his grandfather. I could see nothing of his mother in him. I knew then that Arthur Holmwood's parentage would be a pivotal factor in solving this case."

"What does it mean?"

"It means that Van Helsing's motives were very personal indeed. For that woman, Elisabet, is his wife."

"Good grief, Holmes."

"Van Helsing must surely know that Mr Singleton here has found some vital clues in the castle. The presence of the Royal Engineers has so far deterred any hostile action, and if Mycroft was right then Van Helsing is not in a position to call upon the German Army—or so we should hope! However, he will stop at nothing to end this once and for all. Now that he knows we are here, he will gather his gypsies in greater numbers, and come for us. But we shall be ready."

"You have a plan, Mr Holmes?" Brownsworth asked.

"I think so. I shall need to speak to the prisoner first, of course."

"As you wish. I shall have a man translate for you."

"Mr Singleton—how much gold was left behind in that antechamber?"

"A small fortune, for these parts."

"Good. A small fortune is exactly what we shall need..."

"Parley! Parley!"

The cry from the battlements rang off the cold rock of the mountain. From our position in the great gateway of Castle Dracula, we peered out into the gloom, through flakes of snow that fell gently upon the plateau outside the castle walls, and to the dark shapes that moved ominously there, amidst flickering lamplight.

Holmes himself was nowhere to be seen. He had spent hours plotting with Captain Brownsworth, and although I had my part to play in my friend's plan, I knew that he was retaining some secrets for himself, until the time was right to reveal his full hand.

We waited for a response to our request. Negotiation of terms appeared to be our only hope, as the sheer number of armed Szgany that had amassed on the slopes of the mountain had taken the Royal Engineers by surprise—they had not realised just what numbers the enemy could bring to bear. Van Helsing, it seemed, had galvanised the local gypsies to unite against us.

A full minute passed, and our man on the wall was about to hail them again, when a horseman, heavily clad in furs, trotted from the enveloping snow, calling to us in thickly accented English. "We will parley. Follow me!"

We had already taken our instruction from Holmes. Now I, along with Captain Brownsworth, and a young corporal named Phillips—fluent in German and Romany—walked out of the castle grounds into the lion's den, trudging down the wide track and onto the plateau. The gates thudded shut behind us, and we heard the sound of the bars being lowered. As I stared at the dark figures ahead of us, their horses, lanterns and many rifles hoving into view, I felt suddenly vulnerable. We were placing our lives in Van Helsing's hands, and trusting to whatever sense of honour he had, that he would not simply take us prisoner or shoot us on the spot.

The enemy doubtless wanted us to enter their encampment, but we stopped halfway, at a point near the track, beside a distinctive rocky outcrop. This was no-man's land, where Holmes had instructed us to wait until Van Helsing came to us, beyond the effective range of either side's guns given the darkness and prevailing elements. As Holmes had predicted, there was an exchange of words in German, and eventually a group of men walked towards us, perhaps a dozen strong. The horseman who had dogged our descent down the track now circled, holding up a blazing torch to light the way of his paymaster.

As the group drew close, the ranks of the flamboyantly dressed gypsies parted, and two men stepped from their midst. One was a large fellow, with tufts of pale hair protruding from beneath a furred hat; his pale blue eyes smouldered with enmity towards me, and I knew at once that the surviving twin had returned to Van Helsing's employ. The other was a small, stout man; though he wore a great fur hat and was swaddled in heavy clothes, Abraham Van Helsing was unmistakeable.

"If my eyes deceive me not, I see Dr Watson," Van Helsing said. "We are some long way from the Royal Society now, no? Now, you are straying into a land most hostile, friend John, brought here no doubt by Mr Sherlock Holmes. And where is he? Where is the man who think to pursue Van Helsing to the end of the earth?"

"Holmes did not think you would be well disposed toward him," I said. "Nor toward Singleton, either. And so I have come to parley in their stead, with Captain Brownsworth."

"Ah, the Royal Engineer. Tell me, Captain, are you finding Transylvania to your liking?"

"It is an education, sir," said Brownsworth, curtly.

"Indeed. Transylvania, she have ways, eh? And they are not English ways. Ha! My people, they see you time and time again, blasting charges, digging trenches, and measuring hilltops. Some say you plan to build a railway through the very mountains. I say this would be folly. Do you not agree, Captain? Is it folly?"

"Lesser men might say so," replied Brownsworth. "I would call it ambition."

"The English, as ever, they overreach. Perhaps I need do nothing to hinder this plan, Captain. It will fail, as all such surveys have past failed. The Carpathians are mistresses most harsh, eh? They will betray; they always betray."

"You would know a thing or two about betrayal," I said. "There is a grave dug on a ridge some way down this trail. A man named Aytown is buried in it."

Van Helsing smiled wickedly. "Then the stakes, they are revealed to you, friend John. You know where you may yet end your days, should you take a foolhardy path."

"I do not threaten," I said. "We have a garrison of trained fighting men, with British rifles and British steel aplenty. We shall not be easily moved from Castle Dracula."

"I expect nothing less! The British are nothing if not belligerent, no? They fight for the pride, for the honour and the glory, like no other. But they can lose all the same. There are, what? Twenty men in the castle? Look about us here. I have a hundred Szgany now, and more to follow. The castle walls, they crumble; we can outlast you, or we can assault you, but the result it is the same. Out here in this land I need nothing but the numbers to defeat you, and numbers I have."

I nodded to Corporal Phillips. He repeated my next words loudly, in the tongue of the Szgany.

"And will the Szgany die for you, Professor? Will they rush the great walls of the most forbidding castle in these lands, for the promise of hunting rights that should be theirs anyway, or for gold that has been promised by a distant government, which they must wait for even as their comrades die upon this ground?"

Van Helsing looked confused for a second. He said something in German to the Szgany, which I understood vaguely as, "Do not listen to these English dogs; the German government has never let you down."

"Why die here today, for gold that you may never see?" I shouted, with Phillips echoing my words. "When instead you could take gold from us, and this land, in fair payment for your service, and never again take up arms for a foreign power?"

At this, I took a large purse from my coat, and tipped a shimmering cascade of gold coins into my palm, which I then tossed at the Szgany nearest us. The gypsy snatched one of the coins out of the air as the rest landed in the snow. He held it up in the torchlight, and then bit it to test its authenticity.

"Pathetic!" cried Van Helsing. "You think you can buy the loyalty of these men? Loyalty that has been owed to Van Helsing for nearly two years? They have seen for themselves my power. They have seen the wealth of my government, and they have been provided for in the manner most handsome. If you have the gold, friend John, then the Szgany can take it after you are dead."

The gypsies laughed menacingly.

"And how many must die to secure it? Are you willing to die first?" I pointed at the big Szgany in front of me. "Or you?" I pointed at the next in line. Phillips translated my words, though I think they understood me well enough. "To storm those walls is madness. We have men with rifles, and grenades. We have machine guns, mortars, and explosive charges set on every approach. We have been busy preparing for a siege, Professor. You may defeat us with numbers, and steal our gold, but you seem to count the lives of these men cheaply. How many are you willing to lose to our guns? A quarter? Half? That is how many it will cost, as I am sure you know.

"Listen to me!" I stepped forward, trying to instil within my voice a strength that I did not truly feel out there in front of a savage foe. "Professor Van Helsing is willing to sacrifice your lives to take this castle. And he claims he does this because his government wants the land, and will by their grace allow you to live and hunt upon it when the deed is done. This is a lie!"

"Silence him!" Van Helsing snarled. One of the Szgany stepped forward, but another held him back, and nodded at me to continue.

"Professor Van Helsing cannot give you this castle. He cannot promise you this land, because his government does not own it. His government does not even want it! The land has already been promised to the British government. These men are here legally, and are the only authority here. If they were trespassers, then surely soldiers would come to remove them. They would not risk your lives in this venture. No! Van Helsing is here of his own volition, pursuing his own enemies. He seeks revenge against Count Dracula, even though the Count is already dead. Would you die for such a man? The kind of man who would dishonour the dead? Would you die for his selfishness? Or would you rather strike a deal with us, and leave here tonight even richer, with no loss of Szgany lives?"

This caused some commotion, and an angry conversation broke out between the gypsies who surrounded Van Helsing. He attempted to convince them of his integrity, and for a moment a couple of the Szgany, aided by Van Helsing's large German thug, seemed to be winning the argument on the side of the professor.

It was then that Holmes's plan came to fruition. Someone shoved Van Helsing hard in the back, and he stumbled forwards into the arms of Captain Brownsworth. The Szgany who had done this deed now threw off his hat and scarf, and drew a pistol, which he aimed at the other gypsies. But of course this was no Szgany at all, but Sherlock Holmes, in the clothes of the captured gypsy from the castle.

As angry eyes settled upon him, Captain Brownsworth backed away to us, dragging the struggling professor with him. Phillips now took up a rifle, and I my pistol.

"Holmes," I muttered. "We are outgunned."

"Corporal Phillips," Holmes said, ignoring me, "translate for me. Professor Van Helsing has no official business here, and no authority. Your former master, Count Dracula, sold this land to the British Crown. Van Helsing was his enemy. Van Helsing had the Count murdered, and made you all complicit in the crime. We know this, and can prove it. Believe me, the blood of Dracula is on your hands, and if there is any curse in these lands brought about by the destruction of such an ancient bloodline, it will be on your heads for your treachery."

As Phillips translated Holmes's words, a few of the gypsies checked their stride, while others spat upon the ground in a superstitious effort to ward off evil. The German tried to spring forward, his hatred of Holmes getting the better of him, but the Szgany pulled him back fearfully.

"And yet all may not be lost for you," Holmes continued. "If you swear to leave this garrison in peace, and grant us safe passage away from here, with this man as our prisoner, we shall reward each and every man amongst you. Once word has reached this fine captain that we are safely away from Bistritz, you may come to claim the remainder of your gold. If you betray us, you will have to fight, and for what? Professor Van Helsing has already showed that you are expendable in his eyes—he will care not if every last one of you dies upon the tip of a British bayonet. So I ask you now—will you fight for him? Or will you take our gold and go in peace?"

Holmes spoke with a passion that did not truly translate, and although Van Helsing struggled and swore throughout my friend's rousing speech, he could break neither the steel of Holmes's grip, nor of his words.

While Holmes had been speaking, many of the gypsies had come closer to our position, and we saw now a good many men, some of whom muttered between themselves, while others merely stared at us with deep suspicion.

The man who had circled us on horseback now swung down from his mount, and pushed through the press of Szgany towards us. He barked something gruffly in his own language—his words were directed at Holmes.

Phillips said, "He asks why they should bargain, and not merely take our gold by force. They would be long gone by the time the soldiers arrived."

"I am glad he asked," said Holmes. "Tell him that, during the past few hours, our men have been laying charges all across this ridge. If the Szgany take any hostile action against us, we shall detonate them and trap them all in a great landslide. None shall get off this mountain alive. But the soldiers shall endure within Castle Dracula. Ask him if he is willing to die tonight. After all, I hear the dead travel fast in these parts."

Holmes referred to an old superstition, which Phillips now translated faithfully. At those words, many of the Szgany began to back away, and the large man who spoke for them looked uncertain.

"Now!" Holmes shouted at the top of his voice.

Upon his command, an explosive charge detonated some short distance to our left, sending showers of dirt and rock cascading over the side of the mountain, and raining down upon us. Men cried out and ran for cover; horses bolted down the trail. I was as surprised as anyone, for Holmes had not told us this part of the plan; I could only hope that the site of the charge had been carefully chosen by the engineers not to cause the very landslide that Holmes had threatened.

When calm was eventually restored, the few gypsies who had remained near to us cursed us, and glared at Holmes angrily.

"Leave as friends, or sell your lives for the Germans," Holmes said icily. "I must have an answer now, or our parley is over and it shall be war."

The gypsies quickly spoke amongst themselves, some reacting with outrage, others more cautiously.

"They are representatives of different groups," whispered Phillips. "Not all of them are warlike—many simply wish to go home."

Sure enough, when the answer at last came, the large Szgany stepped forward, spat into a gloved palm, and held it out to seal the bargain.

My friend clasped the large man's hand firmly, saying, "You shall not regret this. A purse of gold for every man here, and more to follow. Return to the castle in three days' time, and your payment shall be waiting. Remember, only when the soldiers receive word from us will the bargain be complete."

Even as Holmes spoke, four men from the garrison emerged from the darkness at our backs, the explosion having been their signal perhaps. They carried with them a large wooden box, which now they placed down before the gypsies, and took away the lid. Within were many hundreds of gold coins, some sorted into cloth bags, but others piled such that they gleamed in the dancing light of the lanterns and torches. The eyes of the gypsies lit up almost as brightly as the shining gold before them.

A few gruff words were exchanged. The big German caused a hue and cry, cursing our names and struggling to get at us, but he was subdued, and dragged away towards the horses. The large Szgany nodded at us, and left our company, whistling to his brethren to gather so that he might impart what had transpired.

Finally, Holmes turned to Van Helsing.

"Professor, your eagerness to complete your personal vendetta has led to your downfall. You are now our prisoner. Every courtesy shall be extended to you, count upon it; but tomorrow morning we leave for London, where justice shall at last be served."

CHAPTER TWENTY-FIVE

VAN HELSING

Our journey back to Bistritz, and then on to Vienna, was by no means a simple one. It took far longer to return than it did to reach Transylvania, for we travelled incognito, with an armed guard and a prisoner in tow. We were forced to wait for trains at unsociable hours in order to assure a quiet passage, and sometimes we had to rely on private road-coaches, providing slow progress across Europe.

It was only upon finally reaching Vienna that Holmes was able to communicate with Mycroft, though at a cost of an extra day's stay. After an exchange of telegrams, Holmes was finally able to secure us passage aboard a train, in a private car reserved courtesy of the British government, and kept secure by a stout Royal Engineer kindly assigned as our escort.

Up to that point, Van Helsing had spoken little, save to taunt Holmes, and to act with bravado, asserting repeatedly that the German government would send agents to rescue him, and that Holmes and I were on borrowed time. Once aboard the train, however, resistance seemed to drain from him. It became clear that no one was coming for Van Helsing—if the Germans knew of his predicament, they had surely deemed him expendable.

The first evening after leaving Vienna, 27 April, we sat for a miserable dinner in virtual silence. Once we had finished, a change came upon the professor, and over cigars he made his confession to Holmes. Yet still he was assured of his own cleverness, believing that Holmes could not possibly have guessed everything about his complex schemes.

"Oh, I have the measure of it now," Holmes said. "Anything I have not yet deduced is surely not worth knowing. And I have gathered enough evidence to present in a court."

"So, you are having the better of me, you think? Go on, Mr Holmes—explain to me that which you think you know. Let us see how clever you are."

"It will be my pleasure," Holmes said. "It began almost twenty-seven years ago," Holmes began, "with a series of events that might appear innocuous to all but those who look for the connections.

"A baby boy was born to your wife, Elisabet, and I imagine that the birth of your first son brought you unimaginable joy. You doted on the child, and even went so far as to leave the German secret service in order that you might raise him without forever looking over your shoulder for enemies. You retired to Amsterdam where you resumed your former occupation as a professor of medicine. I imagine from your family name that your father was Dutch, or at least half Dutch, and so it was natural for you to make your home there. Although you struggled in the post due to your medical knowledge being woefully out of date, the influence exerted by your old office ensured that the university turned a blind eye to your failings as a teacher. I suppose the German government wanted to keep you happy, firstly so that you might never be tempted to reveal the intelligence you had gathered over the years, but also so that they might one day call on your assistance without fear of ill-will between you."

"Excellent, Mr Holmes."

"Thank you. Now, the boy. His name was Arthur or, more likely, Artur. He was a bright lad, and at first he brought great happiness into your life. But as he grew a little older—perhaps when he was four or five—you started to suspect something was amiss. The boy did not really resemble you at all, but instead had the refined features of a man you knew—a man who had once vied with you for the affections of Elisabet. Count Dracula.

"You had supposed that their affair was long over by the time you married, but now you knew that you had been cuckolded by Dracula. He had remained a family friend, and often visited you in Amsterdam. The jealousy and anger you felt festered each time he was near, and you began to transfer those feelings to your boy.

"I cannot know exactly what happened next, Professor, so perhaps you would be so kind as to help me. I am sure that you faked the death of the boy—perhaps you even intended to kill him but could not go through with it—and in the end placed him in the care of an old contact, not in the German government, but the British one. Lord Godalming."

"That is close enough to the truth," said Van Helsing, his antagonistic smile fading, his tone becoming clipped and severe.

"The only reason I can think of that you would do this is because of Germany's close ties to Transylvania and, especially, Bistritz. You needed the boy far away from Dracula and anyone who might tell him the truth.

"You told Dracula not only that the boy was dead, but that you knew Arthur was his child. Your wife, in the throes of grief, would offer Dracula no succour, and so he swore never to bother you again, and returned to his castle a broken man."

Van Helsing nodded.

"Your terrible deception, however, did not remain a secret," Holmes said. "Years later, Dracula somehow discovered that his son was alive. He sent agents to find out more, and these agents came back with news. His son, Arthur, was alive and well in England. I confess the details are incomplete, Professor. I can only assume Renfield played some part in bringing Arthur's survival to his attention, as Dracula was a notorious recluse, wild in his ways, while Elisabet was mad from her loss, and from your own uncaring attitude towards her."

"Ah, but how cruel you are, Mr Holmes. Cruel, and yet astute. Elisabet's friends, they pry and they pry, until I am force to act, to secure their silence. By then, it is too late—rumours are sent to Dracula, for those who love Elisabet knew that he love her also, and might come to save her. But he did not. He hear the name of Lord Godalming, and he begin to plot. Dracula, perhaps mad himself, he contact Lord Godalming, inviting him to visit Castle Dracula, and to survey it for his great railway."

"Ah. Godalming was too old and frail to travel," Holmes said. "And so a solicitor was dispatched instead: Renfield. Let me guess—he had photographs of the Godalming family?"

"In a newspaper, brought at the specific request of the Count. Dracula, he recognise the boy, just as you did."

"So Count Dracula made a deal with the British, and they snapped up the land he offered in order to build a railway across the Carpathians before Germany could even begin their great Baghdad project. In return, through a long and meandering legal process, Dracula arranged to transfer his assets to London, sending his family heirlooms abroad in great boxes, perhaps to protect his fortune from the enemies who would certainly come calling once his deal with the British became common knowledge. Enemies such as yourself, Professor.

"When finally he managed to visit England and discovered the new identity of his son, he found that you had pre-empted his movements, and had set yourself against him. He contacted

Arthur's fiancé, Lucy Westenra, but you killed her for what she knew and blamed her death on the Count. The loss made a broken puppet of Arthur Holmwood, whom you controlled utterly. You vilified Count Dracula, and found an unwitting crew of assistants, galvanised by Lucy's death, who would later serve as reliable witnesses in your complete assassination of him—both figuratively and literally. After dragging Dracula's name through the mud, you pursued him all the way back to Transylvania, using his own gypsy servants to hound him, and to murder the one man who saw the truth at last: Quincey P. Morris."

Holmes was not a man to gloat in his moment of triumph. If his eyes blazed now, it was not with smugness or superiority, but with a righteous zeal. Van Helsing, on the other hand, bore a severe expression of hatred for his opponent. He clapped his hands slowly.

"Remarkable, Mr Holmes," he said, upon ceasing his facetious applause.

"It seems that Count Dracula, the man you painted as a monster, is the most truly noble figure in this sorry tale," Holmes said. "He surprised you. You did not think Dracula had it in him to leave Transylvania—to wake up from the endless cycle of grief and misery in which you had placed him. But when he found out about your schemes—at least in part—something stirred in him. Dracula rode out against you like his ancestors rode out against the Turkish army."

"He was defeated in the end." Van Helsing allowed himself a rueful smile.

"But at what cost, Professor Van Helsing?" Holmes asked. "The Count was surely right. You have become an embittered, lonely old man. Your wife, whom I am sure you loved once, is lost to you as surely as if she too were dead. Her son, whom I am certain you love still, despite yourself, is set on the same path of misery and possibly madness. And you shall stand trial for the many crimes you have committed."

"Stand trial? Oh no, Mr Holmes. Men such as me do not stand trial like the common criminal."

"We shall see. Regardless, your crimes will be made known to those whose lives you have ravaged. There will be a comeuppance for the Harkers, and Seward, and Genevieve Holmwood—I doubt we can prove irrefutably that she was your 'bloofer lady', but I am certain that, should we make a thorough search of Ring, we will find that she is drugging Lord Godalming, will we not?"

Van Helsing only smiled.

"When he has recovered—if he recovers—Lord Godalming will learn of the chaos you have wrought, and why. Perhaps then he shall know peace."

"It is not your place to speak with Arthur." Van Helsing's voice was a quiet snarl.

"It may not be my place, but it is the right thing to do."

"Your so-sanctimonious morality, it sicken me! You sit in judgement over Abraham Van Helsing? I am your prisoner now, yes, but not for very much longer, I think. I still have the friends, no? Powerful friends, Mr Holmes. When they learn of what you do, there will be much trouble between our nations. For the price of one backward, inbred nobleman from the mountains, who do no good in his life, you would risk war?"

"There will be no war, Professor. Your own crimes, and the evidence I have collected, shall see to that. You do not know, of course, that a certain German agent in London has already learned of the affair and has disavowed your actions. No, I rather think a truce shall be signed over this railway enterprise, and one or both of our nations shall withdraw from the venture. Your greatest mistake is in thinking that your own life is worth more than the safety of every other citizen in Britain and Germany. If there is one thing I can tell you from personal experience, it is that we are all of us expendable."

The defiance drained from Van Helsing's features. He turned to stare out of the window, as the snow-covered hills gave way to green-black forests that stretched for as far as the eye could see. Finally, he nodded slowly.

"I am hearing enough. Mr Holmes, you have been an adversary most worthy, but the end has come now. Will you permit me to be sleeping? I have nowhere to run, nowhere to hide from your so-cruel justice. At least afford Van Helsing some privacy to his thoughts, eh?"

Holmes acquiesced, and showed Van Helsing to his compartment.

"You understand, of course, that you will be under guard?"

"Of course."

Holmes slid the door shut, and Van Helsing, secured inside, drew the curtain across the window.

At Holmes's nod, an Engineer came and stood by the door.

A gunshot rang out behind us, muffled, but unmistakeable. I turned in shock, to see the guard pushing into Van Helsing's compartment. Holmes did not flinch, and so I rushed back without him.

Within the confines of the sleeper compartment lay the professor, dead. A tiny pocket-pistol was discarded beside him. He must have had the weapon concealed all this time, but never used it to attempt an escape; rather, he had saved his one bullet for a much more desperate contingency. Blood ran from the ugly wound at the side of Van Helsing's head. About him were scattered a multitude of papers, most now bloodstained.

I looked back along the aisle, to where Holmes stood gravely. He merely nodded, as though he had predicted this outcome all along.

AUTHOR'S NOTE: DATING DRACULA

Scholars are in debate about the timing of Dracula. For my money, it is obviously set in 1893, backed up by many details in the text. But there's an epilogue that states "seven years later", although the book was published in 1897. Rather than accept that the "seven years" is a typo or a fiction, various academics have set about proposing alternative dates (usually 1886 or 1888), despite the fact that these aren't supported by the text. 1888 is also favoured by scholars because of the mysterious foreword to the Icelandic edition of *Dracula*, which makes allusions to the fact that Dracula and the notorious Jack the Ripper were one and the same. There is very little in the text to support this reading, however, and thus I have put this down to a little retrospective cashing-in on Stoker's part.

So, this book assumes that the events of *Dracula* occur between May and November 1893, and that Sherlock investigates early the following year, 1894. This dates *A Betrayal in Blood* shortly after the events of "The Adventure of the Empty House". Holmes hasn't yet encountered the Sussex vampire, but he has defeated Moriarty and the forces behind the hound of the Baskervilles. He also has an ally in Langdale Pike, to whom readers were first introduced in "The Adventure of the Three Gables".

ABOUT THE AUTHOR

Mark A. Latham is a writer, editor, history nerd, frustrated grunge singer and amateur baker from Staffordshire, UK. A recent immigrant to rural Nottinghamshire, he lives in a very old house (sadly not haunted), and is still regarded in the village as a foreigner.

Formerly the editor of Games Workshop's *White Dwarf* magazine, Mark dabbled in tabletop games design before becoming a full-time author of strange, fantastical and macabre tales, mostly set in the nineteenth century, a period for which his obsession knows no bounds. He is the author of *The Lazarus Gate* and *The Iscariot Sanction*, published by Titan Books.

Follow Mark on Twitter:

@aLostVictorian

SHERLOCK HOLMES

THE PATCHWORK DEVIL
Cavan Scott

It is 1919, and while the world celebrates the signing
of the Treaty of Versailles, Holmes and Watson are called
to a grisly discovery.

A severed hand has been found on the bank of the Thames,
a hand belonging to a soldier who supposedly died in the
trenches two years previously. But the hand is fresh, and
show signs that it was recently amputated. So how has it
ended up back in London two years after its owner was killed
in France? Warned by Sherlock's brother Mycroft to cease
their investigation, and only barely surviving an attack by a
superhuman creature, Holmes and Watson begin to suspect a
conspiracy at the very heart of the British government…

"A thrilling tale for Scott's debut in the Sherlock Holmes world."
Sci-Fi Bulletin

TITANBOOKS.COM

SHERLOCK HOLMES

THE THINKING ENGINE
James Lovegrove

It is 1895, and Sherlock Holmes is settling back into life as a consulting detective at 221b Baker Street, when he and Watson learn of strange goings-on amidst the dreaming spires of Oxford.

A Professor Quantock has built a wondrous computational device, which he claims is capable of analytical thought to rival the cleverest men alive. Naturally Sherlock Holmes cannot ignore this challenge. He and Watson travel to Oxford, where a battle of wits ensues between the great detective and his mechanical counterpart as they compete to see which of them can be first to solve a series of crimes, from a bloody murder to a missing athlete. But as man and machine vie for supremacy, it becomes clear that the Thinking Engine has its own agenda…

"The plot, like the device, is ingenious, with a chilling twist... an entertaining, intelligent and pacy read."
The Sherlock Holmes Journal

"Lovegrove knows his Holmes trivia and delivers a great mystery that fans will enjoy, with plenty of winks and nods to the canon." **Geek Dad**

TITANBOOKS.COM

SHERLOCK HOLMES

GODS OF WAR
James Lovegrove

It is 1913, and Dr Watson is visiting Sherlock Holmes at his retirement cottage near Eastbourne when tragedy strikes: the body of a young man, Patrick Mallinson, is found under the cliffs of Beachy Head.

The dead man's father, a wealthy businessman, engages Holmes to prove that his son committed suicide, the result of a failed love affair with an older woman. Yet the woman in question insists that there is more to Patrick's death. She has seen mysterious symbols drawn on his body, and fears that he was under the influence of a malevolent cult. When an attempt is made on Watson's life, it seems that she may be proved right. The threat of war hangs over England, and there is no telling what sinister forces are at work…

"Lovegrove has once again packed his novel with incident and suspense." **Fantasy Book Review**

"An atmospheric mystery which shows just why Lovegrove has become a force to be reckoned with in genre fiction. More, please." *Starburst*

TITANBOOKS.COM

SHERLOCK HOLMES

THE STUFF OF NIGHTMARES
James Lovegrove

A spate of bombings has hit London, causing untold damage and loss of life. Meanwhile a strangely garbed figure has been spied haunting the rooftops and grimy back alleys of the capital.

Sherlock Holmes believes this strange masked man may hold the key to the attacks. He moves with the extraordinary agility of a latter-day Spring-Heeled Jack. He possesses weaponry and armour of unprecedented sophistication. He is known only by the name Baron Cauchemar, and he appears to be a scourge of crime and villainy. But is he all that he seems? Holmes and his faithful companion Dr Watson are about to embark on one of their strangest and most exhilarating adventures yet.

"[A] tremendously accomplished thriller which leaves the reader in no doubt that they are in the hands of a confident and skilful craftsman." *Starburst*

"Dramatic, gripping, exciting and respectful to its source material, I thoroughly enjoyed every surprise and twist as the story unfolded." **Fantasy Book Review**

"This is delicious stuff, marrying the standard notions of Holmesiana with the kind of imagination we expect from Lovegrove." **Crimetime**

TITANBOOKS.COM

SHERLOCK HOLMES

THE SPIRIT BOX
George Mann

German zeppelins rain down death and destruction on London, and Dr Watson is grieving for his nephew, killed on the fields of France.

A cryptic summons from Mycroft Holmes reunites Watson with his one-time companion, as Sherlock comes out of retirement, tasked with solving three unexplained deaths. A politician has drowned in the Thames after giving a pro-German speech; a soldier suggests surrender before feeding himself to a tiger; and a suffragette renounces women's liberation and throws herself under a train. Are these apparent suicides something more sinister, something to do with the mysterious Spirit Box? Their investigation leads them to Ravensthorpe House, and the curious Seaton Underwood, a man whose spectrographs are said to capture men's souls…

"Arthur Conan Doyle was a master storyteller, and it takes comparable talent to give Holmes a second life… Mann is one of the few to get close to the target." **Daily Mail**

"I would highly recommend this… a fun read." **Fantasy Book Review**

"Our only complaint is that it is over too soon." **Starburst**

TITANBOOKS.COM

SHERLOCK HOLMES

THE WILL OF THE DEAD
George Mann

A rich elderly man has fallen to his death, and his will is nowhere to be found. A tragic accident or something more sinister? The dead man's nephew comes to Baker Street to beg for Sherlock Holmes's help. Without the will he fears he will be left penniless, the entire inheritance passing to his cousin. But just as Holmes and Watson start their investigation, a mysterious new claimant to the estate appears. Does this prove that the old man was murdered?

Meanwhile Inspector Charles Bainbridge is trying to solve the case of the "iron men", mechanical steam-powered giants carrying out daring jewellery robberies. But how do you stop a machine that feels no pain and needs no rest? He too may need to call on the expertise of Sherlock Holmes.

"Mann clearly knows his Holmes, knows what works… the book is all the better for it." **Crime Fiction Lover**

"Mann writes Holmes in a eloquent way, capturing the period of the piece perfectly… this is a must read." **Cult Den**

"An amazing story… Even in the established world of Sherlock Holmes, George Mann is a strong voice and sets himself apart!" **Book Plank**

TITANBOOKS.COM